Praise for
DIME DETECTIVE

"The new breed of retro authors isn't getting paid by the word and, therefore, isn't padding thin stories; instead, they're crafting their books with considerable care and quality, and this novel is every bit a winner. Chandler introduces PI Joe Dall in a slick, atmospheric work that captures the underbelly of the 1950s with a sharp eye for detail and a flair for the sinister."

—*Booklist*

"With the publication of his latest novel, Randy Chandler gives modern readers a truly wonderful taste of a bygone age complemented by today's views on women and minorities ... From Dot Barker, a kind of big sister, to Valentine Cooper and her shotgun, Chandler's characters go beyond the stereotypical dames, dolls, and broads that filled the pulps for a cast of strong, multi-dimensional, and entertaining characters. Readers can only hope to see them again in a sequel."

—*ForeWord Reviews*

"To find a wonderful example of hardboiled detective noir today, you need not look any further than Randy Chandler's latest novel *Dime Detective* ... *Dime Detective* is both an homage and a love letter to the genre, but in many ways, an interesting and original departure."

—Walt Hicks, *Hellbound Times*

DIME DETECTIVE

by **Randy Chandler**

WWW.COMETPRESS.US

About The Author

Randy Chandler is the author of *Bad Juju, Hellz Bellz*, and co-author of *Duet for the Devil*. He is also the author of the novellas *Dead Juju* and *Howler*. Randy is a frequent contributor to Comet Press anthologies. He lives north of Atlanta.

For Cheryl Mullenax, editor extraordinaire

CHAPTER ONE

Joe Dall was all set for another numb night on the edge of Dead City.

But the night had other plans.

A sultry breeze hummed through the rusty window screens of the Sundown Lounge, ruffling the tissue-thin pages of Dot's *True Detective*. Caught between the force of the breeze off the lake and the pull of the ceiling fan over the bar, the smoke curling from her cigarette twisted into wispy swirls that disappeared from Joe's unfocused gaze. She was at her usual place behind the bar, and he was on a barstool, facing her. The jukebox was spinning a new Fats Domino platter. The throbbing backbeat rattled the bottles behind the bar.

"Get a load of this," Dot said, tapping a blood-red fingernail against the page of her magazine. "This meat market butcher murdered his wife, chopped her up, put her through a meat grinder and sold her as ground beef."

"Huh," Joe grunted. He didn't share Dot's passion for grisly details of sensational murder. She routinely read every word of every crime rag on the newsstands, but her real joy seemed to come from telling him about each and every twisted case. Some of that stuff turned his stomach, but what could he do? She was his boss. When his job selling insurance went bust, she'd hired him as bouncer/handyman for the Sundown Lounge, Dodd City, Florida's number-one watering hole—number-one because there was no number-two or -three, unless you counted that rat-hole joint downtown, Bill's Bar. Joe had come to think of Dot Barker as something of a big sister, but her constant riffs on criminal degradation rubbed him raw, and he was afraid he might end up telling her what she ought to do with her sleazy magazines. He'd never had a real sister, so he wasn't sure how much blunt honesty was permissible.

"And when they arrested the guy," she went on, "he told the cops his regular customers said she was the sweetest hamburger they ever ate." A big smile crinkled her sun-leathered face, and she snorted a sardonic laugh. Dot's age was her most closely guarded secret, but Joe placed her in the vicinity of forty, give or take. She wore it well, having been blessed with a face that always looked several years younger than it really was, in spite of the sun's damage. She still cut a shapely figure, and her robust bosom did her pink halter-top proud.

Joe paid her scant attention at the moment. He was eyeballing the two rowdies swilling brew in the corner booth and generally making life miserable for Tina the rookie waitress. He'd never seen them before, and with any luck, he'd never see them again, but right now they were making trouble on his turf. It was time to earn his wages. "Excuse me," Joe said to Dot as he slid off the stool. "Duty calls."

Tina walked past, shooting him a look of desperation, eyes brimming with tears. A cute blond with a ponytail and a budding figure, she was barely out of her teens. Joe could see that she wasn't cut out for this waitress gig. Empty beer bottles rattled on her tray as she made her way to the bar, and when he heard the sob catch in her throat, he knew things were about to get out of hand. He patted the leather sap in his hip pocket as he zeroed in on the two mooks hunkered in the corner booth.

The one with a buzz-cut and ears like wings on a coconut looked up at Dall and said, "What's your beef, buster?"

"Time to go," said Joe. "The bar's closed."

The guy with a quart of 30-weight on his Elvis-the-Pelvis pompadour looked at his watch, blew smoke in Joe's face and said, "Like hell. Whadda you, the bouncer for this shit hole?"

Joe didn't answer. He stared into the guy's beady eyes.

"Why don't you go bounce your balls off that old broad behind the bar? You sure as hell don't wanna fuck with us. Right, Ralphie?"

"You said it, Slick," Ralphie guffawed, then he went back to picking his teeth with the corner of a soggy matchbook cover with the inevitable Draw Me challenge.

On a good night, Joe Dall might've had more patience, but this was already a bad night on its way to worse, and he used up the last piece of his patience when he said, "Last chance to walk outta here."

Slick's smirk turned into a mean sneer as he started to get up. Joe knew he wasn't getting up to ask him to dance, so he slipped the sap from his hip pocket and whacked the guy's coconut with it, just above his left ear. He went facedown on the table.

Ralphie came charging out of the booth like a gone-to-seed middle linebacker. Joe sidestepped and blackjacked the back of his head as he went by, and Ralphie ended up on his elbows and knees, stunned and trying to shake it off. Joe bent over and smacked the back of his cranium once more and he dropped like a dead-eyed cow in a slaughterhouse.

Coming out from behind the bar, Dot said, "God, Joe, can't you be a little more diplomatic? Jeez Louise."

Tina rushed to his defense. "They asked for it, Dot. I swear they did. They said really ugly things to me."

Joe pocketed the lead-weighted leather and dragged the sap-sedated boys outside and dumped them in their battered '49 Ford. He was sorely tempted to push the ten-year-old heap into the lake. Instead he paused a peaceful moment to listen to the wind rattling the palm fronds and humming through the tall pines. A sea breeze would have been better, but the Atlantic was nearly a hundred miles east of Dodd City, and the Gulf of Mexico was more than thirty miles west.

Back inside, Joe lit a smoke and sipped from a bottle of mineral water to cool off.

"I should call the cops," said Dot. "Those apes are liable to be plenty teed-off when they wake up. If you didn't kill 'em."

"They're still breathing, but I don't think they'll feel much like going another round tonight," he told her. "You ever seen 'em before?"

"Nope." Dot fired up another Camel and blew smoke out of the corner of her mouth. "Probably just making a pit stop on their way to somewhere else."

"With a detour to Dream Town," Joe threw in. In the six months of his career as a bouncer, this was the first time he'd ever had to use the blackjack.

A party of four regulars arrived and piled into a booth. Tina bopped over to take their order, smiling real big for the two middle-aged men who would be dropping her tip.

Dot inclined her head in Joe's direction and whispered conspiratorially, "Thank God they didn't come in any sooner. Don't think they would've appreciated your little rumble."

"Aw for Christ's sake, Dot, what did you expect me to do? Spank their wrists?"

"No, no. I'm just saying I'm glad no customers had to see it. That's all. You did fine, Joe. Just fine. Don't be so touchy." She reached across the bar and patted his arm.

Half an hour later two cops swaggered in, decked out in Boy Scout khaki and Sam Browne belts well-hung with nightsticks and pistols.

"Well, if it ain't Dead City's Finest," Dot said in dubious greeting.

"That's *Dodd* City," snapped the younger officer, as if he had been personally insulted.

"Seems pretty dead to me," Dot shot back, waving a hand at the empty booths and tables. "As usual."

"Hello, Dot," said the stocky cop. He scrunched up a big grin, his face exhibiting more ruddy lines than a road atlas.

"Gus." She gave him a wary nod. "What can I do for you gents?" They walked up to the bar and Joe scanned their name tags (a habit he'd acquired in the Marines). Grinning Gus was Hardy. His partner's tag was Blue and he had eyes to match his name—especially if his first name happened to be Cold. Blue gave Joe a good going-over with those frosty blues. Joe saluted him with a raised brow.

Officer Hardy was more interested in giving Dot's cleavage a good going-over. For starters. Then he raised his gaze to her face and came to the point of their visit. "You got a guy the name of Joe Dall working here?"

Dot didn't look Joe's way. She was not one to tip her hand too early in the game. She nodded. "Yeah, so?"

"We need to talk to him," replied Hardy, hands on his wide well-padded hips.

"He's not in any kind of trouble, is he?" she asked.

"Depends on what he has to say for himself." Hardy was having a hard time keeping his eyes off Dot's mammaries.

Officer Blue was growing impatient, drumming his stubby fingers against the butt of his billy club. "Where is he?"

Joe was as impatient as the cop was. "Right here," he said, striking a note of belligerent defiance. "What's the deal?"

"We're bringing you in for questioning," Blue said. His steely blues went several degrees colder. "Stand up and put your hands on the bar."

Joe shrugged and did as told.

"Spread your legs," said Blue, his mouth inches from Joe's ear.

Joe did that too. The cop frisked him and removed the sap from his hip pocket. He whacked it against the bar, just missing the little finger of Joe's right hand. "What the hell's this?"

Before he could answer, Dot said, "He's my bouncer, for Christ's sake. I gave it to him. Goes with the job."

Blue grabbed Joe's right wrist, pulled it behind his back and snapped on the cuffs, then he did the same with his left. His thick hand latched onto the back of Joe's neck and he spun him around. "Let's go, big man."

Joe was two inches over six feet, giving him about four inches over Officer Blue. He could see that the guy was the type to take an instant dislike to any man taller than he was. Some short guys were like that. Maybe there was something to that old Hitler Complex idea.

Still talking mostly to Dot's tits, Hardy said, "Sorry to leave you without a bouncer. Give us a call if you have any trouble. But it don't look like you will tonight."

They took Joe out to their prowl car. The beat-up '49 Ford was gone. Joe wondered if Ralphie and Slick had set the cops on him, but he didn't really think so. They didn't seem the type to go crying to the cops.

The wind had calmed and the palm trees in front of the lounge were as still as a picture-postcard. As Joe was about to slide into the back of the black-and-white, Blue drew his billy club and jammed its business end into Joe's gut. "I saw what you did to that poor girl," he said, snarling. "Sicko shit heel."

Bent over and gasping for breath, Joe was slow in connecting the cop's words to his own pain. "What?" He gasped for a breath. "What girl?"

"The one you murdered, you son of a bitch. Lizabeth Tibbedeaux."

"That's crazy! I didn't—"

Blue gave him another jab with his stick, then pushed him

into the back of the prowl car and slammed the door. Shock made Joe oblivious to the physical pain. Lizabeth murdered? No way. He didn't believe it. He *couldn't* believe it.

Lizabeth Tibbedeaux was his ex-wife.

He was still crazy in love with her.

* * *

Bull Kelso was a local legend, a bona fide hero of World War II and a decorated veteran of the Korean War. Discharged from the army in 1954, he had been Dodd City's police chief ever since. He was a take-no-prisoners kind of guy—a fact that spelled big trouble for anybody who ended up in his jail. Dall wasn't there yet, but he was only a few steps away, in what they called the "hot box," and that was exactly what it was: a small, stuffy room with olive-drab cinderblock walls, a scarred cigarette-scorched wooden table and two ladder-back chairs.

They left him alone in there long enough to work up a good sweat, and when they figured he was sufficiently basted in his own juices, Chief Kelso came in to grill him. Officer Blue tagged along behind the chief like an attack dog on a short leash. Joe could tell by the way Blue glared in his direction that he wanted another shot at him.

Kelso was out of uniform, decked out in loud Bermuda shorts and a knit pullover shirt that showed off his massive arms and hulking belly. "Take the cuffs off him," Kelso told Blue.

Blue went behind Joe's chair and removed the cuffs. He tossed them onto the table, where they landed with a threatening clatter, and Joe got the message they special-delivered: a set of steel bracelets could turn a man's face into raw meat in nothing flat.

Kelso didn't sit down. He propped one foot on the seat of the empty chair, rested an elbow on his bent knee, leaned his big head halfway across the table and gave Joe a hard stare. "Joseph Dall," he said with considerable distaste. "Marries into one of the richest families in Florida and winds up a charity case of a soft-hearted club owner who don't know her ass from first base."

"I earn my pay," Joe protested.

Officer Blue rewarded the protestation with a backhand smack to the side of Joe's head. "Nobody told you to talk."

"Tell me something, Dall," said Kelso. "You banging that dried-up broad's box?"

"Who? Dot? No, I'm not *banging* her. She's like a big sister."

Blue chuckled. "Hell, you know what the perverts say. 'Incest is best.'"

"At ease, Blue," Bull said. "Keep your white-trash wisdom to yourself."

"Sorry, Chief." Blue tried to look humbled but couldn't quite pull it off.

"You were in Korea," said Kelso. "A Marine."

"Yes, sir."

"Killed a lot of slants, did you?" His eyes brightened. His weathered face became more animated and his close-cropped iron-gray hair seemed to stand at attention.

"Got my share."

"Don't be modest, son," he said. "I know your military record."

"Nothing compared to yours," Joe said, then added, "sir."

"All that killing . . ." Kelso rubbed his chin thoughtfully. "How did it make you feel?"

Joe knew Kelso was baiting him. He answered with a shrug.

Kelso hammered the tabletop with a beefy fist, making the table jump. His eyes smoldered. He leaned on the table with both hands and said softly, "Listen up, son. When I ask you a question, you damn well better give me an answer. You got that?"

"Yes, sir." Joe exhaled sharply. "I don't remember feeling much of anything except . . . scared. Then after a while I didn't feel anything at all. What's a carpenter feel when he hammers a nail? I was just doing a job. Nailing as many as I could before they could nail me."

Kelso nodded, apparently satisfied with the answer. "When was the last time you saw your ex-wife?"

"Couple of weeks ago. I ran into her downtown. She was coming out of Belk's department store."

"You speak to her?"

"I said hello. She said hello. That's about it." There had been a little more to their encounter than that, but Joe couldn't see that it was any of the cop's business.

"You've been divorced how long?"

"Almost a year."

"She dumped you, right?" Kelso made it sound like an accusation.

Joe felt his eyes misting up, and he looked down at the table. He didn't want Chief Kelso to see the raw pain bubbling up just below the surface. "Right," he said.

"On what grounds?"

"Her lawyer claimed mental cruelty, but that was total bullshit. The only cruelty came from her father. Monroe Tibbedeaux never approved of me. He thought I wasn't good enough for his daughter. Hell, maybe he was right. But he should've let Lizabeth make up her own mind instead of constantly running me down in front of her. After a while she started to believe I was the bum he made me out to be."

Kelso folded his arms across his barrel chest. "Fact is, Joseph, you *are* a bum by Tibbedeaux's standards. How much you make at the Sundown?"

"Thirty bucks a week. Plus a place to live. Dot lets me stay in the bungalow there at the lake. She doesn't want the place to stand empty. She pays the utilities and I do the upkeep."

"So, you're thirty years old with no place to call your own, making chicken-scratch wages as a bouncer with no prospects of a bright future. That about right?"

He had him cold. Perfectly pegged. No point in arguing with the sad truth. Joe was a bum, all right. A real sad sack. He nodded: affirmative.

Another cop appeared in the doorway. He had a manila folder in his fist. "Chief, here's the crime-scene photos." Kelso took the folder, opened it and flipped through the thin stack of 8" x 10" glossies. He did it with the nonchalance of a man paging through a magazine at a newsstand. He grunted, then came over to the desk and slapped down a black-&-white death shot of Joe's ex-wife.

Though it sickened him, Joe couldn't take his eyes off it. Up until then, he hadn't really believed she was dead. He had been clinging to the crazy idea that her father was orchestrating an elaborate hoax just to punish him for defiling his precious daughter. Tibbedeaux certainly had the political clout to pull those strings. But the grainy photograph was no hoax. The dead wear a look that can't be faked, and the Lizabeth in this photo was unmistakably dead, her face a rictus mask of lifeless flesh, her eyes bugged and staring at nothing in this world. Her nude body was stretched out on the floor at the foot of a brass bed—the same bed they had shared during their brief marriage. She was lying on her back, arms akimbo, one knee slightly bent. A twisted brassiere was wrapped around her neck like a scarf. Her skin was pale and stark, and her natural-blond hair looked like a platinum dye-job in the photographer's harsh flash. Her breasts were not heavy enough to sag to either side with the pull of gravity; they stood firm even in death. Out of decency he avoided looking directly at the blond thatch between her legs. A tear or a bead of sweat—he wasn't sure which—slid off his face and fell onto the photo, making a tiny splatter on her belly. He was suddenly struck by the idiotic urge to apologize to her.

"Why'd you do it, son?" Kelso said, his voice almost a purr.

Joe tried to speak but his mouth and throat had gone dry. What came out was a froggy croak. He tried again. "I didn't do it."

"Sure you did, Joseph. She dumped you and she wouldn't take you back. She even went back to using her maiden name. A man can only take so much. We all understand that. Tell us exactly what happened."

"I didn't kill her." The sick feeling in the pit of his stomach was becoming a seething knot of anger. He clenched his fists and glared at Kelso.

Kelso tossed another photo in front of him. A close-up of Lizabeth's face. "Strangled her to death with her own bra strap." Kelso's soothing purr had become a growl. "Did you rape her before you killed her or did you stick it to her after you made her a corpse? You a corpse-fucker, Dall?"

Joe shot out of the chair and went over the table after him. He got his hands around Kelso's bull neck before Officer Blue rained a flurry of kidney punches on his back. Kelso countered with an uppercut to Joe's chin that crumpled him crosswise over the table. Joe hung there with arms outstretched and head bobbing groggily.

Kelso's voice seemed to echo from a deep, dark pit. "He's our boy all right. Goes for the throat on instinct." Then Joe was *in* that dark pit, so deep no sound could reach him.

Somebody threw cold water in his face. He sputtered and spat, swimming back to unforgiving reality. He was back in the chair, hands cuffed behind his back.

"Scrappy son of a bitch, ain't he."

"Rape-o strangler's what *he* is."

Joe blinked his eyes until they were cleared of water. Blue banged his billy club on the table to make sure he and the chief had Joe's full attention. They did.

Kelso said, "Fun's over, asshole. Time to 'fess up. Start by giving a moment-by-moment account of your movements and whereabouts last night. And take us all the way up through this morning."

"And if you even *think* about lying," warned Blue, "I'll crack your skull."

Joe nodded. A white bolt of lightning flashed behind his eyes and pain thundered in his head. He grimaced, then said, "That's easy. I was at the lounge till we closed at midnight, then I went back to the bungalow, read a little and fell asleep. I, uh, slept till nine or so this morning, went for a swim in the lake, then went back to the bungalow and cooked breakfast. After that, I walked over to the lounge to let in the beer deliveryman, Teddy Simms. I think that was around eleven, eleven-thirty. Then I swept up, dumped the trash and restocked the bar. That's what I was doing when Dot got there about noon."

"So you were alone from midnight until almost noon," Kelso said.

"Yeah," he said, resigned to the fact that he had no alibi. "I think I need a lawyer."

"A lawyer won't do you no good, son," said Kelso. "You're under arrest for the first-degree murder of Lizabeth Tibbedeaux. Print him and cage him, Blue."

"Hold on, Chief," called a voice from the doorway. Monroe Tibbedeaux strolled into the room. He moved with the confidence of a man accustomed to having things his way. He was wearing his trademark custom-tailored white suit which complemented the golden glow of his golfer's tan. His white hair was combed straight back from a high forehead, and you could see the cunning behind his hard gray eyes. He didn't so much as glance in Joe Dall's direction as he approached Bull Kelso.

"Before you book him, you'd better take a look at this," Tibbedeaux said casually. He handed a small spiral-bound notebook to Kelso. "It's a preliminary handwritten report. I can give you the official typed version later."

"What is this?" asked Kelso, puzzled but taking care to show proper deference to the illustrious Monroe Tibbedeaux, the Orange Juice King of Pasco County and one of the most powerful real estate barons in the state of Florida.

Tibbedeaux folded his arms across his chest and acknowledged Joe's presence with a neutral glance. "That's the eyewitness account of a private investigator I retained to keep tabs on Joseph. As you can see, it details the subject's activities for the past three days—and nights. It does in fact provide the lad with an alibi. *Ironclad,* I believe they say."

Kelso scanned the notebook's pages. A pregnant silence filled the room. Then Kelso snapped the notebook shut and handed it back to Tibbedeaux. "So why did you have him tailed?"

"That is a private matter." A trace of a sly smile played on Dall's former father-in-law's lips. If he was upset over the murder of his daughter, he sure as hell wasn't showing it. "That's why they're called *private* investigators, Chief."

Bull Kelso was clearly steamed. He'd thought he had an open-and-shut murder case all sewn up, only to have it unraveled by a nickel notebook filled with ballpoint chicken-scratch. "I suppose you can produce this private dick as a witness?"

"Certainly. His name is Homer Dix. He's across the street, having a late supper at the Dodd City Cafe. Here's his card."

Kelso took the business card, holding it delicately with his stubby fingers, and gave it the once-over with a modicum of interest. "Private dick out of Tampa. Huh."

"So. If you are through questioning Joseph, I'll take him off your hands."

Bull Kelso turned his frustration on Joe. He walked toward him on thick bowed legs like a sumo wrestler stalking an overmatched opponent. "I could book you for assaulting an officer of the law, Dall. A few months on the chain-gang might do you good. But seeing's how Mr. Tibbedeaux has taken such an interest in you, I'll let you off this time." He craned his big wrecking-ball head right down in Joe's face. "You ever cross me again, tough guy, I'll rip you a new asshole and jam your fucking head in it. Now get the hell out of my sight."

Officer Blue removed the cuffs, gave Dall what he probably thought was an evil look, and shoved him toward the door.

"Come along, Joseph," said Tibbedeaux. "I'll give you a ride home."

As eager as Joe was to escape the clutches of the Dodd City cops, he wasn't keen on the idea of leaving in the custody of Monroe F. Tibbedeaux. The man had always given Joe the same regard he might give to something stuck to the sole of his Florsheim shoe. He had done his best to break up Joe's marriage to Lizabeth because he didn't think his son-in-law was good enough for his precious little jewel of a girl. So why was he rescuing Joe from a murder rap? Maybe he really believed Joe killed her and he was going to take him out on some country road and shoot him. That business about the private dick might've been a clever ploy to spring him for the kill. Joe held that thought just long enough to see that it wasn't plausible. If Tibbedeaux wanted him dead, he wouldn't come anywhere near him. He would hire a pro to do the dirty work and Tibbedeaux himself would have an unshakable alibi. Joe followed him out into the muggy night, determined to find out all the man knew about Lizabeth's murder. And to find out why the hell he had put a private detective on his tail.

Barry Keefer was leaning against Tibbedeaux's Lincoln Continental, smoking a cigarette and absently fondling his pumped-up muscles. When he saw them coming across the red-brick street, he tossed the butt and stepped on it. He opened the front passenger door for his Lord & Master, and ignored Joe.

"We'll ride in the back," Tibbedeaux told him. "We're taking Joseph home to the Sundown Lounge."

"Yes, sir." Keefer nodded and clicked his heels together. He was Tibbedeaux's all-purpose flunky. Though he didn't look particularly dangerous or menacing in his white Chauffeur's cap and baby-blue blazer, Joe knew he was packing a Colt .38 in a shoulder harness and that he was a crack shot with it. He also knew Keefer was strong enough to break an average man in half without breaking a sweat. Some guys hit their peak early in life and spend the rest of their years coasting the downside. Keefer was one of those guys. He achieved glory as a high school football star, a punishing fullback for the Pasco Pirates, and he subsequently worked his horny way through the energetic cheerleader squad and various long-legged majorettes, only to become the chauffeur/bodyguard for the richest man in the county, reduced to flexing his prized muscles in relative anonymity. Joe knew how it was. He was on the downside too. He'd peaked when he married Lizabeth. After she dumped him, there was nowhere to go but down. The only question was: How far?

Keefer opened the rear door and Tibbedeaux motioned Joe in first. He slid into the plush interior of the back seat. His ex-father-in-law slid in beside him.

"Joseph," he said, putting a well-manicured hand on Joe's knee, "I want you to find out who killed my little girl."

Joe stared at the man's delicate hand and at his diamond-studded wedding band. The hands looked like they belonged on the wrists of a concert pianist, or maybe a surgeon.

"I'll make it worth your while," Tibbedeaux said, removing his hand from Joe's knee to unbutton his coat. "Money-wise."

In the semi-darkness of the back seat, his white suit seemed to glow with otherworldly light. He adjusted his tie and flashed a ghoulish smile. "What do you say, Joseph? Will you do this for me? For Lizabeth?"

"I don't get this," Joe said. "What makes you think I can find out who . . . did it? I'm no detective. I wouldn't know where to start."

"It's very simple," he said, folding his hands in his lap. "You're still carrying a torch for Lizabeth. Even the divorce couldn't make you let go. You never lost your determination to win her back. You held on like a wolverine, no matter how hard she pushed you away. I know all about it, Joseph. Believe me, I understand how love can become an obsession."

"You do, huh?" Did he understand how badly Joe wanted to punch his lights out?

"Oh, yes. And that obsession can be your best asset now. I want you to carry the torch for Lizabeth a little longer. And know this: That torch is now the flame of justice. It must not be extinguished before we find her murderer."

Joe stared at the man, scarcely believing what he'd just heard him say. Then he said, "While she was alive, you did your best to get me away from her, and now that she's dead, you want me to be her . . . her—"

"Champion. Yes, I see your point. It's well taken. But I hope to offset any hard feelings you might have with a very generous remuneration."

The car took a curve too sharply and Joe bounced against the door's armrest. "Goddammit, Keefer," he shouted at the driver, "this ain't a race track."

Keefer swiveled his big head around and gave him a murderous look, his craggy jaw backlit by the glow of the dash lights. Joe immediately regretted his outburst, realizing that his anger was misdirected. He turned it on Tibbedeaux and said, "You got a lotta damn nerve, Pops, trying to buy me off with this cockamamie 'flame of justice' crapola."

"Now listen, lad—"

"You listen. And don't call me *lad*. I wouldn't take money from you if I was starving on the street. The only thing I want from you is the truth. First off, why did you have a detective following me?"

"All right. When I heard that you had recently accosted Lizabeth on the street, I decided to take matters into my own hands. I hired Mr. Dix to dig up dirt on you. There have been rumors floating around town that you might be involved in illegal activities, so I wanted to know if they were true. If they were, I was going to see that you were put away for a long time. And out of my daughter's life once and for all."

"What illegal activities?"

"Peddling illicit drugs. Reefer, pep pills."

"That's total bullshit. You probably started those rumors yourself."

"Think, Joseph. If I started the rumors myself, why would I spend good money to find out if they were true?"

"Then who did? Why would they? I'm not a dope pusher. I've never even seen the stuff."

"I'm sure I don't know. But there is dope in Dodd City. Chief Kelso confirmed that his officers arrested two men for possession of marihuana. Out-of-towners, all the way from California."

"That's got nothing to do with me. I don't know anybody from California."

"Kelso said they were lowlife Hollywood types, visiting Laura D'Amore."

Laura D'Amore was a former screen actress who lived in a Spanish-style mansion halfway between Dodd City and Zephyrhills. The reclusive Miss D'Amore was seldom seen outside her home, and rumors about her mysterious early retirement from the movie business abounded. Hollywood sex scandals, real or imagined, spiced up the otherwise dull lives of housewives everywhere, and the women of Dodd City were no exception. Joe recalled that Lizabeth had been fascinated by the enigmatic Laura D'Amore. Her favorite film of all time was the 1947 melodrama, *Torrid Town,* featuring the raven-haired star. They had watched it on the late show one night, holding hands and munching popcorn in front of the black-&-white television set. Lizabeth knew some of the dialogue by heart and spoke the choice lines with the actress. Joe suspected that she saw the D'Amore character as her alter ego, a dark-haired and dangerous vamp whose power over men bordered on the supernatural. He didn't care much for the movie, but it made Lizzy happy, and that was reason enough to sit through the hokey melodrama with some scenes so dark it was hard to see what was going on.

"But that's neither here nor there, given the current circumstances," Tibbedeaux said with a throwaway shrug. "The fact is, my detective saved you from a murder charge. I should think you would be grateful."

"Yeah? Well, pardon me if I don't bend over to kiss your ass."

Tibbedeaux shook his head disgustedly. "For the life of me, I don't know what my daughter ever saw in you. Her mother and I raised her to have a healthy aversion to such crudity."

"Maybe that's what she liked about me," Joe shot back. "Maybe she was sick of smooth-talking back stabbers and rich-bitch phonies."

He sighed. "Perhaps you're right. It's pointless to discuss

it now. Let's put all that aside. Please. I am asking for your help. Will you find Lizabeth's killer?"

"This is nuts," Joe said, more to himself than to his ex-father-in-law. Then he addressed the dapper man directly. "You can afford to hire an army of private detectives, and the police are already hot to find the killer, so what the hell kind of sense does it make to ask me to play detective?"

"That's a fair question. And here's the simple answer. Private investigators specialize in divorce cases. Unlike their romanticized Hollywood counterparts, they generally don't work homicides. Neither do the local police. What you saw firsthand tonight was Bull Kelso trying to upstage the county investigators. County Homicide will conduct their usual by-the-book investigation. Strictly drudge work. And that's just not good enough. Lizabeth deserves better than that. You lived with her. You know little things about her even I don't know. You won't be bound by a by-the-book approach. And you loved her. That's why you'll do it. You'll do it as a true labor of love. You'll do it because you can't bear the thought that the person who snuffed out her life might get away scot-free. I am right, aren't I, Joseph? You *will* do it."

He had Joe dead-to-rights and they both knew it. "I'll do whatever I can," he grudgingly admitted. "For *her*. Not for you."

"Yes, of course." He smiled an undertaker's smile and gave Joe's knee a paternal pat. "For Lizabeth."

* * *

Joe must have looked as badly shaken as he felt when he returned to the lounge, because Dot tossed her magazine on the bar and said, "My God, Joe, what did they do to you?"

He wove his unsteady way to the bar and climbed onto a stool, rubbing his jaw. Bull's uppercut had clipped him hard enough to loosen a tooth and give him a dizzying headache.

"Roughed me up some," he said. "Give me a smoke, will ya?"

She produced her deck of Camels from behind the bar and shook one out for him, then lit it with her Zippo. He sucked down a good lungful, then exhaled with a heavy sigh.

"So? Give," she said. "Why'd they roust you?"

He looked around and saw that they were alone, then glanced at the Pabst Blue Ribbon clock on the wall behind the bar. It was five past midnight. "Lizabeth's been murdered," he said thickly, avoiding Dot's eyes. "They tried to pin it on me."

"No! Sweet Jesus!" She took a backward step.

He nodded. "They showed me pictures. Of *her*. Ah Christ, she's really *dead*."

Dot covered his knuckles with her hand and gave him a sympathetic squeeze. "I'm so sorry, Joe. I know how you felt about her."

He noticed the already forgotten cigarette burning between his fingers, took another drag, then stubbed it out in an ashtray because the bad taste in his mouth spoiled the smoke's flavor. "I'd be in jail now if old man Tibbedeaux hadn't showed up to alibi me."

"Why would he do that? I thought he hated your guts."

"He does. Or did. Hell, I don't know. He's got this crazy idea that I can find out who killed her."

"He doesn't think you were involved, does he?"

"No. I don't think so. I don't know. I can't think straight right now."

"Let me fix you a drink," she offered. "Seagrams?"

"Yeah. Just give me the bottle." He stood up. "I'll take it with me."

"You want me to stay with you tonight?" Sisterly concern lined her face and made her look closer to her true age.

"No thanks, Dot. I'll be okay."

"At least let me stay till you fall asleep." She set a fifth of Seagrams on the bar.

"I just . . . I need to be alone now."

"Sure, Joe. I understand. But if you need me, give me a ring. I don't care if it's the middle of the night."

"You're a sweetheart," Joe said. The words came out of his mouth but it felt like somebody else was saying them. He was looking at Dot but he was seeing Lizabeth's corpse, frozen forever in grainy black-&-white. He grabbed the bottle of booze and headed for the door.

"Joe?" Dot's voice was a hollow echo coming from a faraway place. "I'm really sorry."

"I know. Thanks." Then he was outside, stumbling through the darkness, shambling toward his bungalow like a weary zombie en route to the refuge of his tomb.

He mounted the wooden steps to the deck built onto the rear of the bungalow and collapsed into the cane rocking chair. He uncapped the Seagrams and took a long pull from the lip of the bottle, the booze burning just enough to let him know he wasn't dreaming. The lake was a dark mirror beneath a starless sky, reflecting nothing but his black mood. Its restless waters lapped the shore with wet whispers, secret intimations of putrefaction and soggy death.

When he was halfway to the bottom of the bottle, the moon broke through the clouds and he saw Lizabeth's face on the lake's looking-glass surface. She was smiling, her eyes full of moonlight and mischief. Joe stood up, leaned on the deck's wooden rail and stared hard at her gently undulating image. "Lizzy," he whispered. "Why?" A gust of wind rippled the lake's inky surface and her youthful face became the death mask he had seen in the crime-scene close-up: eyes swollen near to bursting; full lips slightly twisted around her tongue as though trying to rid the mouth of something distasteful; cheeks hollowed by the horror of violent death.

Then she winked a dead eye at him, chilling him to the bone.

He felt her presence all around him, enveloping him in a soft, feminine mist. With tears rolling down his cheeks, he reeled backward and fell into the rocker. Even as Lizabeth's ghostly presence deserted him and her face became nothing more than the reflection of the moon on the water, he knew beyond any doubt that her wink *meant something*. She was teasing him with ghostly secrets.

Still tingling from her misty embrace, he closed his eyes and sank into a mournful stupor.

CHAPTER TWO

Morning found Joe Dall sprawled facedown on his bed, with no memory of how he got there. He rolled over and sat up. He was still dressed, wearing one shoe. He didn't know where the other one was. He stripped and took a cold shower. He kept his head under the cold spray until the throbbing headache backed off some, then he wrapped a towel around his waist and went into the kitchenette and got the electric percolator going on a pot of strong coffee. He watched it, finding homey comfort in seeing the brown liquid bubble up inside the little glass knob on top of the appliance, turning darker with each perk. When it looked strong enough, he poured himself a cup and went out on the deck to see if the daylight world looked different now that Lizabeth was no longer in it.

The sky was overcast and dreary, a sympathetic backdrop for his sorrowful hangover. He slurped some of the steaming coffee, then sat in the rocker. He didn't rock; he knew the to-and-fro motion would set off more throbbing pain. The coffee gave him enough of a jump-start so that he could think rationally again, and he revisited last night's conversation with Liz's father. After Joe had agreed to help find her killer, Tibbedeaux promised to back him with the full weight of his considerable resources. "Anything you need, you just let me know," he said, but when Joe asked what he already knew about the murder, the man put him off, promising to provide copies of the police and autopsy reports as soon as they were available. Joe pressed him and Tibbedeaux said, "All I know with any certainty is that she was found in her bedroom, apparently strangled to death. Tomorrow I'll meet with the coroner and get the official cause of death and any other relevant details."

A light rain began to fall. Joe went inside, threw on some clean clothes, drank another cup of coffee, then picked up the phone and dialed Monroe Tibbedeaux's residence. The Negro housekeeper answered.

"Hello, Ginny," Joe said. Before the divorce, he'd come to feel a close kinship with Ginny, probably because the master of the house treated them both as second-class citizens.

"That you, Mistuh Joe?" Her voice was a warm rumble.

"It's me. Is Mr. Tibbedeaux there?"

"No, suh, he gone out. Left 'bout an hour ago."

"Do you know when he might be back?"

"He didn't say."

"Thanks, Ginny."

"Mistuh Joe? You all right?"

"Yeah, more or less. How about you?" He knew she had thought of Lizabeth as her own Godchild and that the loss had to have hit her hard.

"Lord knows, I'm so aggrieved I can't hardly stand it," she said, her voice trembling. "That poor girl . . . she in the Lord's hands now. Alls we can do is keep on doin', I reckon."

"Amen to that," he said. "How's Mrs. Tibbedeaux taking it?"

"The Mistuh had Dr. Loftin come out yestiddy and give her a knockout shot and some horse pills. She sleepin' like a baby now. Before that, she wuz out of her mind, screamin' and cryin' for her little girl."

"I know you've got your hands full," he sympathized. "I'll let you go, Ginny. You take care of yourself."

"Yes, suh, Mistuh Joe, I surely will."

He hung up, rubbed his sore jaw and realized he'd forgotten to shave. After he downed a couple of aspirin, he went into the bathroom, lathered up and shaved, nicking his chin only once with the straight razor. He splashed on some Old Spice. The cooling sting felt good. His reflection in the bathroom mirror looked back at him with eyes badly bloodshot. He shivered, remembering Lizabeth's spectral death's-head winking a cold eye at him. A knowing wink, teasing and taunting him with cryptic knowledge only the dead possess. She was a flirtatious wraith, daring him to uncover her darkest secrets. He shook off the shivers and rose, as best he could, to her challenge. "Okay, Lizzy," he said as if she were in the room with him, "you're on."

He went back to the phone and dialed the same number. "Ginny, it's me again. Listen, I need to know if you saw much of Lizabeth in the last few weeks."

Ginny made a rumbling sound in the back of her throat to let him know she was thinking it over. He clamped the phone so hard to his ear it hurt. "I didn't see much of her," she said at last. "She come by to visit a few times. And she never missed Sunday supper with the Mistuh and Mizzus."

"Did you notice anything unusual or different about her? Something she might've said or done that struck you as odd? Anything at all?"

She made that rumbling sound again. "Naw suh. Just that she wuz too skinny. I scolded her for eatin' like a bird."

"Are you sure there was nothing else?" Joe persisted. He didn't like pushing the woman but he had little choice.

More rumbling. Then: "Well, she did ax me 'bout this fortuneteller I go to sometime. I reckon that wuz unusual for her. She said she wanted to have her future told, so I told her where Sister Ruth stay."

"Sister Ruth," he echoed.

"That's right. Out on the highway like you goin' to Zephyrhills? She got that sign with the big red hand in front of her house. She a palm reader, but she reads more'n palms."

"Yeah, I know where that is. I never knew Lizabeth went in for that sort of thing."

"Naw suh, me neither. That's why I say it wuz unusual."

"Do you think she went to see Sister Ruth?"

"I don't know, Mistuh Joe. Alls I know is she wuz mighty curious 'bout her."

He realized he had a death-grip on the phone and relaxed a little. "I guess I'll have to go see her myself."

"Whatcha gone do, Mistuh Joe? Have your fortune told?"

"You read my mind, Ginny," he said in a feeble attempt to brighten the somber mood.

Ginny humored him with a sad, rumbling laugh. He thanked her again and hung up. He looked at his watch: 10:45. He wondered if Sister Ruth was open for business this early in the morning. After a trip to the bathroom to spring a coffee leak, he sprinkled some Vitalis on his hair and ran a comb through it, then climbed into his '55 Buick Roadmaster and set out to see the fortuneteller. He broke the speed limit all the way there, feeling an urgency he didn't fully understand.

* * *

Fat drops of rain splattered on the windshield as he pulled up on the shell-and-sand driveway beside the wooden sign with a big red hand painted on a white background. The universal sign of the palm reader. The house was a small A-frame in need of a new coat of paint. The rain-hazed windows were hung with red lace curtains, and a little colored boy appeared behind the screen door, his eyes wide and fixed on Joe.

He got out of the car and walked up to the door, giving

the boy a smile. "Hi there," said Joe. "Is Sister Ruth here?"

The boy studied him for a long moment, then turned his head and yelled: "Mama! They's a white man here." He gave Joe another inquisitive look before fading into the dim interior of the house.

Joe waited on the front stoop, catching raindrops with his head and shoulders and sniffing the aroma of baking biscuits wafting through the screen door. Preceded by a whisper of unseen movement, a slender almond-skinned woman appeared at the door and regarded him impassively. Her yellow sundress showed off a fine womanly physique, and the multicolored scarf wrapped carefully around the crown of her head made Joe think of an African queen.

"Sister Ruth?"

"Yass."

"Are you open for . . . uh, can you give me a reading?"

Her expression—or absence of same—did not change. "Come back after noon. I'm busy now." Her voice was smooth, yet sharp-edged.

"Ginny sent me. She said you could help me."

She furrowed her thin brow suspiciously. "Ginny who?"

Joe silently cursed himself for not knowing Ginny's last name, then answered as best he could. "The Ginny who works for Monroe Tibbedeaux."

"You cain't come back this afternoon?"

"No. I'm sorry, but this can't wait."

She relented. "Come on in then. But I'll have to watch my biscuits."

"Thank you."

She led him through the living room where the little boy was playing with toy soldiers, then down a short hallway and into a gloomy parlor. She waved him to a chair pulled up to a small, round table, then sat opposite him.

"Five dollars," she said. He gave her a five-spot and she tucked it down the front of her sundress, securely between her cocoa-colored breasts.

Reaching her left hand across the table, she said, "Give me your right hand."

Joe's simple plan was to let her tell his fortune as sort of an icebreaker and then hit her with questions about Lizabeth. He gave her his hand, palm up. He'd never been to a palm-reader before; he was surprised at his sudden apprehension. He had always thought fortunetelling was a lot of bunk, but something about the regal Sister Ruth seriously challenged his belief. He suddenly feared that she actually could divine his future.

She cradled his hand in her long fingers and began to trace the lines of his palm with the fingernail of her other hand's index finger. Ghostly goose feathers fluttered up his arm and tickled the back of his neck and he shuddered.

She examined his palm the way a lost motorist studies a roadmap. "Hmm," she sighed. "You have a very specific question in mind. About someone you love. Umm-hmm. Someone who has left you behind. A woman."

"Yes," he whispered. He felt tears welling up in his eyes.

"You want to find her . . . but this is a dangerous path for you. You should not—" Sister Ruth closed her eyes and stiffened her spine. "A violent death. Someone . . ."

"What? Go on."

She opened her eyes and let go of his hand. "That's all I can tell you now."

He left his hand on the table, a useless slab of pale meat. "Wait a minute. You can't just stop there."

Her fingers fished in the bosom of her dress and extracted the fiver. She put the folded bill in his open palm, her brown eyes avoiding his. "My biscuits are burning," she said, standing.

Joe turned his hand over and dropped the money on the table. "I'll wait. I need to ask you something."

"I cain't tell you nothin'. The psychic waves were all mixed up. Like static on a radio, when one station comes in on top of another? You're too *staticky*. Just forget everything I said. None of that was about you."

He knew she was lying but he let that pass. It was time to lay his cards on the table. He said, "My ex-wife was murdered and I think she came to see you recently. That's what I want to know about. Go see to your biscuits. I'll wait right here."

Sister Ruth folded her arms across her chest and jutted her sharp chin at him. "I don't know nothing about that. You leave now."

"Look," he said. "I don't want to make trouble for you, but if you don't talk to me, you'll end up talking to the police. I think you'd rather talk to me."

She looked at him as if he were a coral snake coiled in her chair. It was a look of angry fear and it told Joe she didn't know he was bluffing about the police. Even a good psychic can be off the beam sometimes. She went to rescue her biscuits and he leaned back in the chair and thought about what she had said when she was reading his palm—or whatever she was reading. *A violent death. A dangerous path.* Lizabeth's death? His? Either way, it was a warning.

She came back into the parlor and sat across from him. She smelled of freshly baked bread and clean perspiration. Thunder rumbled in the distance and rain drummed on the roof.

"I'm Joe Dall," he began. "My ex-wife is . . . was Lizabeth Tibbedeaux. Monroe F. Tibbedeaux's daughter. You've heard of him, right? Ginny, their maid, said she thought Lizabeth might've come to see you last week or the week before."

"Lots of folks come to me. They don't tell me their names."

"Lizabeth was very attractive. Shoulder-length blond hair,

deep blue eyes. She had this cute little mole over the corner of her mouth. Twenty-six years old and so full of life . . . If you saw her, you would definitely remember her."

"I remember her," she said. "And her friend."

He moved to the edge of his chair and propped his elbows on the table. "Tell me about the friend."

"She was wearing a wig and sunglasses but I knew she wasn't no redhead. I knew who she was. I seen her movies. It was that actress. Laura D'Amore. She was the one wanted her fortune told."

Laura D'Amore. As soon as Sister Ruth said the name, it snapped into place. Lizabeth and the former movie star came together to form a small portion of the puzzle for which he as yet had no other interlocking pieces.

"I reckon she liked what she heard," Sister Ruth said. "She gave me fifty dollars."

"So Lizabeth didn't want *her* fortune told."

"No. She just brought Miz D'Amore to me. Sometimes Fate needs a little help bringing people together. Your young lady was just the help."

Joe rubbed his chin. It was still sore from Bull Kelso's beefy fist. "So you can't really tell me anything about Lizabeth. I mean, you didn't pick up any . . . psychic signals or anything?" The skeptic in Joe knew he was grasping at improbable straws, but those otherworldly straws were all he had at the moment.

She shook her head, no. "She was . . . hazy. Like dirty glass. Her light didn't shine through."

"What about Laura D'Amore? What did you pick up from her?"

"That ain't your business."

"My business is finding out who killed my wife and why she was killed. If Laura D'Amore played some part in that, I need to know about it."

"Weren't nothing like that. That's all I can tell you."

"Okay." He stood up and looked down at her. He believed that probably was all she knew. "Thanks for your help."

"Uh-huh." She remained seated.

Joe considered asking her about the "dangerous path" she had mentioned, but nixed the idea. It didn't matter. No amount of danger was going to keep him from finding Lizabeth's killer. Of that he was certain, though he was certain of little else. He dropped an extra fiver on the table and went out into the rain.

* * *

He stopped at The Hilltop Drive-in Diner for a burger and a coke, and wolfed them down on the drive back to the lake. The rain had slacked off but the dark sky was ominous with the promise that worse weather was yet to come.

Dot was already at the lounge. Her Studebaker was parked in its usual spot in the rear of the long weathered-wood building. He parked next to it and went in through the back door.

"I was getting worried about you," she said through a haze of cigarette smoke.

"I had to run an errand," he said, licking burger grease from his fingers. "You're here early."

"Eleven-thirty's not so early." She took a sip of coffee from a cream-colored mug, and stubbed out her cigarette. She gave him an appraising look through squinted eyes. "So, how're you doing?"

He shrugged. "Okay, I guess. A little hung-over."

"What was that about Tibbedeaux wanting you to find the killer?"

"That's what he said." Joe went behind the bar and poured himself a cup of java. "He thinks I know things about Lizabeth nobody else knows and that I'm so 'obsessed' with her that I'll just naturally be able to solve the murder and nail the killer. Hell, she's been out of my life for a year."

"Out of your life maybe, but not out of your heart. She's the only reason you're still here. Except for her, you'd be back home in Georgia now. Or anywhere but here. Am I right?"

"Yeah." With Dot the short answer was the best answer. Like a good trial lawyer, she rarely asked questions she didn't already know the answers to. And sometimes she seemed to know Joe better than he knew himself.

"So," she said, lighting another smoke. "Are you going to do it? Are you going to look for her killer?"

"You're the crime expert, not me." He tried to grin but it felt like an ugly grimace. "Can you see me playing detective?"

"I can see you turning this town upside-down to find the son of a bitch who killed Lizabeth. And God help him if you do."

He slurped some coffee and said nothing. In his mind's eye he saw his hands wrapped around the throat of a faceless man, choking the life out of him. Balancing the scales, the killer's life for Lizabeth's. And the guy was getting a bargain because—whoever he was—Lizabeth's life had to be worth ten of his. Then the faceless man dissolved and Joe was choking nothing but air.

"I want to help you do it, Joe." She was as earnest as he'd ever seen her.

"Sherlock to my Watson, no doubt." He rubbed his hands together and noticed a slight tremor in his fingers.

He pointed at her pack of Camels, she nodded and he shook one out and lit it, inhaling deeply. He'd been trying to quit smoking but wasn't having much success. He hadn't had much success at anything since Lizabeth gave him the boot. "I told Tibbedeaux I'd do what I could. For Lizabeth. Sure as hell not for him."

Dot nodded. He could almost see cerebral cogs spinning

wheels behind her eyes, her brain gearing up for great feats of detection.

"What do you know about Laura D'Amore?" he asked.

"The movie star? What's she got to do with anything?"

"Maybe nothing," he said, watching the smoke streaming up from the ember-and-ash end of his cigarette "Lizabeth went with her to see a fortuneteller. Sister Ruth, a palm reader out on the Zephyrhills highway."

"Interesting," Dot mused. "They say D'Amore keeps to herself. That she has little to do with the locals. Why would she have been keeping company with Lizabeth?"

"I don't know. But I think I should look into it. "

"Definitely," she agreed. She raised a single finger. "Rule number one of The Detective's Handbook: *Even the smallest piece of information may be important. Don't overlook anything.*"

"You've got a handbook?"

Dot tapped the raised finger to her head. "Up here. Based on hundreds of cases I've studied over the years."

"Oh." Joe tried not to let his disappointment show. Dot surely meant well, and she probably really believed that reading all those detective magazines made her some kind of authority on crime, but Joe knew better. The articles he'd seen were nothing but sensationalized police-blotter reports written to titillate voyeuristic readers with a taste for morbid sleaze.

"I'll give you the other rules as they come up." She flashed a Cheshire cat's smile.

As soon as you make them up, he thought. He said, "Okay."

He finished his coffee and cigarette, then fell into his usual work routine. He restocked the bar, swept the floor, cleaned the bathroom, inventoried the supplies and took out the garbage. There was more to the job than giving unruly drunks the bum's rush. He had to be pretty handy with a toilet brush too.

A couple of hours later a rumpled man in a gray light-weight raincoat sauntered into the lounge. A cold cigar stub rested securely in the corner of his mouth and a leather valise dangled less securely from his left hand. He wore a narrow-brimmed brown hat with a red band and a little feathered thing sticking out of it that might've been a fishing lure. He was a chunky man of medium height, with deep-set eyes in a cratered moon-face. His gray eyes locked onto Joe as he waddled toward the bar. "Joseph Dall," he said, his voice a wet rattle in the back of his throat.

"Yeah." Joe did a slow spin on the barstool to face him.

"Homer Dix," he said with an air of boredom. "Mr. Tibbedeaux sent me."

Remembering the name, Joe said, "You're the private detective."

Dot's eyes snapped up from her magazine to focus on an honest-to-God flesh-and-blood private dick.

"Right," he said, swinging the valise up onto the bar and hiking his broad butt onto the stool next to Joe. "Got some goodies for you." He unlatched the valise and pulled out a manila folder. "This here's the copy of the autopsy report and homicide investigator's report. Read 'em and weep."

"What kind of crack is—"

"This," he said, tossing a laminated card on the bar, "is your private investigator's license, issued by the licensing board of the state of Florida. When Tibbedeaux pulls political strings, the government humps start dancing, from the governor on down. Talk about cutting through your red tape."

Dot's jaw dropped and her eyes bugged out. Joe stared at the ID with his name and photo on it. The photo had been cropped from a studio portrait he and Lizabeth had sat for in the first month of their marriage.

Dix took off his hat, ran a hand over his sweaty balding head, then put the hat back on.

"I'm no detective," Joe protested.

"You are now, pal," said Dix with a cigar-stuffed smirk. Then he put another official document in front of Joe. "This is your permit to carry a concealed weapon. Keep that and your PI license in your wallet at all times."

Dix cast a furtive glance around the lounge and saw that the scattered handful of customers paid him no attention. He reached into the valise once more and pulled out a pistol in a brown leather holster and a small box of ammo. "This here's your weapon. Colt .38. Compliments of Monroe Tibbedeaux. It ain't loaded. Put five in the cylinder and keep the hammer on the empty chamber. But you probably know that, right? Being a war vet and all." He closed the valise and snapped down the latches. "I wear mine in the small of my back where it don't show. Them shoulder rigs are for the birds. In this heat those straps will give you a bitch of a rash in a Florida flash."

He put the holstered pistol on top of the manila folder, reached inside his raincoat and extracted a white envelope and placed it in Joe's hand. "One thousand dollars cash," he said. "Five hundred retainer and five hundred to cover expenses. Walking-around money. If you need more, let Tibbedeaux know."

"I . . . I wasn't expecting all this," Joe said lamely.

"When you work for Tibbedeaux, you go first class."

"I'm not working for him."

Homer Dix chortled, shifting his cigar to the opposite corner of his mouth. "You're on his dime now, kid. Way I see it, that makes you his *dime detective*." He slid off the stool, gave a nod to Dot, then fixed his eyes on Joe. "Good luck, laddy buck. Congratulations on your new career."

Joe followed Dix outside and caught up with him as he was sliding his bulk behind the wheel of his '54 Plymouth. Dix swatted at a horsefly in front of his face and looked as if he might want to swat Joe out of the way too.

"Dix, are you, uh, working the case? The murder?"

"I'm looking into it. But that's not your worry. You work your angle and I'll do what I do. Tibbedeaux wants us working independently of each other. Figures the chances of coming up with something are better that way, he says. He likes dealing from a full deck. I'm the Jack and you're the Joker."

Joe rested a hand on the top of the open driver's door as he looked down at Dix, who was sticking his key in the ignition. "I hardly know where to start," Joe told him. "I could, uh, sure use the advice of a pro like you, Dix."

Dix laughed, almost dislodging the cigar from the corner of his mouth. "My advice, off the record, is to bank that cash and forget the whole thing. I got a nose for nasty cases," he tapped his bulbous nose with a stubby finger, "and this one already stinks to high heaven. Do a little digging, there's no telling what kind of dirty crap you'll turn up, but you can bet it'll be something you'll wish you never found. Trust me, Dall. Keep your snozz out of it. You were married to the victim, for shit's sake. That means you're screwed right outta the gate. You can't do good solid detective work if you're emotionally involved. Even if you know what the hell you're doing—which you don't."

Joe said nothing. Dix tried to close the door but Joe held it in place, unyielding.

"All right," Dix said with a ponderous sigh. "Here it is. Start with what you already know and go from there. Talk to the victim's friends and family, boyfriends, anybody she had recent contact with. Find out all you can about how she spent her last days. Do it right and a picture will begin to take shape. A picture of her world. Then put yourself in the middle of that picture, and—if you can—put yourself in her skin. Get what I mean?"

He nodded.

"Get your hands on any paperwork you can. Phone bills, credit card receipts, canceled checks, stuff like that. People leave paper trails. Find hers and see where it leads. Okay? Can I shut my door now?"

Joe let go of the car door. "Thanks, Dix."

Dix slammed the door, hit the starter and cranked the Plymouth's engine. He leaned his head out the window and said, "One more thing. If you get lucky and find something, that's the time you start watching your back. The closer you get to the killer, the better your chances of being dead."

Dix slapped the gearshift into first, popped the clutch and drove off, leaving a little cloud of black exhaust. Joe went back inside. Dot was hanging up the phone, cigarette dangling from her lips. He could tell by the expression on her face that the phone call had tweaked her in some way.

Shaking her head with eyes wide in wonder, she lowered her voice and said, "That was Monroe Tibbedeaux. He said he's sending me a check to cover your rent on the bungalow and to hire somebody to temporarily replace you so you can devote all your time to the 'special job' you're doing for him. A check for one thousand simoleons."

"No kidding," Joe said. "The same figure he gave me. I guess the man doesn't deal in amounts less than a thousand."

"Damned if we ain't making out like a couple of bandits on this deal. It's just a shame it has to be at poor Lizabeth's expense."

"Yeah." He sat heavily on the stool and massaged his temples. His headache was making a comeback and his tongue couldn't seem to stop worrying his loose tooth.

"So, shamus, what's your first move?" Dot asked.

He scowled. "I don't know. All I feel like doing is crawling back into bed. I killed half that bottle of Seagrams last night. Dumb move."

"You needed it." She stubbed out her smoke, filled a shot glass with whiskey and set it in front of him. "Hair of the hound that nipped you. Drink it down. It'll level you out some." He tossed it back and swallowed it down. "Thanks."

"What was that little tête-à-tête outside with the dick?" she asked.

"He gave me a few tips on detective work."

Of course Dot was hot to know what Dix had told him, so he hit the highlights for her (leaving out Dix's advice to bank the money and forget the whole thing). She nodded her approval, then said, "He's probably right, you know. About the danger. You best start packing that hardware." She shot a glance at the pistol on the bar. "And watch your back, starting right now."

Joe took the "goodies" Dix had given him and went to the bungalow. He unsnapped the holster, drew the .38 and acquainted himself with the blue-steel beauty; he spun the cylinder, sighted down the short barrel and dry-fired it a few times. Its heft felt good and natural in his hand. A good fit. He opened the box of ammo and snugged five 158-grain cartridges into five chambers, and as soon as the pistol was loaded, he got that thrilling little flutter in his chest that comes with knowing you're holding an instrument of death. This was the first time since his discharge from the Corps that he'd held a loaded weapon, and it unlocked a door deep within that had been shut and sealed with the close of the war. He turned toward the mirror on the bedroom wall and aimed the gun at his reflection—at the stone-faced warrior that had re-emerged through that shadowy inner doorway. He cocked the hammer and drew a bead on the center of his chest. The urge to squeeze the trigger was nearly overpowering, but the warrior came forward to exert discipline and Joe lowered the pistol and gently thumbed the hammer down. He shuddered as if suddenly chilled as he slipped the .38 back into the holster, recalling vivid moments of deadly combat.

He took off his belt, ran it through the slots in the leather holster and strapped it on with the pistol at the small of his back, as Dix had suggested. Then he pulled his shirttail out of his pants so that the pistol was hidden from sight, and he drew the weapon several times to get the feel of the behind-the-back draw. It was not as awkward as he'd thought it would be. He wondered if Dix had ever had to use his gun on the job. Somehow Joe couldn't picture the man firing his weapon in anger; he was willing to bet that Dix did all his shooting with a hidden camera.

Leaving the pistol on just to get used to it, he went into the kitchenette and sat down at the Formica-topped table to read the carbon copies Tibbedeaux had sent him. He opened the folder and started with the crime-scene report. It was short, and the county investigator who had written it speculated that the murder might have been committed elsewhere since the bedroom where the body was found contained no evidence of a struggle, nor anything out of the ordinary (except, of course, for the victim's body and the brassiere twisted around her neck). The bed covers had been turned down but the sheets were free of any stains a sexual encounter would likely have left. The house showed no signs of forcible entry, no evidence indicating burglary.

Joe read ahead to the coroner's report. Stark phrases jumped out at him: ". . . the body of a well-developed white female . . . asphyxia due to ligature strangulation . . . no spermatozoa in the vagina . . . no vaginal abrasions consistent with forced intercourse . . ."

He got up and rushed to the kitchen sink to throw up. He gagged a few times but nothing came up. He splashed cold water on his face, toweled dry, then went back to the table to finish reading the autopsy report. As he read the clinical details of the coroner's dissection of Lizabeth's body, he could *see* her laid out on the steel table, cold flesh on inanimate bone—a lifeless shell containing non-functioning biological systems. He tore his eyes from the page; he didn't want to think of her that way. He got up and walked around the room, feeling claustrophobic. He was suddenly flushed with heat and sweating, so he went to the jalousie windows and cranked open the slats of frosted glass and stood there staring out at nothing in particular. The air from outside was sultry but it was freshened by the scent of the lake and surrounding vegetation, and he stood there letting the gentle breeze wash over him until the claustrophobia passed. Having lived in Florida for two years, he was completely acclimated to the tropical climate, and he actually liked the heat; he had come close to freezing to death in a foxhole in Korea, so two eggs over easy on a hot Florida sidewalk were fine with him and sure as hell beat diarrhea frozen in your undershorts in the Korean cold.

He went back to the table, took a deep breath and resumed his required reading. The coroner's examination of the body revealed no defensive wounds, nothing under the deceased's fingernails to indicate that she had scratched her attacker, nor evidence of any kind that Lizabeth had resisted her strangler. Her blood alcohol content was zero and there were no traces of any known drugs. The murder weapon was almost certainly the size-34 B-cup brassiere found around her neck.

It didn't make sense that she didn't try to fight off her attacker. How could she have remained passive while someone was strangling her to death? Could she have grabbed the killer's hands or wrists without scratching and clawing his skin? Maybe the killer wore gloves and long sleeves.

The only real surprise in the coroner's report was the description of a tattoo on the inside of Lizabeth's left thigh.

She hadn't had any tattoos when he was married to her, and he couldn't imagine her getting one. The Lizabeth he had known and loved wouldn't have allowed a tattoo artist to defile her flawless skin with a crude ink drawing, but there it was in the coroner's report, a description of a black rose the size of a silver dollar. A black rose within a red triangle, etched on her inner thigh. Joe went back through the photos and found the tattoo in one of them, just as described.

He needed a smoke. He went into the bedroom and rummaged in his sock drawer until he found an old unopened pack of Lucky Strikes. He ripped opened the cellophane, jammed one in his mouth and lit it with a match, savoring the first inhalation the way a thirsty man savors a mouthful of cold beer on a hot day. As he tried to make sense of the rose-and-triangle tattoo, he closed his eyes and saw it again on the milky flesh of Lizabeth's thigh.

A death-glazed eye appeared in the center of the rose.

The eye winked.

* * *

He described the tattoo to Dot and asked if it meant anything to her. He couldn't bring himself to show her the grim, grainy photos.

She shook her head. "It's nothing I've ever seen before. But . . ."

"But what?"

"I don't know," she said, sketching her version of the tattoo on a cocktail napkin. "It looks familiar. Like something I *should* have seen somewhere. You know what I mean?"

"No." He stared dumbly at the sketch.

She studied her drawing for a long moment, then said, "Like something that's there right in front of you all the time but you don't notice it—and then it jumps out at you and you say, 'Oh yeah, I knew that was there all along.'"

He shot her a look of bewilderment.

"It's very womanly," she said, turning pensive.

"Womanly," he echoed.

"Yeah. The flower of womanhood. And the triangle . . ." She tapped her sketch with the pencil point. "When I was in high school, there was this boy who sat next to me in class. Luther Fox. Poor old Luther, he was ugly as sin but he sure could draw. Anyway, old Luther liked to draw naked women. Big-breasted babes like those calendar girls you see on auto shop walls. He put so much loving detail into those bosoms they almost leaped off the page, but when it came to the lower anatomy, all he did was draw a triangle between their legs. I used to wonder if Luther was preserving their modesty or if he didn't know what women have *down there*. Anyway, thanks to ugly old Luther, every time I see a triangle I think of a woman's crotch."

"Damn, Dot," he said, blushing.

"Don't be such a prude, Joe. I think we're mature adults by now, don't you?"

"Yeah, okay. So the rose and the triangle are symbols of womanhood. Why would she have them tattooed on her thigh? I mean, why do you need a symbol of something right next to the real thing?" His cheeks flushed with heat again.

"Why did she get a tattoo in the first place? You don't see many women with tattoos these days, outside a carnival or a brothel. Certainly not on someone like Lizabeth." Dot furrowed her brow and tapped her pencil on the bar's buffed mahogany.

"Well, there's only one tattoo joint in Dodd City. I know the guy who runs the place. If she got it done there, maybe he can tell me what the hell it means."

"You should talk to her friends too," she said. "I'll bet she didn't go alone to get herself tattooed. Considering *where* the tattoo is, she most likely would've wanted a chaperon along."

"Yeah," he said, trying not to think about another man touching Lizabeth there.

"You do know who her friends were, right?"

"I know who they were when we were still together," he said. "But obviously she made new ones I know nothing about. Like Laura D'Amore."

Dot held the pencil to her pursed lips. "You have to talk to her, you know. Miss D'Amore."

"I know. She probably won't give me the time of day. Being a big movie star and all."

"Former movie star. And don't take no for an answer. Turn on the old Joe Dall charm. She'll talk to you."

"Yeah, sure." He cracked a wan smile. "I'm ready for my close-up, Miss D'Amore," he said, bastardizing a line from another of Liz's favorite films.

Dot chuckled. "That's the spirit."

Joe slid off the barstool. "I'm off to see the tattoo wizard," he said, alluding to Dot's favorite movie, *The Wizard of Oz*. Given her obsession with crime and detection, Joe would've figured her favorite to be something like *The Big Heat*, or *The Maltese Falcon*, but it was the munchkin-land fantasy that won her hardboiled heart in the end. She wasn't so hardboiled after all. She just talked a tough game.

She wished him good luck, then added, "I'm going to see what I can dig up on Laura D'Amore. I know some beauty-shop gals who keep up with all the local gossip and they're bound to have some tasty tidbits on our resident celluloid vamp."

"Great," he said, marveling at her way with words. He figured she was good enough to write for those crime rags she so eagerly devoured. "I'll be back in a bit."

As he started out the door, she said, "Hey, Joe? When's the funeral?"

"I don't know. I'll find out this afternoon when I get Liz's house key from her old man. I want to nose around in the house, see if I can find anything."

"You're going, aren't you? To the funeral?"

"Yeah, I guess. I hate funerals, but I think I should be there."

"I'll go with you, if you want me to."

"Yeah, sure. Thanks, Dot."

She waved off his thanks with a cigarette between her fingers. "They say killers often show up at their victims' funerals. We'll keep our eyes peeled for suspicious-looking characters. Who knows? We might turn up a lead."

Joe nodded. "I wonder if Laura D'Amore will be there. Or if she even knows Liz is dead."

"We'll see," she said with a restrained smile. He could see she was thrilled for the chance to play detective. But for Joe this was no game. It was something he had to do for the sake of the only woman he'd ever really loved.

He walked out to his car. The grease and onions of the Hilltop burger were talking back to him, telling him he wanted a cigarette, but he hadn't brought his pack with him. On the way to town he stopped at a gas station and spent some of the money Tibbedeaux had sent him. While the pump jockey filled up the tank with ethyl, Joe went inside and bought a pack of Luckies and a pair of aviator type sunglasses. He put them on, then tipped the jockey a quarter for checking the oil and water. The guy touched the brim of his cap in a non-military salute, and Joe drove on to the tattoo parlor.

He couldn't get the image of Lizabeth's ghostly wink out of his mind.

CHAPTER THREE

The Salty Dog Tattoo Parlor was a cracker box of a room interconnected with the larger Black Cat Gun Room, both run by "Captain" Eddie Wilcox. The "Captain" was a bogus rank, as Eddie's bum heart had kept him out of military service. The dual shop was on the corner of Palmetto and Palm, with the entrance to the gunroom on Palm and the storefront of the tattoo parlor on Palmetto. If you liked one-stop shopping, Wilcox was happy to oblige; he'd tattoo your ass, sell you guns and ammo, then send you on your way, packing heat and engraved with manly skin art.

Joe knew Eddie from his short-lived stint as a life-insurance salesman. The only tattoo Joe had was the Marine Corps insignia on his upper arm, acquired back in his *Semper Fi* boot camp days, and Eddie was always hot to cut him a new one.

When Joe walked into the Salty Dog, Eddie came ambling out of the gunroom and immediately started running his usual needling spiel. He reeked of sour sweat and gun oil. "Whaddaya say, Big Joe? You finally gonna let me do that bare-ass arm?"

"No thanks, Eddie. I just need to ask you a few questions. You remember my ex-wife Lizabeth, right?"

"Yeah, sure." He looked puzzled, no doubt wondering why Joe was bringing up his ex. Apparently he hadn't heard the news.

"Did she ever come to you for a tattoo?"

"Hey, now, Joe, I just give the customers what they ask for. I never—"

"Relax, Eddie. I'm not here to give you any grief. I just want to know if you tattooed her."

"Yeah, about a month ago, I guess it was. She came in with a drawing of what she wanted. A rose in a triangle. A black rose." Eddie wiped beads of sweat off his bald, deeply tanned head. His handlebar mustache was waxed and sculpted, tapered to high, wide points.

"Anybody with her?"

"Yeah, an older lady. Queer-looking duck. Dark glasses, scarf around her head, like she was going for incognito. Pretty sure the hair was a wig. Spoke in whispers to your ex. Never said a word to me. Real cold fish. Something spooky about the broad."

"Spooky?"

"Uh, shit, you know, uh . . . hell, I don't know . . ." Eddie hemmed and hawed. "Something about her gave me the creeps, that's all. I just got the feeling I didn't want to turn my back on her. I was glad as hell *she* didn't want a tattoo."

Joe was quiet a moment, digesting Eddie's take on the mystery woman.

"What's the deal, Joe?" he asked. "Why the first degree?"

"Lizabeth was murdered," Joe told him. His voice was surprisingly steady when he said it. "I'm hunting down whoever did it."

"The hell you say! Murdered? Jesus Christ!"

Joe pushed on. "You ever see a tattoo like that one before? The rose and triangle?"

"Naw. Not that I remember. I know I never did one like it—till I did that one for your ex."

"How did she act with this woman? Did they seem like . . . close friends?"

Eddie nodded. "The way that woman was whispering and cooing in her ear and touching her, I'd say they were pretty fucking cozy, yeah. She held Lizabeth's hand while I worked on her."

Liz had never liked needles, and Joe had no trouble seeing her in need of a friendly hand to hold. He went on with the Q & A. "You know what that movie star who lives out on the Zephyrhills highway looks like? Laura D'Amore?"

Eddie shook his head. "Unless she's been in war movies or westerns, I wouldn't. Why?"

"She was probably your spooky woman."

"No shit? A big Hollywood star in my little old shop. Ain't that a kicker." He grinned, showing bad teeth. Then his grin collapsed, bringing a mustached curtain down on his unsightly dental display. "They say she's some kind of weirdo, don't they? Some kind of degenerate?"

Joe shrugged. "I don't know. I'm not really up on Hollywood gossip."

"Commies and leftwing perverts," he said, "Hollywood's full of 'em. Thank God for John Wayne and Audie Murphy. Right, pal?"

"Yeah, sure, Eddie." Joe headed for the door.

"You still out at the Sundown?"

"Yeah."

"I'll come out some night and we can drink some brewskies and you can tell me how you wasted them slant-eyed Commies."

"I'm not much for war stories."

"Don't be so goddamn modest. If I was you, I'd be bragging my ass off, but—" he thumped his chest, "—this bum ticker kept me out of the fun."

"Shit I saw over there was nothing like the movies. And it sure as hell wasn't fun. Anybody who brags about killing other soldiers is a first-class asshole."

With that bit of hard-won wisdom, Joe left "Captain" Eddie Wilcox to his wartime fantasies, his tattoos and his shop full of guns. He drove out to the Tibbedeaux mansion at the edge of town, used the intercom at the wrought-iron gate and asked Ginny if the Lord and Master was home. She said he was spending the day at his Tampa office and wasn't expected back until later in the evening. Joe told her he needed the key to Lizabeth's house and asked if Mrs. Tibbedeaux would know where the key was. "She don't hardly know where *she* at, Mistuh Joe, the way the doctor got her doped up. I reckon the Mistuh got it." Joe thanked her and started back to the car, then turned around and raised her on the intercom again.

"Ginny, do you know when the funeral is?"

"Day after tomorrow," she said, her deep voice rattling the intercom's little speaker. "Over to the First Methodist Church. Eleven o'clock. I wisht I could go, but you know how that is."

He knew all right. No way would Tibbedeaux allow a Negro at his daughter's funeral. Never mind that Ginny had practically raised Liz from infancy. "Yeah. That's a shame. I know Lizzy would've wanted you there. Thanks, Ginny."

Determined not to be put off by his lack of a key, Joe drove to Lizabeth's house on Shady Lane and used his pocketknife to pick the lock on the back door. It took a while, as his lock-picking skills were a bit rusty, but the lock tumbled and the door swung open, and he crept into the house where his former wife had been found strangled to death.

The big house had been a bone of contention between them. He'd been against moving out of their modest little duplex and into this sprawling Spanish-style abode because her old man paid for it. Joe hadn't wanted to take handouts from her father. He was sure it was the old man's way of undermining him and their marriage, but Liz had been raised in the proverbial lap of luxury and thought nothing of it. They'd had more than a few heated exchanges over this house, and in the end, Joe gave in. Lizabeth was accustomed to having her way, and he wasn't strong enough to deny her anything she wanted. Standing up to her old man was no big deal, but Joe had seldom stood up to Liz on major issues because he was afraid of losing her. In the end he lost her anyway.

The house had been just one of many contentious subjects, and they growled at each other and worried over those otherwise insignificant bones like junkyard dogs in an on-going turf war. The turf was their marriage—a marriage measured in months, not years. The months of rancor piled up. Each year thinned like a calendar down to its last few months, until the last page of their flimsy union was torn off and tossed away. The love that had first bound them together was buried somewhere down at the bottom of the trash bin, covered over with the litter of lost months and disputed bones. With her father subverting them every step of the way, their marriage had never really had a prayer. Somehow his love for Lizabeth had survived. Her love for him apparently hadn't.

So here he was, rummaging through the house where they had lived together in connubial sorrow, looking for some clue that could lead him to her murderer—and to an explanation of why someone had wanted her dead. The bedroom was the worst—not because it was the room where she had died, but because it was the place where they had made love despite all their differences. In those bouts of shared passion, all the arguments and hostilities had fallen away and they had touched, if only briefly, the heart of the mystery that bound them together. Call it love. Call it mutual need. Call it blind. Whatever you called it, it had been real. Of that, he was certain. Considering that she was the spoiled brat and only child of a rich and powerful man, and Joe was a screwed-up war veteran from an unwashed working-class family, it was amazing that they got along as well as they had. And in spite of all the odds, he'd never given up the hope of someday getting back together with her. Who said a battle-hardened Marine couldn't be a moony-eyed dreamer? Liz always said he was a walking contradiction. He figured she'd had it about right.

Now there was zero hope of reconciliation in this life, but still he was haunted by that provocative wink from Lizabeth's eerie image on a moonlit lake, determined to find out what it meant.

He stood at the foot of the bed and stared down at the stain on beige carpet. He knew what had left that stain. He had seen enough death in Korea to know that the bladder and bowels usually let go when the body expires. No matter what anybody might tell you, there is no dignity in dying. The flesh-and-bone vehicle that carries you through life betrays you, shuts you down and casts you adrift. It's the ultimate divorce. And the best lawyers or doctors in the world can't make it go down any easier.

He got a sick feeling in his belly that didn't go away until he left the bedroom. But what the hell? He figured it was better than bawling like a baby with a full diaper. He went to the roll-top desk in the den, sat down and went through the drawers, reading over the bank statements and miscellaneous paperwork he found. Nothing jumped out at him as significant. He found a bundle of letters bound by a yellow ribbon, untied it and thumbed through them. Letters and birthday cards to Liz from well-wishing friends and ingratiating relatives wishing to stay in the good graces of the wealthy Tibbedeaux family. All in all, Liz hadn't left much of a paper trail. Joe knew from experience that her father handled the important financial and legal matters. Her palm-size address book was in the drawer where she'd always kept it. He thumbed through the small pages, then stuck it in his pocket. He'd give it a close reading later.

Next he checked the bathroom adjoining the bedroom. He looked through the medicine cabinet and found prescription medicine for a urinary tract infection and a bottle of tranquilizers dated a week before her death. To his knowledge, she had never needed tranquilizers before, and he wondered why Dr. Simpson had seen fit to prescribe them for her. What had been going on in her life to give her a case of nerves? She was always a bit high-strung, but never to the point of needing pills. Had she told Simpson what was making her nervous? Would he tell Joe if he asked him? He would if Monroe Tibbedeaux gave him the nod. At this point, it was the only possible lead he had, other than her relationship with Laura D'Amore.

He spent another half hour rambling through the house, but turned up nothing else of real importance. He went back into the bedroom, opened the walk-in closet and buried his nose in her clothing, catching the scent of her favorite perfume on some of them. He went through her drawers and resisted the impulse to fondle her folded panties, figuring that would make him some kind of pervert. He left, feeling as empty as the unoccupied house.

* * *

He drove back to the lake, went into the bungalow and called Tibbedeaux's Tampa office. His secretary answered and told him to wait while she located him. A few minutes later, he came on the line.

"Hello, Joseph," he said. "Mr. Dix tells me you're a full-fledged private eye now. Have you turned up something already?"

"I just came from Liz's house. I found a bottle of tranquilizers in the medicine cabinet. Did you know she was taking nerve pills?"

"No, I didn't."

"Dr. Simpson prescribed them, and I was thinking that if you give him a call and tell him to talk to me, he could tell me why she was taking them. Maybe she confided—"

"I'll ask him myself," he said. "Give me your number and I'll call you back."

Joe gave him his number. He didn't like being cut out of the play, but Daddy Warbucks was dealing the cards. Joe had no choice but to trust him to pass on whatever the doctor might say.

"Good work, son," Tibbedeaux said. "This should be illuminating."

"Yeah, maybe."

He hung up. He lit a Lucky, downed a glass of orange juice and sat down at the kitchen table to wait for Monroe F. to call back.

Dot rapped softly on the door and came on in, saying, "Knock, knock."

"Hey, Dot. What's up?"

Her face was animated as she held up a magazine and said, "I found something in this old issue of *Confidential*. And you make fun of me for collecting these."

"What is it?"

She slapped the magazine down on the kitchen table, opened it to a dog-eared page and pointed out the article in question. "Right there in black and white. It says Miss D'Amore was blacklisted in Tinsel Town as a Communist sympathizer with unusual carnal appetites. She sued the magazine in 1955 and lost the suit. And the *Police Gazette* ran a story the same year, 'Torrid Town Vamp Swings Both Ways,' calling her a 'bisexual built for two,' and alluding to her indecent personal practices and subversive politics."

Cold fingers crawled up Joe's spine. "Is this stuff true? Is it gossip-column crap or is it for real?"

"She lost her lawsuit," said Dot, sitting opposite him at the kitchen table. "Think about it."

"So she's . . . a homo?"

"A bisexual," she corrected him. "Swings with the boys *and* the girls."

"But Liz wasn't . . . that way. She never . . ." He remembered how much she had loved *Torrid Town* and how she had idolized Laura D'Amore. Had the glamorous star seduced her? "That bitch," he said.

"Which bitch?" Dot gave him a crooked smile.

"D'Amore. If she corrupted Lizabeth . . ."

Dot folded her arms and propped her elbows on the table. "It wouldn't be the first time a big star took advantage of a starry-eyed fan. Usually it's the man enticing the innocent young girl, but it would work as well for a woman working a woman."

"Sickening," he said, staring at the magazine photo of Laura D'Amore. It looked like they had used a studio's publicity shot from *Torrid Town*, but the magazine's poor reproduction gave the photo a chintzy look and turned the alluring dark-haired vamp into a tawdry tramp. "I don't like thinking about it."

"Hey, it takes all kinds, you know? There are lots of lezzies and queers in Hollywood, but most of the big-name stars manage to keep it secret. Or if it comes out, it's only whispered about around rumor mills. Take Rock Hudson. Word is, *he's* a fag. Good-looking hunk of beef like that, people don't want to believe it. They'd rather believe what they see up on the big screen. But when politics comes into it, you get people with axes to grind, hot to expose Reds. The sex scandals are just icing on the cake. Chances are, if Laura D'Amore hadn't been associated with pinko political types, her sex life would've remained just a rumor. Like the whispers about Katherine

Hepburn and Joan Crawford. But after Joe McCarthy and the Red Scare, Communism was the kiss of death in Hollywood. The stakes were too high. The game got rough and they played it for keeps."

"So it's all dirty pool," Joe said. "Give me a good old-fashion shooting war any day. At least you know who the enemy is."

Dot pointed at his pack of smokes. "May I?"

"Sure. I probably owe you a pack anyway."

She shook one out and he lit it for her.

"Thanks," she said. "So what do you make of this sexual intrigue, Joe Detective? How does it help you find the killer?"

He shook his head. "Nothing's clicking."

"Think motive."

"Motive," he said. Still nothing clicked.

"Yeah. Why would somebody want Lizabeth dead?"

"Hell, if I knew that—"

"If Miss D'Amore had the hots for her, we could have ourselves a crime of passion."

"You think *she* killed Liz?"

Dot shrugged. "She certainly has to be considered a suspect."

Joe was out of his league and knew it. Dot, on the other hand, seemed like a seasoned pro, on top of things and in the know. "So we need to find out all we can about the movie star," he ventured.

"And her circle of friends. We need to know who all's living out there at Chez D'Amore."

"I'll bite. How do we do that?"

"Very carefully," she said, "since somebody there might be a murderer."

The phone rang. Joe's nerves jangled. It was Monroe Tibbedeaux. "Joseph? I'm afraid Dr. Simpson wasn't much help," he said. "Lizabeth was very tightlipped about herself.

She told him she was feeling anxious because of personal problems, the nature of which she chose not to divulge."

"That's it? That's all he said?"

"He said she did seem somewhat nervous, but that was all. Other than that, she was in good health."

Joe looked at Dot, who was all ears. He asked Tibbedeaux if he knew Liz had been associating with Laura D'Amore.

"She did mention that they had met and become friends. She thought very highly of the woman, you know. Perhaps too highly. I think she was star-struck, if you know what I mean."

"Yeah, I do."

"Why do you ask? Are you on to something?"

"I'm looking into a few things," Joe said, trying to sound like he knew what he was doing. "I'll let you know if anything pans out."

"See that you do. By the way, Lizabeth's at Bridges Funeral Home, if you want to pay your last respects."

"Right. Thanks." He hung up.

Dot asked, "What was that about?"

"That was the Orange Juice King himself. He checked with Dr. Simpson to find out why Liz had a prescription for tranquilizers. The doc didn't know anything. Just that Liz complained of bad nerves."

"Hmmm." She crushed out her butt. She *hmmed* again.

"What?"

"Another interesting piece of information. Liz didn't take pills when you were with her?"

"No. Not that I know of."

"So something was upsetting her to the point of needing sedatives," Dot mused. "Or . . ."

"Or what?"

"Or the pills were for someone else."

"But why would she get pills for somebody else?"

"We don't know that she did. The point is, don't accept anything at face value. Things aren't always as they appear on the surface."

"You're making this more complicated this it is," he said in frustration.

"No, Joe. I'm just trying to get you to think like a sleuth. You know for a fact Liz had a prescription for tranquilizers. You don't know that she actually took any. Do you?"

"No." He recalled that the autopsy report said there were no known drugs in her system.

"There you go. Like Joe Friday says, 'Just the facts, ma'am, just the facts.'"

"Okay, I get it. I'm a piss-poor detective."

"No, honey, you're just learning, that's all. You've already dug up some solid information. With me as your mentor, you'll become a first-class shamus." She smiled and batted her eyelashes.

"A regular Fearless Fozdick," he joked, making reference to the kiddy-show puppet that pompously called himself America's Number One Private Eye.

"Hah! I was thinking more along the line of Dick Tracy."

"Yeah?" he said, standing. "Well, I'll see you in the funny papers."

"Where you going?"

"Funeral home. I want to be alone with Liz one last time."

CHAPTER FOUR

The funeral home was two blocks west of the town square. It was a stately brick building with a well-manicured lawn and a couple of mature palm trees standing tall and sentry-like in front of the crescent driveway. The driveway was lined with flowering hedges, carefully trimmed. The late-afternoon sun winked through breaking clouds.

Joe parked in front and remained behind the wheel of the Buick, questioning the wisdom of going inside to view Liz's embalmed remains.

He wanted to see her.

He didn't want to see her.

Would she have wanted him to? Would she have cared one way or the other? The last time he'd seen her alive, she had been angry with him, her brow knotted in displeasure and her eyes flashing fire—not the way he wanted to remember her. And he sure as hell didn't want to remember her the way she was in those crime-scene photos. He climbed out of the car and headed up the walkway to the mortuary's main entrance.

The air inside was frigid. His sweat turned cold, quickly chilling him. A man in a somber black suit gave him a solemn nod.

"Lizabeth Tibbedeaux?" Joe whispered.

The man led him to a viewing room where an open casket sat amid a jungle of flowers. "The family requests that you please sign the register before you leave," the man told him.

Fuck the family, Joe thought as he approached the casket like a condemned man taking his last steps to the gallows. As soon as her profile came into view, he froze. He stuck his hands in his pockets. He rocked on his heels. He glanced around to make sure he was alone. Alone with Lizabeth's corpse. The corpse of the former Mrs. Lizabeth Dall. Finally, he moved forward and stepped up to the casket.

The cloying scent of flowers was so strong he found it hard to breathe.

"Lizzy," he said, choking on the word.

But this wasn't Lizabeth. This was a life-size doll, a cold-flesh replica of the woman he'd loved.

She was gone. Gone forever from this spiffed -up cadaver.

She was *out there*, somewhere. Hidden from sight, waiting to show herself on moonlit water or in dim mirrors in empty rooms. Waiting for him to solve the mystery of her death, the mystery of her life, and to bring her killer to justice.

Feeling no emotional connection to the corpse in the box, he turned and walked away. He didn't sign the guest register.

* * *

Dot was behind the bar, talking to a heavyset man hunched on a bar stool with a mug of beer in his fist. Joe recognized him as a regular, though he didn't know his name. The man nodded amiably as Joe slid onto a stool at the other end of the bar. Joe nodded back. Dot glided down to Joe's end of the bar.

"Did you see her?" she asked in a quiet voice.

He nodded.

"Need a drink?"

"No thanks. I'm okay. I just wanted to let you know I'll be here tonight. You haven't had time to find a replacement for me."

"Don't worry about it," she said. "I'll be all right. It should be a quiet night. And Tina's coming in an hour early. You go on and work the case."

Joe sighed. "You make it sound like I know what I'm doing. I don't. Having a private detective license and a gun doesn't make me a detective."

"Think about it, Joe. You've only been at it one day and you've already turned up some good leads. Laura D'Amore, the tranquilizers, the tattoo. Did you go to the tattoo parlor?"

"Yeah. I didn't tell you about that?" Joe pulled a long face. "Captain Eddie tattooed her all right, and he said an older woman in dark glasses, a wig and a scarf was with Lizzy. He didn't know the woman but he said he thought she was trying to go incognito."

"Laura D'Amore." Dot's eyes suddenly shone with a granite glint.

"That's what I'm thinking."

"She's in this up to her neck. She should be the focus of your investigation."

"Yeah, but I don't know how to approach her. I go knock on her door and start asking questions and she'll tell me to get lost, drop dead. Especially if she's got something to hide."

Dot rubbed her chin. Her fingernails were painted bright cotton-candy pink to match her pullover blouse. "You have to make her want to talk to you," she said, her eyes dancing.

"How?"

"You tell her you have information linking her to Lizabeth's murder and you want to give her a chance to explain herself before you go to the police and the newspapers with it."

"Why would I do that? If I had information like that, why wouldn't I go straight to the police?"

"Because you think you can turn a tidy profit."

"Blackmail?"

"Yes. And because you're the ex-husband, she'd believe it."

"I don't know, Dot. I don't want to do anything illegal. I'm already on the cops' shit list. Chief Kelso would jump at the chance to come after me."

"You don't actually ask her for money. You just make her think that's the deal. You only hint at it."

"But she'll want to know what I have on her. How can I make her believe it without telling her what this information is? At some point, I'd have to lay my cards on the table. Cards I don't have."

"You keep bluffing. Raise the ante and hope she tips her hand."

"I was never any good at poker. I don't think I could pull it off. She's an actress. And I'm no actor. She could bluff me out of my socks."

Dot frowned. "Maybe you're right. But if you don't come up with a better idea . . ."

"I'll think of something."

"There you go. Think positive."

Joe glanced down the bar at the beer drinker. "I think I will have a drink," he said.

*   *   *

After downing a bottle of beer and burning two smokes, Joe walked back to the bungalow and scrambled himself some hen fruit and made an egg sandwich for supper. A good breeze was coming off the lake so he ate out on the deck. The sandwich was too bland and he wished he'd put ketchup on it, but he didn't feel like going back inside to add it now. What was the point? What was the point of anything? There was a terrible emptiness in his chest, as empty as the surface of the lake out there, and he didn't think he could do anything to fill it. Lizabeth was gone, and her absence made a big hole, dead center, inside his ribcage—where his heart used to be.

He tossed the remainder of his sandwich toward the lake. Let the ants have it. The birds or a stray dog or cat. Scavengers of the world, come and get it. The Lord gives, the Lord takes away. Mysterious ways, blah blah blah . . .

He wanted another beer to wash down the dry bread and overcooked egg that seemed stuck in his throat. He got up, went down the deck's steps and walked along the stepping-stone path toward the lounge. It was twilight and the neon sign out front came on. SUNDOWN LOUNGE in glowing red. It looked good against the dark wood of the long building. Its homey warmth was welcoming. A place you could go to forget the world's troubles, at least for a while. The closest thing he had to a home.

Two twilight shadows came out of the tall pine trees to Joe's right. The shadows rushed him and he threw up his hands for protection. The lead shadow plowed into his midsection and knocked him down. The other shadow stood over him with a baseball bat.

"Get out of the way, Slick," said the man with the bat. "I'm gonna teach this asshole a little baseball."

Joe gritted his teeth as Slick dug both his knees into Joe's gut and pushed off.

Slick and Ralphie, back for revenge. Joe knew he should've seen it coming. He should've known these two redneck rowdies would reappear for some payback. Guys like them, what else did they have to do besides swill beer, pick their teeth and abuse women? Batting practice, maybe? Shit.

Ralphie stepped up and cocked the bat over his shoulder, bending a little at the knees to give his swing extra power.

Joe rolled onto his left side, reached behind his back with his right hand and drew the .38 out of the holster. Ralphie checked his swing when he found himself looking down the barrel. "Whoa, wait now," he said, tossing the bat to the ground and holding up his empty hands. "You ain't gotta shoot me."

Joe got to his feet and pointed the pistol at Slick's belly. "Pick up that bat," he said.

"Huh?" Slick gave him a stupid look.

Joe clicked back the Colt's hammer. "Pick it up and break your pal's arm with it."

"What? I can't do—"

"Do it or I'll shoot you."

"You're crazy, man," Ralphie shouted, backing away from his pal.

"Hold still or I'll shoot *you*," Joe told Ralphie.

"Come on, buddy," whined Slick, "just let it go. We won't bother you no more, I swear to God."

"Yeah, we were just pissed off, that's all," added Ralphie. "Let's forget the whole thing. We're sorry, man. We screwed up. Our fault."

"You've got three seconds to pick up the bat," said Joe, "and break his arm. If you don't, I'll just shoot both of you assholes. One . . ."

Slick snatched up the baseball bat.

"Two . . ."

Slick said, "Sorry, man," cocked the bat and swung it hard into Ralphie's left upper arm.

Ralphie yelped, grabbed his bashed arm and stumbled to the ground, cursing.

Joe trained the .38 on Slick and said, "Get your broke-ass pal and get outta here. I ever see you again, I'll shoot you on sight. No more games."

"You broke my fuckin' arm," Ralphie raged at his comrade. "You stupid sonofabitch."

"I had to, man," Slick said as he bent down and pulled the injured man to his feet. "You heard him. He woulda shot us. He's nuts."

Joe watched the two men walk arm-in-arm like a couple of drunks toward the parking lot. "Hey, Slick," he called after them. "If I were you, I wouldn't turn my back on Ralphie for a while."

He holstered his pistol and watched the bickering chumps drive off into the growing darkness. The emptiness in his chest was less acute now. The dustup with Slick and Ralphie left him charged with adrenaline, giving him hope that he could beat back the empty-hearted blues by staying on the go. All he had to do was maintain momentum.

Now that he had the impetus, he figured it was time to pay a visit to Laura D'Amore.

* * *

Joe lost some of his mental momentum when the police car tagged him with its gumball flasher at the edge of town. As he pulled to the side of the road, he cursed himself for carelessly breaking the speed limit. He'd been too anxious to get to the D'Amore place, and his anxiety had found expression on the gas pedal. He had proved Homer Dix right in his assertion that he, one Joseph Dall, was too emotionally involved in the case to be effective. If he wanted to do more than just spin his wheels, he would have to pull back an objective distance and stop acting like a hot-headed kid in a hotrod. He shut off the engine and waited for the cop.

Officer Blue sauntered up to the Roadmaster and rapped the window with his nightstick—no doubt the same stick he'd used on Joe last night. The prowl car's headlights were glaring, slicing at Joe's eyes from the rearview mirror.

He rolled down the window, knowing his resolve to be coolheaded was about to be sorely tested. If he blew it, his resolve was out the window and in the wind.

"Well, look who it is," Blue said in a mocking singsong.

"The war hero with the dead wife. *Ex*-wife."

Dall looked up at Blue. He squeezed the steering wheel and kept his lips tight.

"Just 'cause Tibbedeaux bailed your ass out of a murder rap don't mean you can speed on my roadways."

Dall nodded, not trusting himself to speak.

"Step out of the car." Blue's lips formed a stiff little smile as he moved out of the way of the door.

Joe took a deep breath, opened the door and stepped out.

"Turn around, spread your legs and lean on the car with both hands," Blue ordered.

Joe complied.

"Back your ass up and keep your hands on the car. That's it. Just like you're gonna take it up the ass."

Blue wanted him off balance for the frisk. If he wanted to work him over with the billy club again, Joe would have to take it. With any luck, he would come out of the beating without ruptured kidneys.

Blue started patting him down, beginning with the ankles and then moving up the legs and to the hips. "Oh ho! What's this? A fucking gun?" He yanked up Joe's shirttail and pulled the pistol from the holster at the small of his back. "A concealed fucking weapon? Thank you, Jesus."

"I've got a license to carry it. In my wallet."

"You better hope you do." Blue pulled the wallet out of Joe's back pocket. "What the hell is this? Private Investigator? You?"

"Yeah. Ain't that a gas?"

"Issued 27 June 1958. That's today. What the hell is this, Dall? What kind of con are you running here?"

"No con. I'm working for Mr. Tibbedeaux."

Blue was quiet for half a minute, then he slipped the wallet back in Joe's pocket and said, "Last night you were a murder suspect and today you're a private-ass dick. Don't tell me, let me guess. You're looking for your ex-wife's killer."

"Somebody's gotta do it. Can I get off this car now? I'm getting a cramp."

"Yeah, go ahead. Turn around so I can look you in the eye."

He pushed off the car and turned around. Blue was pointing Joe's .38 at him.

"I don't like you, Dall. I don't give a shit who your rich friends and ex-relatives are. You so much as even bend the law and I'll bust your ass up but good. This time all you're getting is a speeding ticket. Next time you won't be so lucky. You got that?"

"I got it, Blue. Now how about giving me my gun."

Blue flipped the pistol and handed it over, butt-first.

"Now sit your sorry ass in your car while I write you a ticket."

Joe flipped him a casual salute and slid behind the wheel, smiling to himself. This private-dick gig did have its advantages.

* * *

Dodd City's radio station W-DCF signed off for the day with the National Anthem. Joe clicked off the radio and lit a Lucky with the dash lighter. He was driving the speed limit on the Zephyrhills highway. Blue had stolen some of his momentum with the traffic stop, and now he wasn't so confident that he was ready to meet Laura D'Amore. Moving slower, he'd let his doubt catch up with him. What the hell was he going to say to the woman? How could he hope to get a foot in her door? She probably had hired help to answer the door, anyway. He probably wouldn't even get to see the reclusive film star. *Former* star. Probable bisexual and Commie. Possible killer? He doubted it, though he didn't know why. Whenever he closed his eyes to imagine Liz's death, he saw a man's hands doing the deed, twisting the brassiere around her neck and choking the life from her. He couldn't see a woman's hands doing it.

The D'Amore house came up on the left side of the highway. It was set well back from the road, behind a row of tall palm trees and surrounded by pale stone walls. Two giant oak trees stood behind the building, their mammoth limbs festooned with Spanish moss. Floodlights gave the place a ghostly aura.

He turned onto the narrow dirt road and drove up to the wrought-iron gate barring entry into the compound. An iron-necked lamp affixed to the stone archway cast a sickly sepia haze over the entrance. Feeling as if he were stepping onto a movie set, he got out of the Buick and walked up to the intercom to the right of the gate. He punched the call button and waited for an answer.

Seeing the house up close, he realized the place was modest in comparison to the Tibbedeaux mansion. Though it brought to mind a small tropical castle, there was a rundown seediness about the place that he hadn't expected. The beige walls looked as though they could use a good scrubbing, and the lawn and flowering vegetation weren't well-manicured. If D'Amore had a gardener, the guy was lousy at his job—unless she wanted the place to have this edge-of-wilderness look. You never could tell about these Hollywood types, he mused. Maybe the broad wanted the place to look like it was in the middle of a jungle, about to be overrun by nature. Maybe she dug the implied melodrama.

He was wondering if she'd ever been in any jungle movies when the intercom crackled with static and a woman with a Spanish accent said, "Jes? Who ees there?"

"Joe Dall. I'm here to see Miss D'Amore."

After a long pause, the voice said, "She ees seeing nobody now."

He spoke quickly, not giving her time to turn him off. "Tell her I'm Lizabeth Tibbedeaux's ex-husband. It's very important that I see her."

Another long pause. Joe figured the Latina was relaying the message to the lady of the house. He listened to the singing insects and bleating tree frogs. A small squadron of bugs flitted and zipped around the crook-necked lamp above him.

The intercom hissed and crackled again. This time a man's voice came out of the hidden speaker, too loud and garbled: ". . . off the property. You're trespassing."

Joe raised his voice: "She can talk to me or she can talk to the cops."

The intercom hummed.

He shouted: "Somebody murdered Lizabeth! She damn well better talk to me!"

With a click the intercom stopped humming. As Joe was reaching out to stab the call button again, he looked through the gate's iron bars and saw the front door swing open. A huge man with a cannonball head came stalking out of the house. Joe was sure he'd seen the guy before. You didn't forget a baldheaded hulk like the guy barreling toward him now, huffing and puffing like a bull in rut. The guy came on like a locomotive building up a good head of steam. Then Joe remembered where he'd seen the man, and his feeling of being on the set of a movie was stronger than ever. Cannonball had played a porky zombie in an old black-&-white horror movie. He ripped people apart with his bare hands and tore heads off shoulders with frightening ease.

He looked now like he was ready to do some serious ripping.

CHAPTER FIVE

The big zombie stopped at the gate and looked at Dall through green wrought-iron bars. He reached into his trouser pocket and pulled out a handkerchief and wiped sweat off his massive forehead, then stuck it into the breast pocket of his Hawaiian-style shirt, garishly imprinted with tropical flowers of every imaginable color.

"There is no need for the police," he said with faultless diction. "Miss D'Amore isn't available tonight, but perhaps you could come back tomorrow for a tête-à-tête. Would tomorrow afternoon be suitable?"

Tête-à-tête? Not exactly words you'd expect to come out of a giant zombie's mouth. Joe made a mental-note reminder that he shouldn't mistake actors for the roles they play. If he was to be taken seriously at Chateau D'Amore, he couldn't act like a bumpkin with a map to the Hollywood stars in his hip pocket. "Who are you, her secretary?"

"No," he said with a miniscule smile on his big face. "Just an old friend. We were in a few films together."

"I saw you in a horror movie but I didn't get your name."

"Oscar Lamont," he said with a slight bow of his head. "The film was *Uncanny Evil.* It was the kiss of death for my career. Before that, I had a bit part in *Torrid Town.* That's how Laura and I met. After *Uncanny,* I was hopelessly typecast as a horror movie heavy, pardon the unavoidable pun. When the studio wanted to put me in a gorilla suit,

I canned my agent, packed it in and called it quits."

"Tough business," Joe commiserated. "Listen, Oscar, are you sure you can't persuade Miss D'Amore to see me tonight?"

"I'm afraid not. She's . . . in a very important phone conference. But she *will* see you tomorrow."

Joe sighed. "I guess that'll have to do. What time?"

"Two o'clock would be fine."

"I'll be here."

"I'll tell her." Lamont smiled reassuringly.

Joe nodded. "Did you know my . . . Lizabeth Tibbedeaux?"

"Yes, I did. She was a delightful girl. It's tragic, what happened to her."

"Yeah. Well, see, here's the thing, Oscar. I'm gonna find out who killed her and I don't care what rocks I have to kick over to do it. If you know anything about anything, you want to tell me right now. I'm not accusing you, I'm just telling you so you'll know. If it comes out later that you knew something and held it back, then God help you. Lizabeth's father is a powerful man with powerful friends. And I'm not somebody you want to lie to."

Lamont's forehead knotted up and his eyes bore into Dall. "You don't need to threaten me," he said, dropping his voice an octave. "I don't know who killed her and I'm sure Laura doesn't either. When you leave here tomorrow, I expect you'll be satisfied that no one here knows anything whatsoever about what happened to poor Lizabeth. Good-night, Mr. Dall."

Lamont turned on his heels and shambled back to the house. Joe watched him go, not sure what to make of the man. He didn't think the former actor had lied to him. The guy probably didn't know who killed Lizabeth, but that didn't give Laura D'Amore a free pass. Oscar Lamont might believe she knew nothing, but that didn't make it so.

As he was turning to walk back to his car, something

caught his eye and he froze, then turned back toward the house. Just before his eyes could latch on to it, it was gone. He stared at the spot in front of the house where he thought he'd seen it. There was nothing there but a tall elephant-ear plant, its leaves waving in the night wind.

He shook his head. Told himself he'd imagined it.

Lizabeth's ghost hadn't been standing there, watching him, *winking* at him.

* * *

Dot was behind the bar, sucking on a cigarette and squinting at him through the smoke when he came through the door. She winked an eye and smiled. Joe wished women—living and dead—would stop winking at him. Tina was unloading a tray of drinks at a corner booth occupied by two young couples with sunburned faces. The jukebox had Elvis Presley crooning: "If you're looking for trouble/Look right in my face."

He sat on a stool in front of Dot and reached for his pack of smokes.

"Two homicide detectives were looking for you," she said. "They want to talk to you about Lizabeth."

"What'd you tell them?" He shook out a smoke and used Dot's lighter to fire it.

"That I didn't know when you'd be back." She stubbed out her cigarette and added, "I told 'em you were a licensed investigator and that you were looking into the matter yourself. I thought that might put you in a more favorable light. Professional courtesy, that sort of thing."

"Humph. I won't hold my breath. That kind of deal only works in the movies."

"If they give you a hard time, just tell 'em you're working for Monroe Tibbedeaux. They'll back off then."

"Yeah, maybe." He took a drag off his smoke and watched

the languid spin of the ceiling fan over the bar. He looked at Dot. "Do you believe in ghosts?"

"Ghosts?" She gave him a quizzical look, then shook her head. "As far as I'm concerned, the jury's still out on that. I've never seen one, but I know people who swear they have. Why in the world do you ask?"

He shrugged. "Just curious."

"Come on, Joe. Tell me." She folded her arms on the bar and rested her breasts on her forearms. Her pink blouse was cut low and her bosom was deeply tanned, the dimpled cleft dappled with sun-made freckles.

"I've seen Lizabeth," he said. "Twice now. Once in the moonlight on the lake and again tonight in front of Laura D'Amore's house."

"Holy . . ." Dot's face crinkled up in a big grin. "You went out there?"

"I was drunk last night when I saw her face in the lake, but tonight I was stone sober."

"Did you see her? Laura D'Amore?"

"No. She's supposed to see me tomorrow afternoon."

"You're making real headway, Joe. Not bad for your first day as a dick. Not bad at all."

"What do you think it means? That I keep seeing Lizabeth."

She fanned her hand as if waving off the possibility of such a notion. "When you lose someone you love, she's liable to pop up in your mind any time. I think it's part of not wanting to accept that she's gone and she's not coming back. It just takes time to sink in."

"So it's my imagination."

"Yeah. Unless you really *did* see a ghost." Dot gave him a dubious look. "Rule Number Three: *Don't let emotional distractions interfere with your investigation.*"

"But I keep getting the feeling that she's trying to tell me something. Or like maybe she's taunting me, telling me I'll never understand what happened."

"She *talks* to you?"

"No. Not with words. She winks at me."

Dot poured a shot of scotch over ice and set it in front of him. "Drink that. Maybe it'll clear your head."

Rather than argue with her, he picked up the squat glass and chugged down the booze. He wiped his lips with the back of his hand. "I'm not a fruitcake, ya know."

She caught his hand as it was coming away from his mouth and held it firmly. "I know you're not, sugar. After the funeral, it will start to go easier on you and you'll begin to accept that she's really gone."

"I know she's gone. I saw the death shots of her body. I saw her in a casket."

"It's not that simple. Or that easy. Time. Give yourself time. And in the meantime, focus on the job, the detective work. Think how you'll feel if you solve her murder." She released his hand. "I believe you can do it, Joe. I really do."

"Yeah?"

"Absolutely." She refilled his glass and poured herself a shot. "Here's to your new job. And to your future success."

They clicked their glasses together and drank.

Joe reached into his back pocket and pulled out Lizabeth's address book and set it on the bar. "I found her address book. I guess I should go down the list."

She picked it up and thumbed through the pages. "Looks like twenty or thirty names. It'll take a lot of time, but yeah, you should get around to all of them. Depending, of course, on what you find out from D'Amore. She has to be your number-one lead. If you can break her, you might not need to talk to all these people."

"*Break* her? I'm not a cop, Dot. She doesn't have to talk to me at all."

Dot shrugged her shoulders. "Finesse her, then. Make her want to open up to you. I'm telling you, she could be the key to this case. Get her on your hook and don't let her off until you reel in the catch. Know what I mean?"

"That I should take her fishing?" He was feeling the booze now, relaxing a little and letting some of the day's tension drain away. His dumb joke struck him as funny. Damned near hilarious.

Dot chuckled and said, "Good to see your sense of humor trying to come back. You'll be fine, Joe. You'll see."

He picked up the address book, pushed away from the bar and slid off the stool. He said, "Think I'll call it a day. Get an early start in the morning."

"Good plan. I'm closing early. Another slow night. If business doesn't pick up, I don't know what I'll do."

"Oh, I forgot to tell you. Those two rowdies I roughed up last night ambushed me outside a couple of hours ago. They were gonna work me over with a baseball bat but I pulled the gun on 'em."

"Jesus, Joe. They didn't hurt you?"

"No. But I'm pretty sure one of them has a broken arm." He grinned. "I don't think they'll be back for round three."

Dot grinned. "Joe Dall, hardboiled dick."

"Damn, Dot," he said with a wince. "Don't put pictures like that in my head."

"Oh." She giggled and covered her mouth with her hand. "You know what I meant."

"Yeah," he said with a nod and a half-smile. "G'night, Dot."

He left the lounge and walked back to the bungalow. All the lights were off inside, and just for a moment he was afraid of going into that crouching darkness. Afraid Lizabeth's ghost might be waiting there for him.

* * *

A click and a harsh blast of light woke him. He sat up in bed, blinking at the big man in the bedroom doorway.

"Keefer? What the hell are you doing here?"

Barry Keefer folded his arms across his chest and seemed to be sizing up Joe's bare upper body—no doubt making a favorable comparison to his own muscular bulk. "Get dressed," he said with an air of bored disgust. "He's waiting for you."

Joe looked at the alarm clock on the night table. He'd been asleep less than fifteen minutes. He threw off the sheet and stood up, straightening his twisted boxer shorts. "He's here?"

"Outside," Keefer said. "On the deck."

"What's he want?" He found his pants on the back of a chair and clumsily danced into them.

"Get a move on and find out." Keefer leaned against the doorframe. "Cozy little dump you got here, Joe."

He ducked his head into an undershirt and pulled it on. He knew Keefer lived in a cramped pastel-green cinderblock building behind Tibbedeaux's mansion, always at the beck and call of the boss. "A little roomier than your digs, huh, Barry?"

Keefer scowled. He stepped aside to let Joe out of the bedroom.

"Make yourself at home," Joe told him. "Just don't break anything."

Monroe Tibbedeaux was standing on the deck, leaning his arms on the wooden rail and staring at the lake. The waxing moon danced on the water's surface. He turned around when he heard Joe's footsteps on the deck's cedar boards. "Joseph. I'm here for our daily briefing. Tell me about your first day as a private investigator."

"Daily briefing?" Joe stopped in the center of the deck. He wriggled his bare toes.

"You *are* working for me now. I require all my key

employees to brief me on their daily activities."

Tibbedeaux wasn't wearing his usual white suit. Tonight he was in casual attire, white buck shoes, tan slacks with sharp creases and a pale-blue golfer's shirt with crossed irons on the breast pocket.

"I wish you'd told me," Joe said. He folded his arms, feeling self-conscious in his ribbed-cotton undershirt. "I would've waited up for you. Or I could've phoned you."

"I don't take briefings over the telephone. I like to look into a man's eyes so I can see if he's dissembling."

"Dissembling?" Joe jutted his chin.

"It's a politician's ten-dollar word for lying." He allowed a wry smile. "So tell me, Detective Dall. What did you do today to earn your pay?"

"I know what the word means," said Joe, feeling a familiar flash of anger. "And I don't like the implication."

Tibbedeaux's eyes widened, just a little. The little smile still played on his lips.

"As for these daily briefings," Joe went on, "you get 'em before I go to bed or you don't get 'em at all. This is the last time you drag me out of bed for your daily goddamn briefing. You wanna fire me, go ahead. Otherwise, listen up and I'll tell you what I did today *for Lizabeth*."

Monroe Tibbedeaux made a lordly hand gesture and said, "Proceed, then."

Joe recounted the events of the day, beginning with his visit to the palm reader and ending with his trip to Chateau D'Amore. He omitted any mention of Lizabeth's ghost.

Tibbedeaux nodded appreciatively. "A full day's effort," he said. "I believe I was right to recruit you to the task. A man doesn't always know if his decisions are sound until after he makes them. I see now that I may have misjudged you when you were married to my daughter."

Joe said nothing. He looked into the older man's eyes and tried to see what might be behind them. All he saw was moist moonlight.

"I think I owe you an apology, Joseph."

"For wrecking my marriage?" He dug his nails into his palms.

"No, son. For misjudging you. Your marriage wrecked itself. It didn't need my help, though I admit I wasn't sorry to see it run aground and break upon the shore."

"You ran me down every chance you got. You poisoned her mind against me. You think that helped our marriage?"

"You overestimate the influence I had with Lizabeth. You really didn't know her that well. She was a complicated young lady." Tibbedeaux turned back to the lake.

"I knew her," Joe said, just above a whisper.

"See the moon on the water?" Tibbedeaux raised his hand to point. "Beautiful, isn't it? Ethereal. Illusive. When there's no wind and the water is still, you can almost believe the moon is floating there on the surface. You might, in a moment of lunar intoxication, try to swim out to it and touch that delicate miniature moon borne upon the lake. But of course you can't, because it's only a reflection of light from the heavens. As you swim to it, you make waves and the image is spoiled before you can touch the place where the water holds the light."

"Yeah, so?"

"Lizabeth was like the moon on the lake. Beautiful on the surface, full of heavenly light, but if you got close enough to touch that light she was already rippling away, and you could never reach what was beneath the glittery surface. She wouldn't allow it. It wasn't her nature to allow it. Her outer beauty concealed darker depths within. I think she was always like that, though I didn't really realize it until she was all grown up. Her mother saw it before I did. I was too busy amassing my fortunes. She even tried to convince me that our daughter needed to see a psychoanalyst. In retrospect, I think maybe she was right, but I don't know if it would have helped much."

"You're saying she was . . . crazy?"

"No, of course not. I would never use such a vulgar word to describe Lizabeth. There was a wildness in her, dark and complex. Unfathomable. And that's the very thing that wrecked your marriage. That wildness would not be tamed. She was never cut out to be the domestic housewife. That's what doomed your marriage from its very beginning. She would've been happier as a world traveler. An adventurer. Had she been born a man, she probably would've gone off on safaris or become a soldier of fortune."

Joe stared at the moon on the lake and tried to find Lizabeth's face in it. It wasn't there.

"Don't feel bad," Tibbedeaux said. "I doubt any man could've reached her."

"You think a woman could have? A woman like Laura D'Amore?"

Tibbedeaux looked solemnly at Joe. The wind ruffled his white hair. "I don't know, but I fully expect you to find out. And whatever you learn, it stays private. Tell no one but me. You're a *private* investigator. Anything you discover must remain confidential. Don't ever forget that."

Joe saw the man's eyes misting up. For the first time, he looked like a bereaved father.

"Somebody took my little girl away from me," he said, his voice breaking.

Joe said, "We'll get him."

He clutched Joe's arm. "Don't let her down, Joseph. You're her torch-bearer."

"I won't," Joe said. Then he cast his eyes back to the moon on the water.

* * *

He was tired but he didn't feel sleepy after Tibbedeaux's surprise visit. He decided to read himself to sleep. There were three books on his night table. The Hemingway hardback Lizabeth had given him for his birthday, a dog-eared Mickey Spillane mystery, and a paperback Western by a Detroit writer, Elmore Leonard. He picked the Western, settled into his pillow and started reading *The Bounty Hunters*. Joe didn't know how a guy from Detroit could write such realistic scenes of the Old West, but by page 3 he quit worrying about it and let the book take him on into the Arizona Territory of 1876. It was good to get away for a while. Ten pages later, he fumbled for the lamp switch, clicked it off and went right to sleep.

CHAPTER SIX

He woke before sunrise after six hours of restless sleep. He couldn't remember what he'd dreamed but whatever it was, it left him on edge and with a nasty taste on his tongue. After a shave and a shower, he fried a couple of eggs and ate them with dry toast and black coffee.

He put on a clean shirt and walked over to the lounge. He used his key and went in the back door, filled the mop bucket and swabbed the floor. Then he restocked the bar with liquor from the storeroom and wiped down the tables. He was standing on a barstool to dust the blades of one of the ceiling fans when three sharp raps sounded from the front door. Knowing no customers would be wanting in this early in the morning, he went to the door with a knot of dread in his belly. He unlocked it and pulled it open.

"Joe Dall?" said the taller of the two men in identical white shirts and thin black ties.

"Yeah?"

"Pasco County Homicide," the man said. "I'm Detective Morris and this is Detective Stevens. We have to ask you some questions about your ex-wife."

"Come on in. We can talk here. We don't open till noon."

They filed inside and Joe led them to a table in the center of the room. The two detectives pulled out chairs and sat down. Joe sat opposite them. He wanted a smoke but he'd left his pack back at the bungalow.

Morris took the lead. "Mr. Tibbedeaux told us he had a private detective shadowing you and he gave us a copy of the written report of your activities on the night of the murder, so it would seem you have the perfect alibi." He paused, letting *perfect alibi* hang out there for emphasis. "Why do you think your former father-in-law had you under surveillance?"

Joe rolled his eyes. "He said he'd heard rumors of somebody selling dope in town and he wanted to hang it on me if he could."

"Why would he suspect you?"

"Wishful thinking? I have no idea. Ask him."

"But you know he wanted to keep you away from his daughter."

"Yeah. He had the idea I was harassing her or something. Maybe he was afraid I would win her back. He would've been as happy as a pig in shit if he could've had me sent off to prison. I think he was just hoping it was me, but since I don't have anything to do with dope dealers, he was wasting his money."

"From your point of view, it was money well spent," Stevens spoke for the first time, his voice raspy from too many cigarettes. "Otherwise, you'd be the prime suspect in your ex-wife's murder."

"Of course we all know," Morris added, "you could've hired somebody to do it for you."

"Why the hell would I? What's my motive? I loved Lizabeth, I didn't want her dead."

"Oldest story in the book, Dall," Morris said. "Jilted lover wants his revenge. If he can't have her, nobody can."

"That's not me. I never gave up on getting her back. And even if I had, I wouldn't want her dead. I loved her. Her old man knows that. That's why he's set me up as a private detective. Because he knows I want more than anything to find out who killed her."

"Yeah, he told us about your private-eye license," Stevens said with thick derision. "Fuckin' amateur shamus. What a joke. Junior Joe Friday."

"Maybe it won't seem so funny when I find her killer." Joe gave Stevens a hard look.

"Hah! Now *that's* funny." Stevens slapped his palm on the tabletop. "Like there's a snowball's chance in hell of you catching a killer. You're a regular fuckin' comedian, Dall. You oughta be on TV, like Uncle fuckin' Milty. Put you in a dress like Berle, you'd get all kinds of laughs."

Joe leaned across the table and said, "Tell you what, Stevens. I'll make you a bet. If you find the killer before I do, I'll treat you to a month's supply of your favorite booze."

Stevens stopped laughing, but he kept a smirk on his lips. "And if you find him first?"

"Then you can kiss my hairy ass. Detective. On Main Street."

* * *

After the homicide dicks were gone, Joe used the phone behind the bar to start calling the names in Lizabeth's address book. April Anderson wasn't home. Mary Battle gave him a quick brush-off, saying she hadn't seen Lizabeth in months and that she didn't want to get involved in "anything like this." Jane Carmichael was eager to chat, but she didn't seem to have any useful information, other than that Lizabeth had stopped attending art classes with her about three months ago. She wasn't sure why that was.

He had his finger in the rotor to dial the number of Val Cooper when Dot came in through the back door. He cradled the phone and gave her a hello wave.

"You cleaned up the place," she said, looking puzzled. "You didn't have to do that."

He shrugged. "It's no big deal."

"You don't work here anymore, remember? You're supposed to be working the case."

"I am. I'm calling people in the address book. So far, it's a washout."

She came behind the bar, poured herself a glass of soda water and lit a Camel. "I think I've found somebody to replace you. You know, temporarily, until this is over. Then again, you might not want to come back to work here. You might decide to hang out your shingle as private detective. Hell, I wouldn't blame you. It's what I'd do if I were you."

"You'd make a good one," he said. "Me, I'm not so sure."

Dot blew him a raspberry, smoke jetting from her mouth. "So who's the guy? My replacement."

"Hubie Horn. You'd know his face. Comes in now and then to drink beer and eat bar nuts. Big guy, quiet, good manners. About your age, maybe a little younger. Always sits at the bar. Last night we struck up a conversation. I think he was flirting with me, but not in a dirty way or anything like that. So anyway, it comes up that I'm looking for a bouncer and Hubie volunteers for the job. I hired him on the spot. He starts tonight, after he gets off his day job at Powell's Body Shop. Seems like a nice enough guy. And he's big enough to handle any trouble here. Nice build, too."

Joe smiled. "Don't let him break your heart."

"Aw, go on." She smiled, embarrassed. She stubbed her half-smoked cigarette. "Well, since you've already cleaned up in here, I'm going on to town. I don't have anything black to wear to the funeral so I'm hoping I can find something at Belk's. You need anything?"

"No. Thanks. I'll be here working the phone."

She touched his shoulder. "I'll see you before your meeting with D'Amore."

"Right." Joe lit a smoke, picked up the phone and dialed Val Cooper's number. She didn't answer, so he went to the next name in the address book and dialed the number beside it.

* * *

Just before noon, he left the lounge and walked down the short stretch of manmade beach to the snack bar at the south end of the lake to get a couple of hot dogs. The snack bar was a sturdy little shack at the shore-end of the weathered-gray pier, offering cold drinks, ice cream, hot dogs and hamburgers. The owner's teenage kids, Gwen and Gene, ran the place in the summertime. They both had red hair, lots of freckles, and their father's gregarious disposition. The snack bar's owner, Gene O'Bannon, Sr., was also the editor of *The Dodd City Star*, the town's weekly newspaper.

Joe wondered how Lizabeth's murder would play on the front page of the next issue, due out today. O'Bannon was the one man in town who wasn't intimidated by Monroe Tibbedeaux's wealth and power. For Editor O'Bannon, a newspaperman's journalistic ethics didn't vary with the size of a city, even if it meant making close-quarters enemies. O'Bannon saw his editorial job as sacrosanct. Tibbedeaux saw the editor as sanctimonious. When the two men were at loggerheads over any issue, Gene O'Bannon's gregariousness would turn into stubborn fury, and Tibbedeaux would privately rail at the "hick-town" editor's audacity and arrogance.

Joe knew O'Bannon wouldn't sensationalize the murder. He wouldn't have to. The murder of a member of a prominent family in a small town was sensational in and of itself. What Joe didn't know was how *he* would play in the story and in the inevitable town gossip to follow. The county detectives made it clear that they still considered him a prime suspect. It was a dead-solid cinch that others would see things their way as well.

In the end, it wouldn't matter. The killer would be caught and Joe's name cleared. If Joe did the catching, so much the better.

He stepped onto the narrow boardwalk leading to the planks of the pier on the left and to the front of the snack shack on the right. Two boys were splashing each other in the shallow water beneath the pier. A couple of bronzed girls were sunbathing down on the pier's end. On the sand, a chubby mother in a frumpy swimsuit was sculpting a sandcastle for her chubby towheaded toddler.

Joe walked up to the snack bar's counter. Gwen O'Bannon smiled and brushed a fly from her face. Gene looked up from the steaming griddle and waved with a grease-dripping spatula.

"Hi, Mr. Dall," Gwen said. "How about a couple of all-the-way dogs and an ice-cold Coke?"

"You're a mind reader," he said.

"It's what you always have." She gave him an odd look. "Gene?"

"Coming up," said her brother.

"I get burgers sometimes," Joe said in his own defense. He didn't like the idea of being too predictable.

"Not enough to count," said the girl, filling an iced cup with carbonated cola.

"Oh. So that's how it is. Swell." Joe smiled at her. "I'm old and set in my ways."

She chuckled and set his drink on the counter. Its foamy head fizzed and spat. He took a sip, the fizzing bubbles tickling his nose. "How's business?" he asked her.

"Picking up some. Pop says we should be making a tidy profit by the end of summer, after word gets around that people can come swim in the lake and sunbathe on the sand and all."

"I think your dad's right. The only other place to swim around here is the Zephyrhills pool. Unless you happen to have your own pool. Most folks don't."

Her brother passed Gwen a paper plate with two hot dogs nestled in buns. She began to dress them with mustard and ketchup.

Joe said, "Hold the onions this time." He didn't want to meet Laura D'Amore with onion breath.

"Got a hot date, Mr. Dall?" Gwen teased.

"No!" His sharp denial startled him. He moderated his response. "No, it's nothing like that."

Truth was, Joe had no idea what it *would* be like, meeting Laura D'Amore. What was worse, he had no idea what he was going to say to her or how he might react in the presence of the silver-screen celebrity.

He sat at a picnic table and absently ate his dogs. The glaring sunlight hurt his eyes as he gazed at the lake's surface. He knew the deepest point of the lake was 30 feet. He had no way of knowing what the depth of his involvement with D'Amore would be, but he had the uneasy feeling that he was about to get in way over his head.

CHAPTER SEVEN

When he drove up in front of D'Amore's estate, Oscar Lamont was waiting at the gate, ready to open it so Joe could drive inside the walled property. The big man waved him through and Joe followed the short shell-and-sand driveway and parked by a tall willow fronting a squat garage with azure double-doors.

"Right on time," said Lamont as Joe stepped out of the car. "She's waiting for you out back, by the pool. I'll show you the way."

They followed the flagstone walkway to the left.

"You live here, Oscar?" asked Joe. "Or just visiting?"

"My home's in L.A. Laura invited me here for a little vacation."

"Nice of her."

"She's a very nice person, Mr. Dall."

"Call me Joe."

"Well then, Joe, since we're being so palsy-walsy, let me give you a clue to what you'll no doubt tumble to in the end."

"Hey, that's pretty good, Oscar. Is that a line from a movie? Some Damon Runyon flicker with shady dames and jamokes on the hustle?"

"You should leave the acting to the pros and drop the snappy dialogue." Lamont's frown started at his mouth and went all the way to the top of his bald head.

"Hey, you started it. Just trying to hold up my end." Joe gave him a wink. He could hear the echo of water splashing around the back corner of the house.

"Here's the thing," said Lamont, suddenly stopping and swinging his bulk half around on a cracked flagstone for dramatic effect. "Laura D'Amore doesn't live in the same world you do. You might see things here you don't see in your little town. Don't judge her too quickly or too harshly. If you do, you'll be jumping to skewed conclusions. And that would be a disservice to everybody. Yourself included."

"I'm an open-minded kind of guy," Joe told him. "As long as nobody tries to run a con on me, I won't queer anybody's deal here."

Lamont looked startled, but quickly covered it up. "Fine, then."

Joe wondered which of his words had provoked that reaction, but before he had time to mull it over, they were around the corner, and he saw Laura D'Amore poolside, sitting with her long legs stretched out on a chaise lounge, a tall glass in her hand. The shade of one of the big oaks shielded her from the sun. A white skin-hugging swimsuit displayed a deep creamy scoop of her bosom. Her legs were crossed at the ankles and her toenails were painted cherry red. A white towel was turbaned on top of her head, hiding her trademark raven hair. Her alabaster skin bore no hint of a tan. She looked up and smiled as the two men approached. It was a practiced smile, enigmatic, packed with mysterious implication.

On the opposite side of the pool, a young blond woman was sunbathing in the nude, her tanned flesh beaded with sparkling drops water. She was lying face down on a beach towel with her arms crooked around her head. Joe couldn't stop himself from staring at the supple mound of her buttocks or at the tempting morsel of her breast flattened beneath her torso.

"Remember what I said," Lamont whispered. "Different world."

"*What* different? Florida has nudist colonies, ya know."

Lamont made a low grumbling sound. Then they were standing by D'Amore's chaise lounge and the big man was introducing the visitor.

Joe gave her a polite nod. She smiled up at him and said, "I feel like I already know you, Joey." He bristled. Liz was the only person who'd ever called him Joey. It had been her pet name for him, often whispered in his ear when they were making love.

D'Amore saw his reaction and arched her plucked-thin brows over her dark eyes.

"Nobody calls me that," he told her.

"Oh? But Lizabeth did." Her tongue flicked out to moisten her lower lip. Or maybe just to tease him.

"Nobody else does," he said.

"All right. Shall I call you Mr. Dall, then?"

"*Joe* is fine."

"All right, Joe. Would you like a cold drink? A screwdriver with fresh-squeezed orange juice?"

"Sure," he said with a gruff edge in his voice. "That'd be swell."

Lamont said, "I'll be inside, Laura."

"Be a dear and tell Frida to bring Joe an ice-cold screw-driver," she said.

Lamont dutifully nodded, turned on his heels and walked toward the house. Joe glanced at his surroundings to keep from staring at Laura D'Amore's famous face and luscious milk-white body. Tiki torches, unlit, stood like skeletal sentinels around the oval pool. An ornate birdbath crouched in the narrow patch of shaggy lawn between the pool and the house. A garden of tropical flowers flourished alongside the west wall and against the back of the house. When his eyes fell again on the nude sunbather, he quickly looked away.

"Betty," D'Amore called across the pool, "we have company. Cover up that enticing body. We're embarrassing the poor man."

The nude blond raised her head, gave Joe a look of irritation and then stood up, wrapped the beach towel around her hips like a sarong and sashayed, pert breasts bouncing in proud defiance, toward the back door.

Joe was irritated too. He didn't like being referred to as *the poor man*.

"Have a seat, Joe," D'Amore said. "*Mi casa es su casa.*"

He sat in a deck chair and angled it toward her. A round table with a green beach umbrella sticking out of it rested on the concrete between them, as if it was meant to keep him from invading the regal lady's space. She set her sweating glass on the table, picked up a gold cigarette case, pinched one out and mounted it in a long cigarette-holder. She lit it with a lighter sticking out of the head of a fat little bronze Buddha. She inhaled deeply, then vented smoke through pursed lips and flaring nostrils. Joe thought that if she held the cigarette any higher, she'd look like a vampish Statue of Liberty holding up a tiny tobacco torch.

She said, "I'm heart-sick about poor Liz. I'm sure you are too."

"Yeah, you look like you're all broken up over it."

She took another draw from her smoke without taking her eyes off him. "Surfaces are deceiving. Don't be fooled by the illusion."

"I guess you should know, since you made a career off it."

"Illusion? Yes, we all use it, in one way or another. It's not exclusive to Hollywood, you know. Everybody's an actor to some extent. Some of us are just better at the game."

"I'm not playing a game." He clasped his hands together and leaned forward. "I'm hunting the killer . . . of the woman

I loved." He was going to say more, but his voice had started to tremble with emotion. He reached into his shirt pocket for his cigarettes. He lit one with Buddha's flaming head.

"And you're here because you think I can help you find him." She took a sip of her drink.

"If it is a *him*. It could just as easily be a woman."

"You really think so?" D'Amore uncrossed her ankles and casually bent one knee, showing off a shapely calf.

"You bet. Like the woman you played in that movie. *Torrid Town*. You were one cold-blooded bitch."

"Liz's favorite movie," she said as an aside. "Yes, Lena Devore was certainly that. Classic *feme fatale*. I really got my teeth into that role."

"You sure you weren't playing yourself?"

She smiled. Without makeup, she looked somehow younger than she had on celluloid, though she was a decade older now. "You come straight out with it, don't you? You don't waste time with subtleties."

"I told you, I'm not playing a game here. So how about dropping the act and telling me what you know about what happened to Lizabeth."

"All right. That's easy enough." She paused to take another drag from the tip of her cigarette-holder. Then she spoke, smoke billowing out with her words: "I certainly didn't kill her. I can't tell you who did. I loved Liz. I would never have done anything to hurt her."

"You loved her." He said it flatly.

"Of course, I did."

"And you knew her how long?"

She smiled and got a faraway look in her eyes, as if remembering something funny. "We first met when you two were still married. She and her friend Valentine showed up at my door like star-struck teenagers, stewed to the gills and silly as hell."

"You knew her *that* long?" Joe found this hard to swallow. Surely Liz would've told him about meeting her screen idol. She would've been too excited not to. Unless she'd had reason to keep him in the dark.

"Cross my heart." She made an X across her bosom, letting her fingertip linger provocatively on the creamy cleft. "You won't like this, Joe, but I knew she was going to give you the heave-ho before you ever saw it coming."

"No." He shook his head, trying to shake off what he'd just heard.

"No? *No*, you don't like it, or *no*, you don't believe it?"

He didn't answer. He was caught in a sudden rush of vertigo, feeling as if the ground beneath him might not be as solid as he'd always assumed. After staring at her for a long moment, he shook his head again and said, "You know how to pull the rug out from under a guy, don't you."

She shrugged her bare shoulders, slowly, seductively, her breasts nuzzling against each other within the skimpy top of her swimsuit. "You wanted the truth. But I'll tell you something, Joe. Sometimes it's wiser to let things lie. No pun intended."

The back door slammed. An olive-skinned petite woman in pink shorts and matching jersey walked toward them, carrying a small tray with a single drink on it. She was barefoot. As she came closer, Joe could see that she wasn't wearing a brassiere. At Chateau D'Amore, even the hired help was sexy; a good set of knockers a prerequisite.

"Here's Frida with your drink," said D'Amore. "She's from Havana and she 'haf leedle English,' as she says. I just adore her accent. If I were still in the movie business, I'd get her a walk-on."

Frida set the tall glass of orange juice and vodka on Joe's side of the table and then did a little courtesy-like dip.

"Thanks," he said. He picked up the glass and took a big swig.

"Thank you, Frida," said D'Amore. "Has anyone called?"

Frida shook her head. She had a pixie face with a small chin. "No ma'am."

"If anyone does, I'm not available."

"Jes ma'am." Frida turned and walked back to the house.

D'Amore removed the butt of her cigarette from the holder and crushed it in the ashtray. Then she reloaded the butt-holder with a fresh smoke and fired it up. She performed the little ritual as if it might have some deeper meaning Joe wasn't privy to. She studied him a moment, then asked, "Why do you want to do this, Joe? Why not leave it to the police? Liz divorced you. Severed her ties to you. You don't owe her anything. It's too late for that."

He weighed the question and gave serious thought to the answer. Then he said, "Maybe I owe it to myself. Maybe I didn't really know her like I should've, and maybe that was partly my own fault, and partly hers. Maybe I want to know who Lizabeth really was."

"Oh, I think I see. You want to understand why she cut you out of her life."

"I wanna know why she was murdered and who did it."

"You're thinking the two are related? Why she left you and why she was killed?"

He shrugged. The vodka was already swimming on strong strokes to his head. The atmosphere inside his skull was changing, high-pressure fronts converging. "And aside from my personal reasons, her father's paying me to play detective. I've got a license, a gun, the works."

She laughed. It was a musical laugh, vamping like a jazz riff. "So you really *are* playing a role. Joe Dall, private eye. You know, you *do* look the part. I can picture you up on the screen as the down-at-the-heels dick, tortured by lost love and bent on revenge. But trust me, Joe, those trite plots always have tragic endings."

"It's gonna end with the killer going down, tragic or not."

He put his glass on the table. It was already half empty. He feared he was falling under this woman's alluring spell. He was here to grill her but she was the one coaxing information from him. And what was worse, she had the advantage of already knowing too much about him and his failed marriage. The woman was cunning and he knew it, yet he was close to spilling his guts and revealing even more of his personal life to her. He *wanted* to open up to her, probably because she'd been closer to Lizabeth during the final months of her life than he had, and that made the woman a kind of a proxy—Liz's stand-in. But D'Amore was holding the high cards, playing them close to that lovely chest, and the best Joe could do was bluff his way to the next hand before getting busted out of the game. He leaned back in his chair and tried to fashion a poker-face.

"May I see it?" she asked. "Your license?"

"What for?"

"I've never seen a real one. Humor me, Joe."

He leaned forward and fished his wallet out of his rear pocket and showed her his spanking-new detective's license.

"Very impressive," she said. "From bouncer to shamus, just like that." She snapped her fingers. "But you were a war hero, too. That gives you extra moxie."

"I wasn't a hero." He stuck the wallet back in his pocket.

"Liz thought you were. She was proud of you for that."

"Yeah? That was probably the only thing about me she was proud of."

"You really have no idea why she dumped you, do you?" A look of concern came into her face. Joe didn't trust it. The woman could run through a gamut of phony emotions in nothing flat if she wanted to. She was the consummate professional.

"Do *you?*" he shot back.

"I think I do." She smiled behind a cloud of cigarette smoke. "When we know each other a little better, maybe I'll tell you."

He snatched up his drink, then set it back down without taking a sip. He squirmed in his chair, caught himself doing it, and remembered he was supposed to be sporting his poker-face—if he even had one. "Look," he said, "this cat-and-mouse racket is getting old. Stop playing with me."

"If I were playing with you, we'd both know it, Joe. The hard evidence of it would be standing straight up between us, at attention like a fine little soldier." She tongued her lips and smiled.

He grabbed his glass and gulped down a couple of good swallows. She had the upper hand again, and he was floundering like a fish on a hook.

D'Amore laughed again, mocking him, he was sure.

Fuming now, he launched a desperate offensive. "Look. I know Lizabeth took you to the fortuneteller. I know you went with her to get that tattoo. I know you got drummed out of Hollywood for . . . God-knows-what. What I don't know is what you were up to with my wife. So why don't you cut the crap and tell me. What were you really after? Her money? Her old man's connections? Go on, I'm all ears."

"Well. That's really not bad work for a novice gumshoe. I'm impressed. But I already told you, I loved Liz. Love was all I was *up to.* I assure you, I didn't need her money. And her daddy's political connections are of no consequence to me. I did flirt with politics while I was in Hollywood, but that's in the past. Politics bores me to tears now."

"Flirted with Communism." He was anxious to press his perceived advantage.

"Yes, I'm sorry to say. Never again. We all make mistakes. That was one of my big ones. You'd think I would've learned a lesson."

"Meaning you didn't?"

"Let me tell you something about me, Joe. I'm the sort of person who's always searching for something, something to give meaning to life. Something larger than myself. Oscar says all true actors are empty vessels, yearning to be filled. I don't know that he isn't right. When politics didn't do it for me, I eventually turned to the spiritual world. Not standard organized religion, mind you. The occult."

"Like the fortuneteller." Good, he thought, now we're getting somewhere.

"No. Well, yes, but I'm afraid I got involved in something much darker than fortunetelling. You don't want to know."

Joe had a sudden hunch. He played it. "You got Lizabeth in it too, didn't you?"

"The less you know about this, the better. It's dangerous, Joe. I didn't know how dangerous until . . ."

"Until it got Lizabeth killed?" He had a queasy feeling in his belly. He'd made a wild throw and he was unexpectedly afraid it had hit the mark.

"I'm sorry," she said, her eyes brimming with tears. "I can't talk about this now."

"The hell you can't." He was sitting on the edge of the deck chair now. He was on the verge of reaching out, grabbing her and shaking it out of her. "Spit it out, sister. And turn off the crocodile tears."

Wiping a tear from the corner of her eye with a fingertip, she suddenly laughed, wet eyes sparkling, and said, "That's awful dialogue, Joe. You want to stay away from those clichés. Rewrite!"

Joe cursed under his breath as he stood up and reached down for her arm.

"Get your hands off her!" Oscar shouted as he burst from the house and charged toward them.

With D'Amore's upper arm in his grasp, Joe yelled over his shoulder: "Butt out, Oscar. This ain't your business."

"Stop it, you're hurting me," she said with too much volume and vigor, like a stage actress in a bad melodrama. Joe caught on that she was playing it up for Oscar Lamont, manipulating the galoot to violence. He let go of her and turned toward Lamont, who was rumbling around the shallow end of the pool, coming on fast for all his hulking bulk.

"Hold on," Joe said. He held his hands up in front of him. "I didn't hurt her."

Then Oscar was on him. He grabbed Joe's right shoulder, gave it a hard jerk and sucker-punched him with a big right mitt to the jaw.

Joe reeled backward into hot darkness.

CHAPTER EIGHT

He came back to the world of light with a start. He was in a dim room with the window shades drawn, lying on a soft bed canopied in frilly red and tented with the same translucent material. He raised his head off the pillow and saw Lizabeth standing at the foot of the bed, her face crimsoned and blurred by the filmy curtain between them.

"Lizzy," he whispered as he sat up for a better look. The act of sitting up so quickly spiked a sharp pain through his skull and sent black waves washing against the backsides of his eyes, blacking out his vision of her and pulling his head back to the pillow as if caught in a tidal backwash. He groaned, pressing his palms to his eyes.

"Easy, big fella," said a girly voice.

When his head stopped swimming dark waves, he glanced to his right and saw Betty the nude sunbather sitting at his bedside. She wasn't nude now, but she wasn't far from it, dressed as she was in a hot-pink French bikini.

"Did you see her?" he asked.

"See who, honey?" Betty had a movie magazine balanced on her bare thigh and a cigarette hanging from her lips. "It's just you and me here. Laura said I should sit with you till you came around."

Joe looked beyond the foot of the bed, where Lizabeth had been standing—or floating—on the other side of the diaphanous red curtain hanging from the canopy of the oversized bed. She wasn't there now. Hadn't been there then. He'd taken too many big-fisted shots to the head these last few days. No great wonder he was seeing things. Lizzy was dead. She wasn't coming back, not even as a ghost.

"How long have I been out?" He rubbed his bone-sore jaw.

"Oh . . . ten minutes maybe. That Oscar packs a wallop, huh? He thought you were trying to hurt Laura, but she told him you didn't really mean to hurt her. You were just upset. Oscar's like her guardian sometimes, you know? Her big lovable watchdog."

"Gorilla's more like it."

Betty chuckled, dropping ash from her dangling smoke. "Shit. I'm not even spoze to be smoking in here. I better duck this butt." She got up and went into the adjoining bathroom. She returned with the sound of the commode gurgling behind her.

Joe's eyes went from her breasts to her belly and came to rest on the tattoo on her inner thigh, just at the edge of her bikini bottom. It was the same rose-in-a-triangle Lizzy had on her thigh. "Nice tattoo," he said, his mind suddenly racing a maze.

Betty smiled. "Thanks."

"What's it mean?"

"It means it hurt like hell going on. That's a tender spot, you know?" Betty's accent suggested New York. Joe had been exposed to all sorts of accents during his stint in the Marines and he'd gotten pretty good at identifying them.

"Yeah, I can imagine," he said. "But what does it mean?"

"It's just one of Laura's quirks, you know? She likes all her girlfriends to have 'em."

"Girlfriends," he thoughtfully echoed. "You must feel pretty lucky, being the girlfriend of a movie star. Having her mark on you."

Betty shrugged. "Yeh, I guess. But the way things are now, I'm not sure the luck's all that good."

"How so?"

"Oh, you know, with that creepy—" Betty broke off in the middle of her sentence. "You don't know about that, do you? About Chago?"

"No. What's that?" Joe was already frustrated with the way the girl flitted from one topic to another without giving him time to get his teeth into any one topic. He'd wanted to find out exactly what Betty meant by *girlfriend*, but now she'd tossed out *creepy* with *Chago*, and he was compelled to go after the toss like a mutt chasing a stick.

"He's this guy," she said, making a sour face to show her distaste, "Laura can't get rid of. He's . . . I better not say. You should ask her. She'll tell you if she wants you to know. It's . . ." She shuddered, then reached for another cigarette.

Joe eased up to a sitting position and swung his legs over the side of the bed. He found his pack of Luckies in his shirt pocket and Betty used her lighter to fire it for him. His jaw made a clicking noise when he spoke again. "Does Laura have a lot of girlfriends?"

"You ask questions like a cop. You're not, are you?"

"No. I was married to Lizabeth Tibbedeaux. You knew her, right?"

"Sure." She pronounced it *shu-wah*. "Sweet girl. So you're the poor smuck she dumped."

"Yeah. I'm the smuck." He dropped his eyes to the rug. Then he looked up again through the bluish smoke. "She had one of those tattoos too."

"Say, what's your deal, anyway? Are you trying to make trouble for Laura or something? 'Cause if you are, you can take a hike. Off a short pier."

"I'm trying to find out who killed Lizzy." His jaw clicked

again. Lamont's fist had done some lasting damage. Trying to keep his jaw from opening too wide when he spoke, Joe said through clenched teeth, "When I do, there's gonna be big trouble for everybody in on it. If the Laura D'Amore Girlfriend Club had anything to do with it, you'll be in the stew too. And I'll enjoy turning up the heat."

"Humph. Big tough guy. I don't think I like you."

"That's okay, you don't have to." Now that he'd unintentionally antagonized her, he figured he might as well go all the way and try a little intimidation. She didn't seem too bright so it might work on her. "I'm also a private detective and I'm pretty good at getting the truth out of people and knowing when somebody's lying. You seem like a nice girl. I hope I don't have to get rough with you."

She responded with an abrasive laugh. Then she narrowed her eyes and issued a brazen challenge. "Go ahead, get rough. I'll yell for Oscar and he'll knock you on your can again." Again with the laugh. Then: "Rough, hah! Don't make me laugh."

He fished-eyed her, giving her what he hoped was a threatening scowl. "Look, toots, I ain't gonna hurt you. But if you know anything about this mess, you're better off telling me instead of the cops. Lizabeth's father is rich and powerful. You get him coming down on you, you'll lose everything. Your good looks will be the first thing to go." Joe was winging it now, zeroing in on what he thought her weakness might be.

Betty jumped up and stomped out of the room. Joe couldn't help admiring the girly-show moves of her near-naked backside. He stubbed his smoke, found his shoes and slipped them on, then went looking for Laura D'Amore.

He walked down a long hallway toward the sound of voices from another room. He'd left his gun at home, figuring it wouldn't be quite proper to bring a weapon to his meeting with D'Amore, but with Lamont the guardian gorilla being so quick to throw punches, Joe wished now he was packing the equalizer so he could wave it in Lamont's face if the guy wanted to start throwing his fat fists around again. When he heard Lamont's baritone voice, Joe picked up a tall vase off an antique table in the hall. He hoped it was hefty enough to do some damage to Oscar's thick skull, but he had his doubts.

The Cuban housekeeper appeared in the hallway in front of him. She pointed a finger at him and said, "Chew put that back! Meez D'Amore! He stealin'!"

Before Joe could deny the accusation, Oscar Lamont came charging into the hallway and brushed past the petite woman.

"Stay away from me," Joe warned, gripping the vase by its tapered neck and cocking it over his shoulder, "or I'll bash your skull."

Oscar halted with a wiseacre smirk on his face. "Put that down, Dall. That vase is worth more than you'll make in a lifetime."

"It'll make an expensive dent in your head too." Joe's jaw clicked as he spoke.

D'Amore appeared behind Lamont. She was wearing a knee-length terrycloth cover-up over her swimsuit. She said, "Go sit down, Oscar. You're frightening him."

"Yeah, Oscar, go sit your ape ass down." Joe shook the vase at him.

Oscar looked like he wanted to start ripping Joe apart, but she tugged his sleeve and pointed him into the other room, and he shambled off like a big sulky child.

D'Amore walked up to Joe and took the vase from him and returned it to its place on the table. "A couple of overgrown boys acting like you're on a schoolyard," she said.

"Hey, he started it. I think he dislocated my jaw. It clicks every time I talk. There. Did you hear it?"

"I'm sorry he hit you. He's very protective of me. You shouldn't have laid your hands on me the way you did."

"Sorry about that. But you shouldn't've been playing so cozy coy with me. What'd you expect me to do? Bow down and kiss your famous feet?"

"What I expect you to do now is leave." She folded her arms across her chest.

"Uh-uh. Not before you get off the dime and tell me what you were talking about out by the pool. About what you got Lizabeth into. That occult crap."

"I didn't say that."

"I read between the lines. I'm not stupid. And you're not that good an actress."

Anger flashed in her dark eyes. Joe smiled, knowing he'd scored with a stinger.

"I'm trying to do you a favor, Joe. Trust me, you do not want to get involved in this. It could get you killed."

"I notice you're still alive and kicking."

"This could get worse than deadly." She said her enigmatic line with such solemn delivery that Joe got goose bumps. She *was* good—or she was telling the truth.

"What's worse than deadly?" he asked, trying to ignore the nagging clicks from his jaw. "How can anything be worse than that?"

She gave him a look of concern. "Your jaw really is clicking." She took his hand and led him into a big sunroom, where Lamont and Betty were sitting near a huge aquarium with drinks in their hands. Jazz played softly on the hi-fi console in the corner. Frida the housekeeper peeked down the hall to make sure the vase was safe, then gave Joe a dirty look and flitted out of the room. One wall was decorated with a dozen or more wooden masks which looked like authentic artifacts of some lost tribe of ancient aboriginal pagans. Each mask was unique, some scarier than others. Collectively, they gave Joe a bad case of the creeps, the way they all seemed to be looking right at him with sinister eyeholes.

"Oscar," said D'Amore, "see if you can fix his jaw. It makes a popping noise when he speaks."

Standing, Oscar smirked and said, "Some guys are always popping off at the mouth."

"He's not touching me," Joe said.

"Relax, Joe," D'Amore said, squeezing his hand. "Oscar's a trained chiropractor. He won't hurt you."

"I don't need a back-cracker, I need a real doctor."

"You need a lot of things," said Lamont. "I'd put etiquette training at the top of the list."

"A back-cracking zombie comedian," said Joe. "You're a regular one-man show."

Oscar smiled weakly. "Look, Joe. I'm sorry I hit you. You were upset, I was upset. It's over. Now come sit in this chair so I can reset your jaw. Laura won't let me hear the end of it if I don't."

Joe backed off a little. "Will it hurt?"

"Just for a second, then it will feel better. Sit."

He sat in a tall wicker chair and looked up warily at Oscar. "Lucky for me you didn't throw all your weight behind that punch or I'd be a dead man."

"That could be an insult or a compliment," the big man said. "Rather than try to decipher it, I'll just ignore it. Now, let your jaw hang open while I have a look."

Joe let his jaw drop. Oscar's thick fingers explored Joe's chin and jaw, pressing here, pinching there, poking tender spots near the ears until he grunted and said, "I should fix that easily enough." Then he moved behind Joe and put one hand on top of his head while reaching around and seizing Joe's chin with the other hand.

Joe knew the brute could snap his neck with little effort, if he wanted to. Had D'Amore already told him to do it? A broken neck was easy enough to explain. They could say he dove into the pool (nude) and hit the bottom. End of sad story.

"You know, Joe, I used to be chiropractor to the stars. That's how I got my first film role. These hands have worked on many famous bodies."

Joe couldn't speak, so he grunted acknowledgment. What he really wanted to do was bolt out of the chair and out of Oscar's powerful grip.

Oscar said, "Okay, relax and hold your breath." He gave a controlled jerk on Joe's chin, keeping his vice-grip on the back of his head. There was a little *snap* just below Joe's left ear, accompanied by an electric current of ear-to-ear pain, and then Oscar released him, saying, "There, that should do it."

Joe tentatively worked his jaw and tugged on his chin. No clicks. Not much pain.

"Better?" asked Oscar.

"Yeah. Thanks."

"I'm sorry I hurt you, but you had no business manhandling a lady."

"Yeah." Joe looked at D'Amore. "I'm sorry about that, Miss D'Amore. I got a little carried away. I let you push my buttons."

"I understand," she said. "No harm done. But it would be best for you to leave now. Better still for you to drop this amateur investigation of yours."

Joe got up. "Who's Chago?" he asked her pointblank.

Now D'Amore's jaw dropped. "How did—" She gave Betty a look sharp enough to peel a grapefruit.

"It just slipped out," Betty said. "He tricked me."

"What did she tell you?" she asked, rounding on Joe.

"That this Chago is a creepy guy. A bad luck kind of guy. Is he part of your occult deal?"

"He's not anybody you want to know," she said, her voice going cold. "Goodbye, Joe. Oscar, would you see him out?"

Lamont nodded and made a move toward Joe. Joe balled his fists, then thought better of it and allowed Oscar to walk him to the door. "Thanks for the drink," Joe said to D'Amore. "I'll be seeing you."

"No, I don't believe you will," she said, lighting a fresh cigarette in her holder and raising it high between two fingers. The classic pose of the celluloid vamp. The one she'd played to perfection in *Torrid Town*.

Oscar walked him to his car and opened the driver's door for him. The sun was hammering heat on the Buick, and a gust of scorched air from the car's interior hit Joe in the face. He stepped back from it and said, "She's scared, Oscar. We both know it. Whatever kind of jam she's in with this Chago, I could help her out of it."

"No, you couldn't. You'd only make things worse if you interfered. For everyone's sake, don't stick your nose in things you know nothing about. Take my word for it. You don't want to get involved in this horrid business. It's worse than anything you could imagine."

"Is that from a movie? Sounds a little too pat. What's the real story on Chago?"

Lamont gave a heavy sigh. "Unless you want to shake hands with the Devil, you don't want to know Chago."

"What is he, a Devil worshipper?"

"Chago *is* the Devil."

"Sure he is," Joe said. He slid behind the wheel, slammed the door and started the engine. "I had hundreds of slant-eyed devils trying to kill me in the war. I don't scare that easy, Oscar."

He put the car in gear and drove off. Despite his boast to Lamont, he was scared spitless. As scared as he'd been during his first taste of combat in Korea.

CHAPTER NINE

On the drive back to the lake, he chain-smoked Luckies and absently listened to the radio. His head was humming louder than the music, tunelessly abuzz with the skinny he'd gathered from D'Amore and company, but he couldn't seem to sort it all out. There were too many tangled leads going off in too many directions. A big balled-up knot had been dumped in his lap and he didn't know where to begin to untangle it.

Aside from the introduction of Chago the mystery man into the mix, the most troubling thing he'd learned was that Lizabeth's friendship with D'Amore predated the breakup of his marriage. Lizzy and her friend Valentine Cooper had crashed D'Amore's party and Liz had been accepted (initiated?) into the Girlfriend Club. Had Val been rejected? Or had she balked at the strange going-ons at Chateau D'Amore? From what he knew of Val Cooper, she was probably too straight-laced for the Hollywood-style morality and would've seen it as depravity, but she might've stayed with it long enough to learn some things that could further his investigation. He would try her number again as soon as he got back to the bungalow. Intuition told him she was going to be important.

Tall tropical clouds were stacking up in the sky ahead. One of them suggested a giant mushroom, the atom-bomb kind. The hot sunny day was turning dark and threatening around the edges, but Joe had a creepy feeling he was heading for the center of a dangerous storm that had nothing to do with the weather.

* * *

It was half past four and raining when he flopped in his easy chair and picked up the phone to try Valentine Cooper again. After the tenth ring he hung up.

Val's family was old money, and she didn't have to work. She was in her late twenties and strikingly beautiful with her pixie face and fiery red hair that would've given D'Amore a run for her money in the beauty department. Like Lizabeth, she had married below her station, but unlike Joe, her husband had achieved dignified status by getting killed in Korea. Joe dug out his phone book and looked up the number for Val's parents. He dialed it.

"Stimson residence," the colored maid answered.

"This is Joseph Dall. I need to get in touch with Valentine about the life insurance policy I sold her. She's not answering at her home number and I was hoping her folks might know how I can reach her. It's very important."

"She in St. Augustine, at the Stimson's beach house."

"Could you give me that number? I sure would appreciate it. And the address too, if you have it. I need to take her some policy documents."

"Reckon I can. Just a minute."

Joe lit another Lucky and waited, listening to the rain drumming on the roof. A couple of minutes later the maid came back on the line and gave him the phone number and address of the Stimson's house on St. Augustine Beach. He jotted down the numbers in the address book, thanked her, depressed the switch-hook and dialed the beach house. After the tenth ring he was ready to slam the phone down in frustration but then she answered. It was a poor connection. The storm's lightning caused intermittent crashes of static.

"Val?" he said above a crashing hiss.

"Yes?"

"This is Joe Dall."

"Joe . . .?"

"Yeah. Listen, I—"

"I'm so sorry about Lizzy," she said, her voice breaking. "I still can't believe it."

She sounded close to tears and he wanted to head off a crying jag if he could. He said, "Listen, Val, I need your help. I'm trying to find out who did it. Lizzy's father is backing me on this. Can I ask you a few questions?"

"I can't tell you anything about that. I don't—"

"You went with her to see Laura D'Amore. I think those people out there know something they won't talk to me about. If you—"

"I'm sorry, Joe. I can't . . . I have to go." The raw fear in her voice was unmistakable.

Val hung up. Joe cursed, convinced she was hiding something. He called her back. This time she didn't answer.

He put on a fresh shirt, grabbed the address book, ran out to his car in the downpour and cranked up. It was a two hour drive to St. Augustine. He could be there by sunset, if the storm didn't slow him down too much.

Whatever Val knew, it was scaring the hell out of her. He was going to confront her face to face, and he wasn't going to leave until she told him all she knew.

*   *   *

It was dark and rainy when he turned off Highway A1A and turned onto Sea Grass Road. It was a narrow tongue of blacktop dead-ending at the edge of the dunes. Rain-beaten sea oats waved in the wind. The Buick's headlights arced over dumpy dunes and faded to black where the Atlantic's waves tumbled ashore with a steady sizzling roar.

He confirmed the number on the mailbox and pulled into

the short driveway of the two-story beach house. There was a flagpole in the backyard, Old Glory flapping and flagging in the windy rain. He parked beside Val's fiery red '57 Thunderbird (the red matched her hair) and killed the engine. The top-floor windows glowed with homey yellow light. Unless she was out on the beach in the night rain, Valentine was inside.

Joe got out and rang the doorbell. A small awning over the door kept most of the rain off him. He heard her thumping down the stairs on the other side of the door. "Who is it?" she called.

"Joe Dall," he shouted back. "Open up, Val."

A latch snapped back and the door swung open. Val frowned, eyeing him with suspicion. She wasn't happy to see him. Dark emotion clouded her fair complexion. "What're you doing here?" she asked, her voice edged with belligerence.

"Like I told you, I need your help. Can I come in? It's sort of damp out here."

She stepped aside to let him in. She had on a pair of black shorts and a white top that looked like a puffy strapless bra, but wasn't. It was apparently the latest in sexy chic beachwear. She was barefoot. Most of the red lacquer on her toenails had flaked off. Her full head of hair was pulled back and fastened in a blowsy tail. She had chimerical eyes that seemed to change color with variations in the lighting. Now they were shining like wet emeralds in pale moonlight.

"You came all this way for nothing," she said, looking down at the sand-smeared doormat just inside the door.

"I don't think so. I talked to Laura D'Amore today. She told me you were there with Lizzy. Did you get the tattoo, too?" He glanced behind her and up the long narrow stairway to the main floor.

"Tattoo?"

"The rose in the triangle like Lizzy had. And Betty, the girl who likes to sunbathe in the nude."

"Come on up," she said in obvious resignation, then started up the stairs ahead of him. He followed her, trying to keep his eyes off the pleasing spectacle of her shapely backside.

She led him to a small pine-paneled living room with a nice view of the beach. Rain pattered and pooled on the wooden deck on the other side of the sliding glass door. A small television flickered in the corner. It might've been a quiz show on the screen but it was hard to tell because the picture was snowy and rolling, and the sound was turned way down. The picture stopped rolling long enough for him to see a quiz show contestant in a soundproof booth. He moved farther into the room and the picture rolled again, his body's electromagnetic charge screwing up the reception even more.

"Have a seat," she said with a wave to the sofa. "Want a beer?"

"Yeah, I could use one." He sank into soft sofa cushions.

She went into the kitchen and came back with two bottles of Carling's Black Label. "Mabel, Black Label," she said, tunelessly repeating the beer's advertising jingle. She gave him one and sat on the other end of the sofa, curling her legs under her. "I don't know what to tell you, Joe. I was out there once or twice, and that's it. I wasn't taken with those people the way Lizzy was. You do know Laura D'Amore was her idol, right? She was thrilled just to breathe the same air, you know? What can I tell you?" Val shrugged.

Joe took a sip of brew. "Does D'Amore like the girls?"

"You mean . . .?"

"Yeah, instead of guys. Did she and Liz . . . uh, you know . . ."

"Oh. Why do you want to know this now? Lizzy's gone. It doesn't feel right to talk about her this way." She clicked her nails nervously against the bottle.

"I need to know," he said. "D'Amore said she loved Liz. Does that mean what I think it means?"

Val solemnly nodded. "They were lovers. Lizzy was really smitten with the woman. She would've followed her over a cliff, no questions asked."

"That's what I thought. But she went over the cliff and D'Amore didn't." He stared out at the rain. A giant fork of lightning stabbed the Atlantic.

"I tried to talk sense to her, but she wouldn't hear it. She was like a lamb among wolves and she knew it but didn't care. It was like she wanted to see how far she could go." She shook her head. "She changed, Joe. I really didn't know her anymore. I didn't *want* to know her. They had these wild parties with illegal drugs and booze. She tried to get me to go to one of their . . . sex orgies. I told her she was nuts. She just laughed and said I was too square."

Joe nodded and worked to keep his face impassive.

"Is this what you wanted to hear, Joe? That she divorced you so she could live wild with those Hollywood weirdos? That she had a colossal crush on Laura D'Amore?"

"I have to hear it," he said, trying to wash the bad taste from his mouth with beer. "Did you know a guy named Chago?"

Val flinched. She seemed to shrink into the sofa. Her mouth worked but no sound came out. Finally, she said, "He's the reason I left town."

"What?" He'd heard her well enough, but it caught him off guard.

"I got scared when I heard about Lizzy. I was afraid he would come after me next."

"You're saying *he* killed her? Chago?"

"I don't know, not for a fact. But he's . . ."

"The Devil."

Val paled—no easy trick for such a fair-skinned redhead. She looked ready to cry.

"That's what Oscar Lamont called him," he explained.

"You know Oscar? Big guy who played a baldheaded zombie in that horror movie? Uncanny something-or-other."

She nodded. "I met him my last night there."

"So you were there more than once."

She nodded. "I was . . . I know I shouldn't have . . ." She got flustered and broke off.

He reached across the sofa and took her hand, surprising himself with the easy intimacy. "Val, you don't have to worry about me. I won't judge you. You know me. I'm no goody-goody angel. Whatever you say stays between us. I promise."

"I'm too ashamed." She looked at her hand in his as if she wanted to be reassured by the contact but didn't think it could really work that way.

"Please, Val."

She gave his fingers a squeeze. "Okay. But you can never repeat this."

"You have my word. Boy Scout's honor."

"You're not a Boy Scout," she said with a hollow laugh.

"Marine's honor. *Semper fi*. Always faithful." He tried to smile but it felt more like a soldier's sneer.

"God, I can't believe I'm doing this. Promise you won't think I'm a slut."

"I promise." He squeezed her hand.

She tossed back a quick couple of swallows of beer. "Okay, here goes. Lizzy and I were three sheets to the wind the first night we went out there. We were like silly little teenagers. We were on the Yellow Brick Road and Laura D'Amore was the Great and Powerful Oz. It was just a lark, you know? A big stupid goof. We had no idea we would run into a real wizard. And even now I'm not sure if Laura is the good witch or the Wicked Witch of the West."

She downed the rest of the Black Label, belched quietly and said, "I need another beer."

"Sit tight. I'll get it." Joe stood up and started for the kitchen.

"Joe? There's a bottle of tequila on the counter. Bring that and two shot glasses. I need something stronger than beer to get all this out."

He came back, set the shot glasses on the coffee table and filled them with tequila. He gave one to her, raised his and said, "Bottoms up."

She downed the shot, then made a sour face and shuddered like a toddler sucking on a lemon. "Ugghh, that's nasty. But it does the trick."

"Take your time. Here, chase it with this." He handed her his beer and she chased the liquor with it. He poured two more shots.

"All right. Now I'm ready," she said with phony bravura. "That first night, we thought for sure she'd run us off or sic the cops on us, but she took us right in like she'd been expecting us. There were a couple of guys just in from California that night and one of 'em obviously had the hots for me right away. Laura was already making the moves on Lizzy, cozying up and pouring booze down her and even getting her to smoke cigarettes. Then Todd—the guy who wanted in my pants—lit up a reefer. You know, marihuana? We were too far gone by then to say no to anything. They passed it around and everybody smoked it. Then we *really* got silly. Next thing I know, I'm in a bedroom and Todd's taking my clothes off. He's already naked and his thing is up and rearing to go. God, I can't believe I'm telling you this."

"It's okay. Go on."

"I hadn't been with a man since the night before Steve left for Korea, and when I saw how much Todd wanted me, I knew it was what I needed to officially end my period of mourning for Steve. I remember thinking, *This will lay the grieving widow to rest once and for all so I can get on with the next phase of my life.* And then we did it. The grieving widow got laid, all right."

She paused to down the next tequila shot. She avoided his eyes.

"Lizzy told me later that Laura had seduced her in the master bedroom. I wasn't really surprised, after seeing them play footsy all night. And Lizzy was so . . . *happy* about it. Like she thought making love to another woman was perfectly normal. And I guess it was, for them. I mean, I tried it the next night we were out there, after Todd and the other guy were gone. It was just me and Liz and Betty and Laura. They fed us pep pills and we smoked a lot of reefer. All four of us ended up in bed together. I guess you'd call it an orgy. I went along with it for Lizzy's sake, but I didn't like it. I mean, it felt okay, you know? But just the idea that it's a woman doing it . . . I mean, *yuck!* You know?"

Joe nodded. He had a yucky feeling just hearing about it, but at the same time it was making him hot. Listening to Val's description of their sexual escapades and picturing Lizabeth in the thick of it aroused him to a startling degree. He hoped Val didn't notice the bulge in his pants. He hadn't been with a woman since Liz dumped him.

"After that, I told Lizzy I didn't want to go out there anymore, that I didn't go for that Isle of Lesbos stuff."

"That *what?*"

"Lesbos. A Greek island where Sappho the poet lived and taught at like this girls' school. Apparently, they did more than write love poems. That's where the word *lesbian* comes from. Lesbos. Laura told us all about it. She's one smart Lesbian. Well, actually she says she's *bi*sexual, that she likes to sleep with men sometimes too, but she likes women best."

"Did Lizzy sleep with men at any of these orgies?" He was

surprised at how easily the question came out.

"Oh, you're still jealous, aren't you? This must be hard for you to listen to." She leaned over and patted his shoulder. "You have to get over her, Joe. Just let her go. It's not healthy the way you're still trying to hold on to her. She used to worry about you for that."

"Did she? Sleep with a man?"

Val's face turned cloudy again. She looked out at the rainy night on the other side of the glass. "Just once," she said, tentative. "With *him*. Chago."

"God*dammit*." He wanted to throw his beer bottle through the glass door. "Who *is* this son of a bitch? And don't say he's the Devil."

"She didn't wanna do it. She was afraid not to. Even Laura was scared of him."

"Why? Why is everybody so goddamn afraid of this shit heel?"

"If you saw him you'd know. Something about his eyes sends shivers and gives you the creeps. He's like some kind of voodoo man, except it's not really voodoo. It's something worse. Laura called it *Palo* or something like that. Whatever it is, it's scary as hell. And so is he."

Joe drained his shot and refilled both their glasses. "If he's such a bad guy, why did she let him hang around?"

"She was afraid of what would happen if she bucked him. Laura was mixed up in this occult stuff, this Palo black magic."

"Yeah, she mentioned something about that. So that's how she met up with Chago?"

"Evidently. But by the time she saw what he really was, it was too late. She didn't know how to get rid of him. Lizzy even took her to a palm reader for spiritual guidance, but of course that didn't do her any good. I think Chago was blackmailing her. No, that's not right, not blackmail. Extortion.

That's when you give somebody money because they threaten you, right? But it's not just money he wants, apparently. I get the idea he wants her to do something for him, but I don't know what, and in the meantime she was paying him off so something bad wouldn't happen to her."

"And something bad happened to Lizzy," he said, suddenly seeing it. "He killed her as a warning to D'Amore, didn't he? To show her he meant business."

"I don't know. Not for sure. But that's what I've been thinking."

"And that's why you left town. 'Cause you thought you might be the next warning."

Val nodded. "I panicked. I couldn't just stay home and wait for something bad to happen. Something *else*."

"So Chago knew D'Amore had a thing for Liz and that's why he killed her. I don't see how that would make you his next target. What about Betty? She's got the mark. The tattoo. You don't have one, do you?"

"Hell no! I wouldn't let anybody take a needle to me. And anyway, Laura didn't ask me to get one. I guess I didn't pass the Lesbos test."

Joe lit a cigarette. He offered one to Val, but she declined.

"So you don't know for a fact Chago killed her. You're just trying to put two and two together."

"Laura believes he did. She called to warn me. She said she didn't like the way she'd seen Chago looking at me. And that he could've killed Liz without even being there."

"How the hell could he do that?"

"Black magic. A curse? I don't know. That's just what Laura told me. Knowing Chago, I can almost believe it."

"She was *strangled,* for Christ's sake. With a bra strap. What's that, *bra* magic?"

"He could've made her strangle herself."

"That's crazy, Val. You make him out to be like some kind of Dracula hypnotizing his victims."

"Yeah, something like that. I don't know how he did it, but I know he did."

"And you came here to hide out. Aren't you afraid being alone here?"

"I have a couple of girlfriends here. Just *friends*. I invited them to come stay at the beach a few days. Susie's coming tomorrow. I'm really glad you came tonight, Joe. I'm sorry I gave you the brush-off on the phone, but I didn't want to face you. But here you are and I feel safer with you here. But when you rang the doorbell I almost wet my pants." She gave him a wounded smile.

"Chago doesn't seem like the doorbell type," he said. "If he's as bad as you say he is, he'd probably just fly up on bat wings and pass through that glass door there."

"If you saw him . . ." She poured herself another shot and downed it.

"Oh, I'll see him all right. I'll look right into his spooky eyes when I drive a stake through his goddamn heart."

"I wish you would," she said. Then she excused herself to go to the bathroom.

Joe got up and went out on the deck. The rain had dwindled to a light drizzle and it felt good on his face. The rhythm of the breaking waves was hypnotic. He stared at the great dark mass of the sea, and the sea and the night became one—the heart of the world beating back at the darkness.

"It's stopped raining," Val said behind him. "Just about."

"Yeah." Joe held onto the deck's wooden rail with both hands. The booze had made him lightheaded. He could feel waves of darkness tugging at him, trying to pull him under with its sinister undertow. He squared his feet and braced himself on the beach-house deck like a seaman in a storm.

Val came to the rail and leaned drunkenly into him. "Will you stay over tonight, Joe? I don't wanna be by myself."

He looked at her. She'd let her hair down so it fell loose on her bare shoulders. Light from inside the house filtered through the glass door. In the semidarkness her luxuriant locks glowed like crimson embers. Her eyes were faint pinpoints of waxy jade.

"The funeral's tomorrow morning at eleven," he said, working out what time he'd have to leave St. Augustine to make the graveside service. "I guess you're not going."

She shook her head. "I can't go back, not now. I want to but . . ."

She sobbed and buried her face in his shoulder. He slipped his arm around her.

"It's okay," he told her. "It doesn't matter. I saw her at the funeral home. That's not her in the box. She's somewhere else now."

"I know," Val said with a sob. "Heaven."

"No. She's still down here with us. I think she's been shadowing me."

* * *

He slept in one bedroom and Val slept in the other. He was pretty sure he could've slept in her bed if he'd lifted a little more than a finger to make it happen. She had enough tequila in her and was so spooked by Chago's alleged mystical powers that she would've been grateful to have Joe snuggle with her for the night, and she *was* damned attractive with her hair loose and wild, that puffy top clinging to her full breasts, her belly small and tight, but Joe wouldn't have felt right doing it—not with her drunk and Lizabeth's ghost abroad in the night. So he'd tucked her in, kissed her safely on the cheek and promised he'd be close by.

He hadn't gotten to know her very well when he was still with Lizabeth, but he always liked Val best of all Lizzy's friends. Though she was from a wealthy family, Val had never come across as snooty or stuck-up. And she'd never looked down her nose at him the way most of Liz's gal pals had. He went to bed thinking he'd like to know her better, and wondering if he would have these same feelings for her when he was sober. But first he had to deal with Chago and somehow lay Lizabeth's spirit to rest. Maybe it was stupid superstitious thinking, but he had the idea that Lizzy would leave him alone and move on to wherever ghosts were supposed to go once he took care of Chago. Wasn't that how it worked in all the ghost stories? Sure it was.

Another thing he liked about Val was the way she'd reacted when he told her Lizzy's ghost was following him. Instead of ridiculing him, she'd been sympathetic and supportive—even though she was far from sober herself.

She'd stiffened against him and said, "Ah, Joe, you've got it bad, poor baby. And here you are, comforting me. Don't do this to yourself. You've got to let her go."

"I keep seeing her," he insisted. "I don't know if she wants something from me or if she's haunting me just to punish me. She sure didn't want anything from me when she was alive."

"It's gotta be your imagination," she said, though she didn't sound all that convinced of it herself.

"A few minutes ago you were saying Lizzy could've been killed by black magic. Why is it so hard to believe in ghosts?"

"Because I know how you are about her. Obsessed."

She had him there. But that didn't rule out the existence of ghosts. "I know what I saw," he said.

Though the rain had stopped altogether, the high humidity was still having an effect on her hair, frizzing it, making it curl and giving it a wild fullness. She was looking more and more like a calendar babe—a redheaded vixen perfect for October, half-naked in a pumpkin patch, say. She leaned her breasts into him, held his hand with both of hers between their bellies and said, "We both loved her, Joe. Now we have to let her go. You were letting her haunt you when she was still alive, you know what I mean? After the divorce?"

He nodded. She had a point.

"Ghost or not, you have to say goodbye and turn her loose."

He told her he knew that, that he was working on it. He added, "Knowing she was in love with D'Amore will make it easier, I think. It helps explain why she jettisoned me. I never could quite understand it before. I knew I was always good to her. I just never knew she was the Lesbos type."

"Lesbian," she corrected him with a downbeat laugh. "Lesbos is the island."

"I wonder if she knew all along. What she was."

"Probably not," Val said. "Not until Laura brought it out in her. It's nobody's fault, I don't think. I'm sure she loved you the best way she *could* love a man. It must've been hard for her too."

"Her old man didn't help things, always bad-mouthing me to her and putting the squelch on me."

"He's always been a ruthless bastard. But he loved his little girl."

"Yeah, the same way he loves his money."

Val said, "The thing you have to remember is that Lizzy didn't know how to let you go. I tried to talk her out of it, but she decided the only way to do it was to turn cold toward you and treat you like dirt, the way you'd run off a loyal dog so it wouldn't follow you where it shouldn't go. That's why she was so harsh. She didn't know how else to do it. You didn't deserve it, but that's what she did. You were too nice a guy to treat that way."

"Thanks. At least I've got one fan." He tried to smile.

"Yes, you do." That was when she stood on tiptoes to kiss his cheek. "You remind me a lot of Steve, before the war. He was a nice guy too."

Sometimes it was hard being a nice guy. Like when Val let him know by the looks she gave him and by the little things she said that he was welcome in her bed. He'd wanted to slide under the sheet with her, but he played the nice guy and tucked her in, told her he'd be close by, keeping the boogey-man away. Then he went out to his car and got his .38 out of the glove box and took it to bed with him, slipping it under the corner of his pillow.

So here he was now, awake in the middle of the night with a loaded pistol, a tequila headache and a loaded hard-on. Mr. Nice Guy, alone again.

In nothing but his boxer shorts, he got up and went to the bathroom to look for a bottle of aspirin. He found a tin of Bayer tablets in the medicine cabinet, popped two into his mouth and washed them down with a handful of water. He relieved himself, turned off the light and was walking back to the bedroom when he heard something—a thump, followed by a faint rattle of metal. Somebody was trying the sliding glass door to the deck. He got his gun from under the pillow and crept around the corner and eased into the living room. He half expected to see a Dracula-like figure lurking on the deck, a bloodless face pressed against the glass, but there was no one out there. Not Chago, not Lizabeth's ghost. Nothing.

He unlocked the sliding door and stepped quietly out onto the deck's wet boards. The rain-soaked flag fluttered sluggishly in the wind, the halyard ticking against the metal pole. The only way onto the deck was from inside the house, unless you climbed up the support beams from the ground. It wouldn't be hard to do. It was less than a twenty-foot drop to the grass. Joe crept to the rail, leaned over and looked down. He didn't see anyone, but somebody could be hiding under the deck, out of sight. He bent over and peered between the floorboards but it was too dark down there to see anything. He could go over the rail and drop to the ground or he could go back inside, down the stairs and out the street door. The door route would give the unseen lurker—if he was still there under the deck—time to slip off into the night. Over the rail would be risky. Joe could snap an ankle that way.

He chose the rail. If the creeper was down there, Joe was not going to let him get away, even if it meant a sprained ankle.

With the gun in his right hand, he hoisted himself over the rail and dropped to the ground. He landed off balance, his right leg touching down first on the wet grass, and he fell backward, throwing his left hand behind him and throwing the weight of the gun forward for balance. Never taking his eyes from the thick darkness beneath the deck, he ended up on his ass, right arm extended, gun aimed at nothing. No human target there.

He got to his feet and went around the corner of the house to the street door. His Roadmaster and Val's Thunderbird crouched in the hazy glow of the streetlight, their grills mocking him with chrome sneers. A night bird glided low in the clearing sky and disappeared behind the beach-house roof.

He looked down the street and scanned the darkened shapes of the neighboring houses, seeing no one. He was turning to head back to the deck when he saw the thing on Val's door stoop. He walked over to it and nudged it with a toe. It was a squat ceramic pot, a miniature cauldron. It was black, about the size of a ripe cantaloupe. There was something long and furry sticking out of it.

He picked up the cauldron and examined its contents in the yellow porchlight. A forked twig of hickory about nine inches long protruded a couple of inches higher than the pot's rim. A thick swatch of blond hair was wrapped around one prong of the crooked V and a few strands of red hair were twined about its opposite tine. The other end of the twig had been sharpened to a point and was embedded in a heart freshly removed from a small animal— perhaps a cat. A glaze of blood covered the bottom of the black cauldron.

A surge of tequila-beer-and-bile burned the back of Joe's throat. He wanted to smash the obscene cauldron on the driveway, but he didn't. It was evidence. Evidence of occult magic. Evidence suggesting that someone—almost certainly Chago—had followed either him or Val here to St. Augustine. Joe didn't know if it was meant as a warning or if it was a part of a dark ritual for marking the next victim, but he figured someone somewhere would know what it meant. All he had to do was find that someone—and in the meantime, make sure Val didn't become the next casualty of this dark and deadly game.

He set the cauldron down on the stoop and went around to the back and climbed up a crossbeam and onto the deck. Then he went down the back stairs, unlocked the door and brought the thing into the house. A light came on upstairs.

Val was at the top of the stairs in a silky green robe. "What's wrong?" she whispered.

"We had a visitor," he said, mounting the steps and holding the gun down by his bare leg. "He left a little party favor."

She crossed her arms defensively. "What *is* that?"

"See for yourself." He took it into the kitchen and set it on the counter. Val approached it warily, then stared into the cauldron.

"My God, that's my hair!" She pointed a finger at the few red strands twisted around one of the twig's prongs.

Seeing the forked hickory in better light, Joe was now certain of what he'd already suspected, and it filled him with black rage. "And that blond hair is Lizabeth's," he said through clenched teeth. "The son of a bitch took a souvenir after he killed her."

CHAPTER TEN

He sat with his feet propped on the deck's rail, sipping coffee and watching the sun ooze up from the cloud-smeared edge of the Atlantic. The smell of sea salt was strong. The pulse of the earth beat at the shore. Joe smoked his last Lucky and was stubbing the butt in a seashell ashtray when Valentine joined him. She was in a V-neck green blouse with a high collar and a pair of matching shorts with roomy pockets. She had her hands cupped around a brown ceramic mug of coffee as if she might be cold. The sea breeze ruffled her hair, which she'd pulled back in a thick ponytail.

She smiled at him and said, "Good morning, Joe."

He nodded at the horizon. "Looks like the clouds will burn off. Probably be sunny back in Dodd City. Fair funeral weather."

Before they had gone back to bed after last night's prowler incident Val had seen the futility of staying at the beach house and had agreed to follow Joe back to Dodd City. She would go to the funeral after all. He'd quizzed her about Chago and his black magic but she said all she really knew was that Palo was more powerful than voodoo—according to Laura D'Amore. Val thought it was some sort of Cuban mumbo-jumbo involving blood sacrifice and powerful curses, but she wasn't sure. D'Amore had been tightlipped on the subject, but she did let it slip that Palo originated in Africa and spread to Cuba. And that it was very dangerous. Nothing to play around with.

Val had seen Chago only once at Chateau D'Amore and nowhere else. She had no idea where the guy lived but if she had to guess, she half-joked, she would say he lived in a graveyard. She was pretty sure he was Cuban, maybe of mixed heritage. He was a wiry man in his mid-thirties, always wearing a dirty white panama hat. He had long black hair that hung out from under the hat in braids, and a ferret face that just missed being handsome. He wore a white shirt, cutoff jeans that showed off hairy, muscular legs, and he strutted around like a bantam rooster. He had a funny odor, a mix of sour sweat and something sweet like patchouli incense.

When he'd listened to Val's description of the guy, Joe couldn't believe Lizzy would've had anything to do with somebody like Chago—unless she *had* been under some kind of spell.

Val sat beside Joe in the other deck chair and gazed out at the surf, sipping coffee.

Joe took up where they'd left off in their middle-of-the-night conversation. He couldn't let it go. "You believed Lizabeth when she told you Chago . . . had her?"

"Oh yes. It's not the kind of thing a girl would make up to impress her friend. It was a shameful confession. She was disgusted with herself for doing it with him. Afterwards, I mean, once the dope and booze had worn off."

"I couldn't sleep last night," he confessed. "I kept trying to picture her with him . . . even though I didn't want to. It drives me nuts thinking about it."

She touched his arm. "Then don't. Don't torment yourself."

He shook his head. "The only thing that helps is picturing what I'm going to do to him when I find what rock he's hiding under."

"I hope you find him before he kills me," she said with bitter humor.

"You should go to the police," he told her. "I'm just one guy. And if D'Amore won't tell me where to find him—"

"I can't go to the police. What would I tell them? Some Cuban hoodoo man threatened me with a hairy stick? Besides, I'd have to tell them the whole story and I can't have that going around town. My parents would just die. And probably disown me. I wouldn't blame them."

"So it's up to me," he said.

"It's up to *us*. I'm not going to just sit back and wait for him to kill me. I'm with you on this, Joe. I can't afford not to be. I won't run from it again. I'm not usually the running type, but after what happened to Liz I just panicked. I'm really pissed-off at myself for that. It's just not me. I'd never backed down from a fight, but this guy spooked me bad. Never again, by God. That's a promise."

He saw that she was in a real jam. Her father was a wealthy man who could afford to hire bodyguards to protect her but she couldn't go to him with the truth and ask for the muscle. Likewise, she couldn't go to the cops. Joe knew he couldn't persuade her to change her mind on that score. The way she saw things, her reputation and her family's good name were worth as much as her life. Maybe more. The country club crowd could be as unforgiving as a hanging judge when anything tainted the hoity-toity membership's public image. And now that she'd confided in him, Joe felt responsible for her safety.

"One thing I don't get," he said. "I can buy that Chago killed Lizabeth as a warning to D'Amore because she loved Lizzy, but why you? Do you mean something to her? Would she really care if you were killed?"

"That's exactly what I asked her when she called to warn me. She said Chago doesn't see things the way normal people do. He does things to appease his 'dark gods.' Apparently he believes he gains more spiritual power by killing off a number of people connected by friendship or circumstance. Laura said it has to do with the orbits we make through life, something about making bigger rips in the tapestry of reality."

"Come again?"

Val shrugged. "I know it's crazy, but that's what she said the guy believes. He's in his own weird world."

"I'll say," said Joe. He thought about it for a minute, then said, "So it's like a game of chess to this freak. He takes your pieces off the board, one by one until you're down to your king. Or in this case, *queen*, the queen being Laura D'Amore. You still lose, but he drags it out to make you suffer longer."

"And to add to his power." After a thoughtful pause, Val said, "She's not necessarily a bad person, you know. Just because she was a screen queen doesn't mean she won't feel bad to see innocent people die because of her. Even if I'm not all that innocent."

"Sure you are. Maybe you made some mistakes, but nothing to get killed over. If D'Amore's such a decent person, why doesn't she just pay the man off? Seems to me she's putting her money over your life, and everybody else's."

"Like I said, I don't think it's really the money he's after. I'm not sure she has that much money left. She hasn't made a movie in years."

"Then what does he want from her?"

"I can't be sure, but from a few things she's said, I think it might have something to do with her Hollywood connections."

"Don't tell me the guy wants to be in pictures."

"No. At least I don't think so. You'd have to ask her."

"I intend to." He polished off his coffee. "Guess we should get on the road."

Val popped out of her deck chair. "I have to walk on the beach before we go. Just for a few minutes. I haven't left the house since I got here. I have to let the waves touch me."

He gave her a screwy look.

"It's just this thing I do. For luck." She smiled apologeti-cally. "Come with me."

He stood, shrugging. "A little luck couldn't hurt."

* * *

They left St. Augustine shortly after eight. The sun was already slamming the day with summer heat. He stayed behind Val's Thunderbird, protecting her flanks. She'd insisted on driv-ing with the convertible's top down. If a shooter up ahead on the side of the road took a shot at her, there was nothing he could do but pray for a missed shot, but he didn't think Chago would go the sniper route. Based on what Val had told him, Joe figured the guy liked his kills up close so he could soak up all the dying soul's power. Up close the way he'd killed Lizabeth. The evil son of a bitch.

On Highway 10 Val gunned the T-bird wide open and would've left him in the dust if he hadn't sat on his horn until she got the message and slowed down to a cool 70 mph. When he pulled up beside her and signaled her to stop at the gas station ahead, she waggled her fingers at him and shot him a lovely smile. With a green scarf holding her stunning red hair in place and catty sunglasses sitting low on the bridge of her pert nose, she could've passed for a movie star herself. She certainly had the looks.

They pulled in at the station. Joe gassed up the Roadmas-ter and went inside to pay and get a pack of smokes. He kept glancing out at Val to make sure she was okay. Each time he did, she beamed him a sunny smile. That told him something. That she felt safe with him. She was trusting him to protect her from Chago's crazy black-cauldron curse. He *couldn't* let anything happen to her.

While he was waiting for the cigar-chomping cashier to make change, an old beat-up black Caddy pulled in at the pumps, blocking his view of Val's T-bird. "Make it snappy, huh?" he urged the cashier, glancing out at the pumps.

The cigar-chomper grunted and slapped down the coins. Joe shoveled the change into his pocket and sprinted outside, his heart thumping with jackrabbit anxiety. A man in a panama hat got out of the black Caddy. The hair on the back of Joe's neck stood erect. He reached behind his back and under his shirttail for the .38.

The panama hat seemed to float above the other side of the Caddy's roof, the man under it approaching Val's convertible. The same hat Chago wore.

The gun was in Joe's hand as he rounded the Caddy's rear bumper. Hearing his approach, the man in the hat turned with a startled expression on his wide pug-nosed face. When he saw the gun, the heavyset man backpedaled, lost his balance and sat on the pavement. He held up his hands as though trying to placate an angry god.

Joe halted and slipped the .38 back in its holster, then fluffed the shirttail over it.

The man on the ground said, "I didn't mean nothin' by it. I's just being' friendly."

Val raised her sunglasses a few inches above her eyes and looked over the side of the T-bird at the man sitting on the ground. She pursed her lips and kissed the air with the sexy flamboyance of a young starlet. Then she laughed and let the catty shades drop back over her eyes.

"Scram," Joe told the man.

The guy got to his feet, fell into his Caddy and drove off with tires squealing.

"What'd he say to you?" Joe asked.

"He said I oughta be in pictures." She giggled. "It was just a harmless pass. You didn't have to give him a heart attack. Goodness, Joe . . ."

"All I could see was that hat," he explained, blushing. He started toward the Buick.

"Joe? Thanks for being so on-the-ball. You make a good guardian angel."

"You're the angel," he said, the words out before he knew it. "I'm just the guy with the gun."

* * *

Joe rode the T-bird's tail all the way back to Dodd City, Val keeping her speed under 70 most of the way. He chain-smoked Luckies and drifted into a reverie of the carefree week he and Lizabeth had spent in St. Augustine when they were still Mr. and Mrs. Joseph Dall.

They'd rented a beach house on Vilano Beach and lived like well-heeled beach bums, taking in all the historic tourist attractions, from the old Spanish fort *Castillo de San Marcos* to the iconic black-and-white-striped lighthouse. Lizzy had loved the mysterious oldness of the city and the sense of touching history, but what tickled her the most was Ripley's Believe It Or Not! The famous castle-like museum of oddities from all the world over. She'd taken in the bizarre exhibits with child-like wonder, and she'd believed them all with the blind faith of a child, though Joe was sure a lot of it was as phony as the junk you might see in any carnival sideshow. Looking back on it now, Joe saw how gullible she'd been and how she'd always been drawn to things dark and bizarre. With the benefit of hindsight he understood how easy it must have been for Lizzy to fall in with Laura D'Amore and become involved with the woman's occult pursuits. But the fall had landed her in the clutches of Chago the Devil, and Joe still had a hard time believing she'd given herself to the likes of him. He didn't want to believe it. Thinking about it—picturing them naked and grappling—tied his gut in knots and made him woozy and nearly nauseous. It was foolish to be so jealous of a dead lover. And probably more than a little crazy.

He pushed the dirty images of Chago out of his mind and tried to remember a pleasanter picture—walking along the sunset beach, hand in hand with his wife, the waves kissing their ankles, the ocean breeze a cooling caress. But then his mind tricked him, and it was Val Cooper who was with him on the sand, holding his hand and holding him in her sea-green eyes.

He looked at her through the Buick's bug-spattered windshield, the tail of her green scarf fluttering from the base of her neck, her hands resting casually on the Thunderbird's steering wheel, her shaded eyes framed in her rearview mirror.

Mentally replacing his ex-wife with Valentine Cooper didn't seem right—not on the day of Lizabeth's funeral.

Val caught his eyes in her rearview and gave him a backward wave of her hand.

He waved back and tried to smile.

*   *   *

He followed Val to her ranch-style house on Hot Springs Road on the outskirts of Dodd City, and nosed the Roadmaster into the carport next to her T-bird. He went inside first and made a run-through of the house to make sure no one was waiting for her, then he sat and smoked in the den while she took a shower.

The attic fan sucked the tobacco haze from the room. The drone of the fan and the hum of water through the pipes soothed him. He shut his eyes and imagined it was Lizzy in the bathtub. In a few minutes she would come strolling out with a towel wrapped around her and ask him to dry her back. Then she would turn around, loosen the towel and he would catch it before it hit the floor. He would gently blot the beads of water from the smooth skin of her shoulders and work his way down to the swell of her buttocks. Going to his knees, he would kiss the cleft of her cheeks and she would slowly turn to him . . .

The phone rang. Joe jumped up and strode into the hallway to answer it. "Cooper residence," he said.

"Joe? Is that you?" He recognized the woman's voice. It was famous for its sultriness.

"Yeah, it's me. What do you want with Val, Miss D'Amore?"

"A more interesting question might be: What are you doing at her home?"

"How did you know she was back in town?"

"Back? I didn't know she'd been away."

"You didn't, huh?"

"No. I've been calling since yesterday. What's going on?"

"You tell me. You know what your pal Chago has been up to?"

"Tell me what's happened, Joe. Is she all right?"

"She's fine. She's getting ready for Lizabeth's funeral."

"What *about* Chago?"

"He tracked Val to her beach house in St. Augustine and left a little present on her doorstep last night. I'll show it to you when I come out to your place this afternoon."

"What is it?" Her voice was grave now, edged with fear. Unless she was using her best acting chops. "Tell me."

"A little black pot with the heart of a small animal in it. A fork of hickory sticking in the heart, human hair wrapped around it. Val's hair. And Lizabeth's."

"Jesus."

"Jesus, hell! We're done playing games here. Tell me where the son of a bitch is before he kills somebody else."

"I don't know where he is."

"I don't know if you're lying," he said, squeezing the phone hard. "What I know is that all this is happening because of you. And you're gonna help me stop it. Unless you want more murders on your head."

"No, I don't want that. I just don't know if he *can* be stopped."

"He's human, isn't he? I'll stop him dead in his tracks."

There was a pause. He heard her lighting a cigarette. He pictured her with the long cigarette-holder between her fingers and he saw himself stuffing it down her throat.

"I don't suppose you're going to the funeral," he said, "being the reclusive movie star and all."

"I'd like to but I wouldn't want to cause a stir. It wouldn't be dignified."

"Getting strangled to death with a bra strap isn't too dignified either, but you didn't let that bother you too much."

"You blame me and you want to punish me," she said. "I understand that. But you can't punish me any more than I've already punished myself."

"I wouldn't bet on that," he said. "I'll be at your place this afternoon. Don't go anywhere."

"Take care of Valentine," she said, and then hung up.

As he was setting the receiver back in its cradle, the bathroom door opened and Val stepped into the hall with a small white towel wrapped around her torso. Steam billowed behind her. She gave a start when she saw him and crossed her hands over the tops of her breasts. "Did I hear the phone?"

"Yeah. Laura D'Amore called. She was worried about you."

"Oh. Well, that's nice to know. I guess."

"We're going to pay her a visit after the funeral. Don't make any plans."

"You're certainly taking your bodyguard duties very seriously." She gave him a self-conscious smile as she slyly glanced down at her skimpy covering of terrycloth.

"Yeah," he said, his mouth going dry.

"I'm not complaining. I'm lucky to have you." She disappeared into the bedroom and pushed the door halfway to.

Joe watched the bathroom steam dissipate in the pull of the attic fan.

* * *

She emerged half an hour later in a long mourning-black dress. Her hair was done up in a tight bun on the back of her head. She had on just the right touch of makeup. "Do I look all right?" she asked.

"You look great," he said, standing.

"I hope I didn't keep you waiting too long."

"You didn't. I had a lot to think about."

She gave him a quizzical look.

"We'll take my car," he told her.

"To your place, right?"

He nodded. "It won't take me long to get ready. Quick shave and shower, throw on a coat and tie."

"Will you be bringing me back here later? I mean, I don't know where . . . You haven't told me the plan. Where am I staying tonight?"

"My place on the lake. Is that okay with you?"

She smiled. "As long as you're close by I'm sure I'll be fine."

* * *

A black wreath on the Sundown's door somberly announced that the lounge was closed out of respect for the dead. As he drove around back to park in the spotty shade of tall pines, Joe figured Dot would probably open for business by mid-afternoon. She couldn't afford to sacrifice a full day's takings. The Sundown's profit margin was too thin.

"It must be nice living on the lake," said Val. "It's so peaceful."

"Let's hope it stays that way," he said, killing the engine.

"I was wondering . . . Do you think Chago already knew I was at the beach house or did he follow you there?"

"Could've been either way. But I don't know why he would've followed me. Your Thunderbird was like a big red arrow pointing at the beach house, saying 'Here she is.'"

They got out and walked across the way to the bungalow. He unlocked the front door and waved her inside. He threw the deadbolt behind them and said, "Make yourself at home. I won't be long."

"Cozy little place," she said, taking in the kitchenette, the modest living room and the deck on the other side of the glass door. "One bedroom?"

"Yeah. You'll sleep in the bedroom and I'll sack out in here on the roll-away."

"I hate to put you out."

"I can sleep anywhere. As long as it's not a frozen foxhole, I'll be happy."

She smiled and sat on the sofa, crossing her long legs in a way they didn't teach in charm school. The thin skirts of her black dress slid off shapely legs sheathed in opaque hosiery. Joe took that tantalizing sight with him into the bedroom and closed the door.

He sat on the bed and dialed Dot's home number. She answered before the second ring.

"Hey," he said. "What time do you want me to pick you up?"

"Where have you been? I was worried sick about you when you didn't come home last night. I kept calling and calling . . ."

"St. Augustine. I'll tell you about it later. I've got Val Cooper with me. I think somebody means to kill her."

"*What?*"

"I'll fill you in on the way to the funeral. I found out a lot of stuff since the last time I saw you."

"Val Cooper? Isn't she . . .?"

"Lizabeth's best friend. Listen, I've gotta get ready. What time?"

"A quarter to eleven would be fine."

"See you then."

He stripped, shaved and showered. As he was drying off, he heard a man's voice in the other room. He slipped into a pair of undershorts, grabbed his gun and went through the door.

Barry Keefer was on the sofa with Val. He was wearing a dark lightweight suit instead of his usual chauffeur's outfit. He grinned when he saw Joe in shorts and holding the gun. "Don't shoot, shamus," Keefer said, holding up his hands. "I give."

"Keefer, what the hell are—"

"You missed your briefing last night. The Old Man ain't happy." He let his hands drop.

"Where is he?" Joe lowered the pistol and glanced out at the deck.

"Relax, Joe, he's not here. He sent me to check up on you while he's getting ready for the funeral. You weren't answering your phone. He can't have his boy dick going AWOL on him."

"I wasn't. Tell the old fart I was . . ." —Joe glanced at Val— ". . . doing what needed to be done."

"Yeah, Miss Cooper was just telling me what a hero you are."

"I was not!" Val came off the couch, put her hands on her hips, and glared down at Keefer.

Joe smiled. If Keefer didn't already know about Val's hot temper, he was about to get his first spicy taste.

"I wouldn't have let you in if I'd known you were going to be such an ass," she sounded off like a female drill sergeant. "Now you behave yourself or I'll show you the door."

"Whoa now," said Keefer, holding his hands up again. "I was just kidding. Don't get your panties in a wad."

Val's right hand came off her hip in a blur and smacked Keefer's caveman jaw. "Don't you even *think* about my panties!" she warned him.

Joe laughed aloud. Stunned by the surprising slap, Keefer said, "Okay, okay, I'm sorry. Sheesh."

Val turned and stalked off into the kitchen to pour herself a glass of ice water, presumably to cool down.

Sheepish, Keefer stood, rubbing his reddened jaw, and said, "Damned if it ain't true what they say about redheads." Under his breath, he added: "Valentine, my ass."

Joe advised: "You better beat it before she comes back for round two."

"No joke." The big man moved toward the door. "That's it, anyway. The Old Man just wanted to know your whereabouts. See you at the funeral, shamus."

The door shut behind Keefer, and Val came back from the kitchen with a frosty glass of ice water. "I'm sorry, Joe. I didn't mean to make a scene. I always feel like he's undressing me with his eyes. I never have cared for that man."

"Ah, he's all right. Can't blame a guy for looking, not when you look like you do."

Her eyes flashed up at him beneath long lashes. "Is that supposed to be a compliment?"

"It's not an insult." He held up his hands, ready to ward off a slap.

She suddenly grinned at him. "You should've seen yourself charging in with the gun, in your boxer shorts."

He chuckled. "Like last night."

Her grin faded. "No. Last night it wasn't funny."

Remembering the pierced heart in the black cauldron, he said, "No, it wasn't."

CHAPTER ELEVEN

Val and Dot took an instant liking to each other and were acting like old friends by the time Joe pulled up in front of the First Methodist Church. He had given Dot an abbreviated version of what he'd learned since he'd last seen her, leaving out details of Val's participation in D'Amore's orgies. Dot was impressed with the progress of his investigation and smugly reminded him that she'd told him he had the makings of a good detective. She turned grim when he told her about the apparent symbolic threat on Val's life.

Joe surprised them when he said he wasn't going to attend the service. "I can't sit there cooped up with all those people," he explained. "I'll pick you up out front when it's over and we'll go to the graveside service."

"Joe . . ." Val started, then let her frown say the rest.

"You'll be safe here. Chago won't try anything with all these people around. And there'll be a police escort to the cemetery."

"What're you going to do?" she asked. "Sit out here in a hot car?"

"I'm going to pick up Tibbedeaux's maid, Ginny. She'll be going with us to the cemetery. I called her before we left home and told her to get ready. She practically raised Lizabeth."

"That's very thoughtful of you," Val said.

Joe shrugged.

The two women got out of the car, smoothed their dresses and diffidently waved from the sidewalk as Joe drove off.

*   *   *

Ginny shut the gate to the Tibbedeaux estate behind her and started to climb into the Buick's backseat, but Joe told her to sit up front with him. She did so reluctantly.

"Mistuh Tibbedeaux ain't gone like me bein' there," she said, wiping sweat from her broad forehead with a lacy hankie that smelled of rose water. She was a big woman with a robust smile and kind eyes. She had on her Sunday best, a navy blue dress with printed flowers and a small blue hat that look like an upside-down basket with a pink plastic flower pinned to it.

"It'll be all right. We'll stay in the background. He probably won't even see us."

"Sho is nice o' you, Mistuh Joe."

"It wouldn't be right for you not to be there. I know how close you and Lizzy were. She'd want you there."

As they pulled away from the Tibbedeaux mansion Joe asked Ginny if she'd ever heard of Palo. "I think it's something like voodoo," he prompted.

"No suh, I don't reckon I have."

"You think Madam Ruth would know anything about it?"

"She might. Did you go see her yet?"

"Yeah, I did, but she wasn't too happy with me asking questions about Lizzy. If you talked to her and put in a good word for me, maybe she won't try to shoo me off next time."

"I'll call her," she said, nodding solemnly. "This afternoon."

"Thanks, Ginny."

"This 'bout Lizzy, ain't it."

"Yeah. I'm afraid it is. It looks like she was mixed up with some bad people."

Ginny made a deep sound of disapproval. "You be careful, Mistuh Joe. Don't you be getting' mixed up in no hoodoo."

He didn't tell her he already was.

* * *

In the cemetery, Joe and his three ladies stood well behind the gathering of family and friends seated in folding chairs in the shade of the funeral home's canvas canopy. Rather than sit in the shade Val and Dot had chosen to stand in the hot sun with Joe and Ginny. They were close enough to hear the minister's eulogy delivered from beside the casket poised above the rectangular trench that would be Lizabeth's final resting place. From where Joe stood, the grave looked like a yawning doorway. A doorway to the underworld.

Ginny's face was streaked with tears. Val was using a tissue to mute her sniffles, and Dot stood stoically, as if she were trying to lend Joe some of her strength, but Joe was unmoved by the solemn spectacle of the graveside service. He was already emotionally divorced from the body in the box. He glanced around, half expecting to see Lizzy's ghost lurking nearby. If she was there, she wasn't showing herself in the bright sunlight.

After the preacher closed the ceremony with a final prayer, Monroe Tibbedeaux stood over the grave and watched as the casket was lowered into the earth. He picked up a clump of gray-black dirt and ceremoniously tossed it on top of the gilded box housing his daughter's remains. His wife wailed a string of unintelligible words. Tibbedeaux ignored his wife's display and stared statue-like into the grave, leaving it to the minister to comfort the grieving mother.

Val's hand found Joe's and she held it tightly. He saw that her eyes were brimming with tears and he gave her hand a supportive squeeze. She gave him a brave smile and squeezed back.

"You want to go say goodbye to her?" Dot asked him when the mourners began to leave the gravesite and head for their hot cars.

"No." Joe knew there could be no real goodbye before he dealt a dead-man's hand to her murderer. Until that happened, Lizabeth's spirit would not be at rest.

"She gone," Ginny said in a hoarse whisper of raw emotion.

Joe wanted to say something to console the woman but the words just weren't there.

Dot came to the rescue and said, "You'll always have her"—touching her fingers to her own breast—"here."

"Yes'm," Ginny said. "I know thass right."

Barry Keefer peeled off from the remaining mourners milling about the canopied plot of earth and started across the lawn to where Joe stood. In his suit and sunglasses he looked like a matinee idol gone to seed.

"What does he want now?' Val said. It was more a complaint than a real question.

"Maybe he wants you to get rough with him again," Joe said. "I hear some guys dig that type of thing."

"Bite your tongue," she said under her breath. She let go of his hand.

"Oh Lawd," Ginny said when she saw Keefer's swaggering approach. "Here come the Mistuh's monkey boy." She immediately slapped her hand over her mouth as if to recall her words.

Dot, Val and Joe exchanged surprised glances, looked at Ginny, and then they all burst into laughter. Ginny joined them with her hearty rumble. It was a welcome release of tension and a much-needed flight from funereal angst.

Joe saw Tibbedeaux glare at them after hearing the unseemly outburst of gaiety.

"Show some respect for the dead," Keefer said as he walked up to Joe.

"It's the living you're worried about, isn't it?" said Joe, nodding in Tibbedeaux's direction.

Keefer jerked his head at Ginny. "What's she doing here?"

"Paying her respects. It was my idea, so if the boss man has a problem with it, tell him to take it up with me."

"I'm sure he will," Keefer said. "He wants to see you. He says you should come to the house in an hour."

"Tell him I can't make it. I'm following a hot lead."

Keefer gave Joe a cool look from behind his dark glasses. "Playing the private dick bit to the hilt, huh? Listen up, Mike Hammerhead. You don't wanna piss the big man off. Trust me on that."

"Trust me on this," Joe told him. "You and the big man don't wanna piss me off." Then he turned to the women and said, "Ladies, shall we go?"

They walked off together, leaving Tibbedeaux's overgrown monkey boy alone among the gravestones.

* * *

After dropping off Dot and Ginny at their respective homes, Joe drove Val back to her house so she could change out of her black dress and pack a suitcase for her stay of indefinite duration at his bungalow on the lake.

She came out of her bedroom with a suitcase in one hand and a shotgun in the other. "I'm ready," she announced.

"I'll say," he said with a wide smile. "That loaded?"

"Mighty right, it is. I'm a good shot too."

"Yeah?" He took the suitcase from her.

"Daddy used to take me skeet shooting. And Steve took me bird hunting a couple of times."

"Then you should know you don't travel with a loaded gun. You wait to load it when you get where you're going."

"I know that. And you should know this is for protection, not recreation. If somebody messes with me I intend to be ready. I'm not going to say, 'Wait a minute while I load my gun, Mr. Voodoo Man.'"

"Okay. Point taken. Just be careful where you point that thing."

"I know how to handle a shotgun. I can shoot a deer rifle and .45 semiautomatic pistol too, for your information."

Joe nodded. "Good. Nothing like being informed before I'm accidentally blasted with a shotgun."

"If I shoot anybody, it won't be an accident."

* * *

When they pulled up to D'Amore's gate, Joe said, "You know you can't go in there with the shotgun, right?"

"Don't tell me what I can't do, Joe. You'll learn that about me. Tell me what I can't do and I'll do it just to prove you wrong. Watch, I'll show you."

She threw the door open and slid out of the car with the weapon in the crook of her arm. "What're you waiting for? Let's go."

"Val, you can't . . ." He saw she was serious about taking the gun inside. "That's childish, you know. Being so . . . obstinate."

"You don't say." She grinned at him as she pressed the intercom's call button.

"I do say." He got out of the car and slammed the door. "It makes you an easy mark for reverse psychology."

"Yeah? While you're going in reverse, I'll be charging ahead and I'll get there before you."

He joined her at the gate, holding a small brown grocery sack containing the cauldron and its disturbing contents. The Cuban housekeeper Frida answered the buzz, and Joe announced himself. Then he lowered his voice and asked Val what she knew about the housekeeper. It might be a coincidence that Frida was Cuban and that the Palo religion had come from Africa by way of Cuba, but then again, it might not be.

"Not much," said Val. "She's quiet, keeps mostly to herself

from what I've seen of her. Stays in the background but she's always there whenever Laura wants something."

"I wonder if she's the one who put D'Amore and Chago together, seeing as how they're both Cuban."

"You're thinking she could be in on it with Chago?"

"It's a possibility,"

Oscar Lamont came out of the front door and waddled toward the gate. He blanched when he saw the shotgun resting in the crook of Val's arm.

"Don't worry, Oscar," Joe told him. "She won't shoot you."

"You can't come in here with that," said Lamont, clearly incredulous.

Joe amended, "She won't shoot you if you open the gate. Otherwise, all bets are off."

"My life's been threatened," Val explained. "By your friend Chago. This"—she held up the Remington—"is for my protection."

"That man isn't my friend," Lamont said. "And I'm sorry, but I can't let you in with that."

Val leveled the shotgun at Lamont's midsection. "I'm already hot and cranky," she said. "If you don't let us in right now I'll blast my way in. And I'm not joking."

The big man glanced at Joe with a raised-brow look that said he didn't know if she was really serious.

"I'd do it if I were you," Joe said.

Frowning, Lamont unlocked the gate. It swung open with an iron groan.

"Laura's going to kill me for this." Lamont arched his heavy brows and made a grumbling sound that reminded Joe of Ginny's expressive rumbles. "Aren't you going to bring your car inside?"

"Nah, it's fine where it is. A nice shady spot."

As they passed into the patchy shade of a palm tree, Joe asked, "How did D'Amore meet Chago?"

"Frida," Lamont answered. "She knew of Laura's interest in the occult so she told her about him."

"Could Frida be in cahoots with Chago?"

"Laura doesn't think so. Frida is terrified of the man. She goes into hiding whenever he comes around."

"That doesn't put her in the clear," Joe said. "It could mean she's afraid enough to do anything he tells her."

"Laura trusts her. That's all I can tell you."

"How often does he come around?"

"Not often. He's been here . . . oh, three times that I know of."

"Does he come by appointment or does he just pop in?"

"He shows up when he feels like it, whether he's invited or not. Laura never turns him away."

Scowling at the shotgun, Lamont held open the front door and Val and Joe stepped inside.

"They're in the screening room," Lamont told them, "watching one of Laura's movies. Have a seat in the sunroom and I'll let her know you're here. You both know the way."

"Which movie?" Joe asked, curious.

"*Torrid Town.*"

"Lizabeth's favorite."

"Yes, that's why Laura's running it now. In memory of Lizabeth. Since she couldn't go to the funeral."

"Swell," said Joe. "Watching herself in memory of somebody else. You can take the broad out of Hollywood . . ."

"But you can't take Hollywood out of the broad," Val finished it for him.

Lamont's scowl deepened and he said, "Please don't brandish that shotgun in front of Laura. She doesn't like guns. Not even when they're props loaded with blanks." Then he walked toward the back of the sprawling house while Val and Joe sat in rattan chairs in the spacious sunroom and stared at the six-foot aquarium filled with tropical fish of various sizes and colors. The assorted tribal masks hanging on the walls gave Joe the creeps, as if they were watching him with evil intent. These masks weren't those corny coconut replicas you could buy in the home-decorating section of a Florida department store or souvenir shop; they were the genuine articles, an anthropologist's dream display.

"I wouldn't mind living in a place like this," Val said as she set the shotgun on the floor by the side of her chair. "But I'd fix the place up some."

"You could start by hiring a good gardener. Unless you like the wild jungle look." He set the paper sack on the floor by his foot.

"It is a tad on the shaggy side," Val agreed. "I guess she wants it that way. Mysterious, like the women she always played in her movies."

"Yeah." Joe looked up to see Laura D'Amore making her entrance, a long and slinky black gown flaring out at the ankles. It was an entrance Loretta Young would've envied if her tastes ran to the dark and mysterious instead of to the bright and cheery. D'Amore's hair was loose on her shoulders, catching the light in a blue-black sheen. She gave them a tentative smile of greeting. Oscar sheepishly followed her.

"You look like you just stepped down off the movie screen," Joe said. He didn't bother to stand up and play the gentleman.

She paused with her cigarette-holder held high, then delivered her line with measured pathos: "Sometimes that's just how I feel. As if all this"—she waved her free hand—"isn't real."

"Maybe that's when it gets too real for you," Joe suggested. "Like when your friend Chago starts killing people you know. Then you escape to your make-believe movies and pretend everything's hunky-dory."

She ignored the comment and said, "Hello, Valentine. I

didn't know you'd be coming with Joe. But of course, you're always welcome here."

Val nodded, her face expressionless. Then D'Amore saw the shotgun.

"You brought a gun in here?" D'Amore said. "Oscar?"

"Save your breath," said Joe. "Oscar was overruled by firepower. Since your pal Chago marked Val for death, we don't go anywhere unarmed. Take a load off. We've got a lot to talk about."

She sat in a high-back wicker chair that resembled a throne, but she seemed suddenly unsure of her role in this impromptu drama. She took a drag off her cigarette and exhaled with a gesture that was probably supposed to be regal, but she didn't quite pull it off. Her eyes flitted about the room and finally settled on Joe. "So. I suppose you know everything now."

"I know you got Lizabeth killed." He waited for her to respond. When she didn't, he said, "Lay it out for me. What exactly does Chago want from you?"

"He wants a foothold in Hollywood," she said. "He wants me to use my influence to get it for him. With my stamp of approval, certain doors would open for him and the bastard would go slithering into the glamour gardens of Tinsel Town to spread his evil. I have a circle of friends there who would welcome him as the dark prince he thinks he is."

"What are they, devil worshippers?"

"Something like that. Dabblers in the occult. Fading stars who believe they might extend their careers with the right kind of magic. Chago could deliver the goods, too, if the price was right. He's not like the West Coast charlatans they're used to dealing with. He's the real thing. But in the end, it would cost them more than money, and their lives would become nightmares."

"And that's why you refused to make the introductions for

him? Out of concern for your nutso Hollywood friends. And at the cost of Lizabeth's life."

"I didn't know he was going to kill her. I thought he was only trying to scare me into giving him what he wanted. Had I known he wasn't bluffing, I would've done everything I could to protect her."

"Like selling out your Hollywood chums?" Joe gave her a skeptical look.

"If there was no other way, then yes."

"So why haven't you already done it? Now that you know he means business."

"I would've done it to save Liz's life, but now it's too late for that."

Val said, "What about my life? Don't I count?"

D'Amore didn't answer.

Then Oscar jumped to her defense. "Put yourself in Laura's place. How do you decide which of your friends to sacrifice to the man? How does anyone with a conscience make that decision?"

"You could go to the police, now that he's killed somebody," said Val.

"With what evidence?" Oscar heaved a grave sigh. "It wouldn't do any good. The only way to stop him is to kill him, I'm afraid."

"Which brings me to my next question," said Joe. "How can I find the son of a bitch?"

"What are you saying, Joe?" asked D'Amore. "That you intend to kill him?"

"If I was going to kill him, you think I would announce it to anybody? Just tell me how to find him. What happens after that, you don't have to worry about."

"Nobody knows where he hides out," said Oscar. "It's as if a secret doorway to hell opens and he appears, unannounced."

"So there's no way to get in touch with him? No phone number to call?"

Oscar and D'Amore both shook their heads.

Joe muttered a curse.

"Show her the pot," said Val.

Joe took the cauldron out of the bag, got up and set it ceremoniously in D'Amore's lap. "Seen one of those before?" he asked.

She nodded. "Lizabeth got one too, just before she died."

"So it *is* some sort of death curse."

"It could be. I don't know that much about Palo—that's this particular brand of magic Chago practices. These cauldrons are used for various purposes. It's primarily a soul-catcher, I think. It can imprison the soul of the target of his magic, even if the victim isn't dead. Chago likes to ransom souls. He says he has one of those things for me, too. But he won't kill me because I'm of no use to him if I'm dead."

"Where's Liz's?"

"Locked in my safe. My first impulse was to destroy it, but I was afraid that would have some disastrous effect on her soul."

"So you've swallowed this jerk's mumbo-jumbo, hook, line and sinker. I don't get it. You're not a stupid person. How can you believe this crap?" Shaking his head in disgust, Joe took the cauldron out of her lap and sat back down beside Val, who was lighting a smoke. Oscar was staring at the aquarium, watching the carefree rainbow-colored fish swim about.

"Voodoo can kill," said D'Amore. "There are cases on record. Palo is no less effective. In fact, it's more powerful than voodoo."

"I think it requires belief on the part of the cursed person," Oscar offered. "Then it becomes a self-fulfilling prophecy. Or so I'm told."

Joe fixed his eyes on D'Amore and said, "Did Liz believe it? Did she believe this bastard put a death curse on her?"

"Not at first," answered D'Amore. "But then she started falling apart. She became a nervous wreck and was afraid he was taking her soul, just the way he said he would."

"He told her that?"

"He told me. I told Liz."

"Why the hell did—"

"Hold on, Joe," Oscar cautioned. "Laura was only trying to warn her."

"Maybe you're dumber than I thought," Joe said to the actress. "Yeah, I think I gave you too much credit. Jesus."

"That's enough!" Oscar shifted his bulk in his chair as if he were on the verge of getting up and coming after Joe.

"It's all right, Oscar," D'Amore said with a wave of her hand. "Joe has a right to be angry. If I had it to do over, I would've given Chago what he wanted to save her."

"But not to save me?" Val's hair seemed to blaze a brighter shade of red. "Just because I don't swing your way in the sack?"

"Valentine, you have to understand. I *loved* Liz. More than I've ever loved anyone else. It's not that I'm willing to sacrifice you, it's just that . . . well, love blinds one to all other considerations. Now I see things more clearly and I have to weigh the options and outcomes. You see that, don't you?"

"I see a selfish bitch," Val snapped, exhaling smoke through flared nostrils. "I see you're not going to help me out of this goddamn jam *you* got me into."

"I'm sorry." D'Amore seemed to shrink a little into her wicker throne. The Screen Queen was sagging, sinking into a kind of despair, but doing it with dramatic flair. Or so Joe thought. He wondered if it was all just an act. He didn't think so, but he couldn't be sure. Not with her.

"*Sorry* doesn't help," Val told her. "Not one damn iota."

D'Amore said, "Nobody made you come to my house in the first place."

Joe said, "If your housekeeper first put you in touch with Chago, she must know how to get in touch with him. Get her in here."

"No, Frida said Chago contacted her," said D'Amore. "She doesn't know how to find him."

"She could be lying."

"You don't know Frida. She's so deathly afraid of the man, there's no way she would lift a finger to find him."

"Get her in here," Joe said again. "She may know more than she thinks she does. Won't hurt to question her."

"He has a point," chimed Oscar. "Couldn't hurt to ask."

"All right," D'Amore relented with a smoky sigh. "Oscar, would you mind? I'm suddenly feeling very tired."

"Maybe the bastard has your soul in his pot already," said Val, still fuming. "You do strike me as a cold fish. Or maybe you were always that way."

Oscar got up and lumbered out of the room, seemingly glad to escape the acidic hostility saturating the room's atmosphere. He obviously took attacks on his queen very personally.

Laura D'Amore stared directly into Val's eyes until a tear trickled down her left cheek, then she looked away as if to hide her pained expression.

"You're good," Val told her. "But save your tears. I know you can turn them on at will. I'm sure you'd cry a river if the bastard murdered me."

"Don't worry, babe," Joe said to Val. "Nothing's gonna happen to you."

Val turned her eyes on him. He thought he saw a hint of amusement mixed in with the anger. "*Babe?*" she said softly.

He shrugged.

She graced him with a tiny smile. "You're sweet," she whispered.

"Oh God!" Oscar's voice boomed through the house. "Betty!"

Joe bolted out of his chair and ran toward the sound of the big man's voice, followed by Val and the lady of the house. Joe ran down the hallway and saw Oscar pushing through the door to the pool area.

Betty was floating naked, facedown in the swimming pool.

Joe knew she was dead before they dragged her out of the water.

CHAPTER TWELVE

Oscar waded into the shallow end of the pool and made his way toward Betty until the water was up to his thick shoulders and he could reach her, then he rolled her face-up and everyone could see death in her half-open eyes and in the bluish pallor of her face. She was naked except for a leather thong around her neck, attached to some sort of small charm of dark wood. Unlike the bleached-blond hair on her head, her pubic hair was a soggy nest of dark brown ringlets

"Oh God," D'Amore moaned. "No, no, no . . ."

Frida came to the edge of the pool, took one look, and then fled back into the house, muttering to herself in Spanish.

"I thought she was a good swimmer," Val said, looking down at Betty's body as Oscar guided it into the shallow end of the pool.

"She was an excellent swimmer," D'Amore confirmed. "*He* did this. He killed her right under our noses, the evil prick. That thing around her neck . . . He put it there so we'd know. God *damn* him."

Joe looked at the thing on the leather thong around Betty's neck. It was a small hand-carved skull. Grinning.

Joe scanned the trees and foliage beyond the walls. "He's out there watching us to get his jollies," he said, drawing the pistol from the holster at the small of his back.

Not missing a beat, Val said, "Shotgun. Wait for me."

Joe was only a little surprised that she'd known what he

was thinking and was eager to join him in chasing down the killer. The better he knew her, the more he realized that she was the toughest woman he'd ever been around. Maybe she wasn't as physically strong as the average male (though she did appear to be in excellent shape), but she was proving to be tough-minded in extreme circumstances—notwithstanding her panicked flight to St. Augustine—and that increased his respect for her. Camaraderie was developing between them, and he was already thinking of her as his comrade-in-arms and dependable partner, an able first-mate on his fledgling voyage into the dangerous undercurrents of mystery and murder.

Oscar lifted Betty out of the water and carried her up the steps and out of the pool. He set her down gently on a lounge chair, then draped a beach towel over her. "We should put her swimsuit on her before we call the police," he said.

"What are we going to tell them?" asked D'Amore, melodramatically wringing her hands.

"That we found her in the pool," Oscar said. "Which we did."

"You're going to tell them about Chago," said Joe.

"Why? We can't prove he did it." She cut her eyes at Joe. "And if we mention Chago, we'll have to tell them everything. I don't want the police and reporters snooping into my private life. I've got . . ." She broke off.

"Too much to hide?" Joe said, his words the stinging jab he'd intended.

She recoiled, then said, "You don't know what that kind of attention does to you. I do. And I won't go through that again. If you tell them anything about Chago, I'll say I have no idea what you're talking about. Then the police will be your problem. Not mine."

Joe fought the urge to throttle her and throw her into the pool. Though he knew it wasn't really her fault that Chago was trying to extort her influence and Hollywood connections by killing those close to her, he was hard-pressed not to blame her for the whole murderous mess.

"And even if we did tell them everything," she went on, "you think *those* Keystone Cops could find Chago? They wouldn't know where to begin. No, Joe. The police can't help us. We have to do this ourselves. *You* have to find him. And then you have to kill him."

Val came jogging up with her shotgun. "Ready?"

"Yeah," said Joe, his eyes lingering on D'Amore's smug expression. "Let's go."

*   *   *

They stood at the edge of the jungle-like wilderness behind the back wall of the property and cocked their ears, hoping to catch the sound of their prey moving through the underbrush, but they heard nothing but a rising wind rustling the trees. The sky darkened as storm clouds scudded directly overhead. A crow cawed forlornly.

"What do you think?" Val whispered.

Joe shook his head, then whispered back: "This is the only way he could've snuck up and climbed the wall unseen. I'd bet dollars to donuts there's a road on the other side of these woods. And that's the way he'd be bugging out of here. You sure you're up for this?"

"Damn right," she said, a little too loud.

"Okay. Stay about ten yards to my left and don't step on any sticks. Be as quiet as you can."

She nodded. They walked into the viny shadows. The wind blew harder, covering the soft sounds of their passage, but also covering all but the loudest noise Chago might make—if he really was there. Joe didn't doubt that the man had slipped over the wall and drowned Betty, but he'd had enough time to be long gone by now, unless he'd stuck around to witness their discovery of Betty's body. Joe hoped he had. He was ready to kill the man. Laura D'Amore knew it as well as he knew it himself. Though he didn't like the idea that she was using him to eliminate the source of her problem, he had his own good reasons for killing Chago. One of those reasons was walking abreast of him with a shotgun cradled in her arms. The other reason was already below cemetery ground. Joe had no intention of apprehending the killer and turning him over to the law. That would be pointless, since there was no real evidence for a criminal case. Killing Chago was the only option, and Joe had no problem with being the instrument of Old-Testament justice. He was resigned to his role as triggerman—executioner of the unofficial death sentence. It was no big deal for a combat veteran. Killing was always the same. The only difference was in the enemies.

Val waved her arm to get his attention. Then she pointed ahead at what looked like a footpath through the undergrowth. She pointed again, more emphatically, at the ground immediately in front of her. Joe went over to see what she'd found.

A footprint. By its size, the print of a man's shoe, captured by a muddy spot of earth on the narrow trail. The toe of the footprint was pointing away from the D'Amore compound. It had to be fresh because the recent heavy rains would've washed away any older tracks.

"We have to move fast," Joe said. "I'm gonna run this trail. Stay far enough behind me so you don't shoot me in the back if you slip and fall."

"I've got the safety on," she snapped. "I told you I know how to handle a gun."

He gave her a nod, then started jogging along the slip of a trail, the .38 tight in his fist. Small branches slapped at his face and briars nipped at his ankles as he charged ahead. He was running at too fast a clip for the measly footpath, but he could *feel* his prey up ahead, and he was determined not to let Chago escape. If he got away now, they would have no choice but to wait for the stealthy prick to show up again, and somebody else might die when he did.

He glanced back over his shoulder to see if Val was keeping up. She was, about ten yards behind him, pumping her legs and holding the shotgun crossways in front of her, a grim expression on her face. Joe suspected she could outrun him in a footrace. His legs were longer than hers, but she was lighter and obviously more agile. She moved like a sleek cat. He was glad to have her backing him up.

The light beneath the broken canopy of trees grew dimmer as the clouds thickened overhead. Thunder rolled and rumbled as they ran on through the darkening jungle. The wind-swollen foliage seemed to be reaching up to charm rain from low clouds. The path veered around an impenetrable thicket of brambles and Joe lost his footing on a patch of mud and went down on one knee, using his left hand to stiff-arm the ground and push off like a halfback going for extra yardage.

A crack of thunder he first thought was a gunshot brought a hot-metal taste of fear to his mouth. Then there was another sound he recognized right away: a vehicle door slamming. Through the trees in front of him he saw a green truck in a black-dirt clearing, heard the motor start up and glimpsed the white panama hat on the driver's head as the mud-spattered vehicle began a lazy turn toward muddy ruts leading out of the woods.

Joe stopped, raised his gun and drew a bead on the white hat. Sudden doubt undermined his determination to shoot. What if the truck's driver wasn't Chago? What if the man had nothing to do with Betty's death? In all likelihood it *was* Chago, but *what if it wasn't?* He remembered the fat guy in the panama hat accosting Val at the gas station, the guy he'd mistaken for Chago.

He lowered his aim to the right rear tire and squeezed the trigger just as Val stopped short and drew up beside him and shouldered her shotgun. The pistol's sharp report was immediately followed by the deep booming blast of Val's Remington. The truck slewed right, rear tires kicking up clumps of damp earth as the driver gunned the engine. Joe fired at the tire again and was sure he hit the mark this time. Jacking another shell into the chamber, Val took a step forward and cut loose with a second scattergun blast, knocking out the back window.

Motor growling, the green pickup righted itself and shot forward in spite of the blown-out tire. The driver hunched behind the wheel to offer a smaller target.

Joe aimed at the back of the man's head and tried to keep it centered in his gunsight as the pickup bounced and rattled away on the ruts. Then he lowered the pistol and read aloud the Florida license-plate number: "13 – 2943." He repeated it three times. Then to Val, "Help me remember it. 13 – 2943."

"You think we hit him?" she asked, breathing hard, face reddened with heat.

"He might've caught a few stray pellets, but not enough to slow him down."

"You could've had him. Why did—"

"I want to look in his eyes before I do it," he said.

"You choked, didn't you." It wasn't a question.

He saw that it was pointless to lie to her. "I can't shoot a man in the back. What if it wasn't him?"

"That was him. I recognized the truck. And his goddamn hat and hair. That was Chago all right."

"We'll get him. Now keep repeating that tag number till we can write it down."

"13 – 2943," she recited. "I've got it. Whatever the hell good it will do us."

"Tibbedeaux can use his connections to get a name and address from it."

Val wiped sweat from her brow and said, "Well, at least the son of a bitch knows he's in for a fight."

"Yeah. C'mon. Let's get back to the house. I've got to call Tibbedeaux."

A hard rain began to fall, but the leafy canopy caught most of it as they trudged through the woods.

"I'm sick about Betty," said Val. "She was no angel but she didn't deserve to die like that. So young."

"No she didn't," he agreed. "But she had the mark."

"The what?"

"The rose tattoo. D'Amore's brand. Goddamn mark of death."

"I'm beginning to hate that woman."

"Save it for Chago."

"Oh, I've got enough hate to go around, don't worry."

"The way you unloaded on his truck? I'm not worried."

"I never dreamed I'd ever shoot at anybody," she said. "But you know what? It was easy. I wanted to blow his damn head off. After seeing Betty like that, I wanted to kill him. I'm sorry I didn't. I don't think I like feeling that way. And yet, I do. Like it."

Joe pushed a small tree branch out of the path so Val could move ahead without stepping into a mud puddle.

"Was it like that in Korea?" she asked. "Did you kill the Commies with hate in your heart?"

"At first, yeah. Especially after losing some of the guys in my squad, but later on I didn't feel one way or the other about 'em. I just wanted to get them before they got me, to get it over with. It got to be a big nuisance. Tell you what, though. There were a few times when I loved it. You're never more alive than when you're caught up in the action and it's life or death in every second that ticks by. It's the greatest high in the world. And then when it's all over, you think it's a miracle you're still breathing. But what it was, was just dumb luck that you lived through it. Nothing but pure dumb luck. That's why so many guys turned so superstitious over there. You don't wanna feel unlucky in combat."

"It's the same with sports. I knew a girl on the tennis team who wouldn't step onto the court unless she was wearing her lucky hair band. That must be how Chago works his voodoo. He plays on peoples' superstition. Some people are ready to believe any damn thing. Not me, brother. That crap won't work on me."

Joe said, "You trying to convince me or yourself?"

"I'm just saying I—"

A clap of thunder interrupted her. She didn't bother to finish her thought.

"It's not that hard to believe crazy things in screwed-up situations," he said. "For a while there, I believed I was really seeing Liz's ghost even though I never believed in ghosts."

"You don't believe it now?"

"No. Not really. It's like Dot said, it was just the shock of knowing Liz was gone. And what happened to her. I wasn't ready to let her go. But I haven't seen her since . . . well, since I started spending time with you."

"I guess that makes me a positive influence." She smiled. "But I'm not sure I like the idea of being some kind of replacement."

"It's not that. It's just . . . I don't know. It's just good to have a friend, somebody you can trust. And depend on. Somebody to watch your back."

"Yes, it is, isn't it." She turned up the wattage of her smile.

They reached the edge of the woods and then ran through the downpour to the swimming pool deck where Oscar was standing guard over Betty's body, unmindful of the rain.

"You get him?" Oscar asked. "We heard the gunfire."

"We shot the hell out of his truck but he got away," Joe told him. "Why don't you come in out of the rain, Oscar?"

"I'll stay with Betty until the ambulance gets here," he said. "She shouldn't be alone right now."

Val and Joe exchanged sorrowful raised-brow glances. Then they went into the house and used pool towels to dry themselves and their guns. D'Amore was nowhere in sight. Joe figured Frida was hiding under a bed somewhere, unless she'd flown the coop altogether.

Suddenly looking sheepish, Val excused herself and made a dash to the bathroom, and as soon as the door shut behind her, Joe heard the sound of puke splattering porcelain. *Poor kid,* he thought. *Sickened by how close she came to taking a life.* He'd known a few guys in Korea who'd had the same reaction to killing Commies or to seeing their brothers-in-arms get blown apart in cold combat. He'd upchucked K-rats himself when he found Charlie Parks with his guts frozen to the side of a foxhole. What had made it so bad was that Charlie wasn't quite dead then, but he died before the medic could thaw his intestines out and stuffed them back in his belly. At least that was the way Joe remembered it. War memories had a way of turning into bullshit war stories. Maybe Charlie's guts weren't really frozen, but they were sure as hell icy; Joe was certain of that much.

He used the phone in the kitchen to call Monroe Tibbedeaux's office at the plant in Dodd City. The secretary answered and put him on hold. Two minutes later, the Orange Juice King came on the line. Joe gave him the Florida plate number (which he remembered without Val's help) and said he needed the name and address of the person it was registered to. Tibbedeaux was anxious to know the story behind the plate, but Joe put him off with: "It might lead me to the killer. It's too soon to tell. You'll know when I know."

"You *are* on to something," said Tibbedeaux. "By God, you are."

"Just put a rush on it," Joe said. "Call me back at this number." He gave him D'Amore's phone number and then hung up before his former father-in-law could hit him with more nagging questions.

Val came out of the bathroom with an embarrassed look on her face, but she no longer looked sick. "Sorry about that," she said, wiping her mouth with a washcloth.

"Don't worry about it. Happens to the best of us." He pulled his pack of smokes from his pocket and fished out two Luckies that weren't saturated with rainwater, passed one to Val and lit them both. "I want to talk to Frida before the cops get here. You know where her room is?"

"Yeah, it's in the rear of the house, just off the utility room. Come on, I'll show you."

He followed her down the hallway, past a room just large enough to contain a washing machine and dryer. She knocked on Frida's door. "Frida? It's Valentine. May I come in?"

Frida opened the door and then stepped back to let them enter. The housekeeper kept a wary eye on Joe as if she expected him to steal something, though there didn't appear to be anything worth stealing in the tiny room. Her eyes were reddened as if she'd been crying.

Val said, "We want you to tell us everything you know about Chago, okay?"

"I dun know no-thing 'bout heem," she said.

Val nodded. "You may know more than you think you do. When and where did you first meet him?"

Frida backed away from her uninvited visitors. The backs of her legs bumped into the kid-size bed and she inadvertently sat down on it. A crucifix hung on the wall over the head of her bed. An expression of embarrassment turned into one of anger. "I dint know thees happen. He follow me. *Mia madre* house, you now? Say something bad happen I dun meet him Miss D'Amore. He watch thees house. He say he help her."

She went on a full minute in broken English mixed with Spanish, but Joe thought he got the gist of what she was saying. Chago scoped out Chez D'Amore long enough to make Laura D'Amore as a prime mark for his hoodoo con. He'd been peeping one of the theatrical rituals D'Amore and friends performed while wearing masks from her eclectic collection of tribal masks and artifacts. Joe wondered if the actress was still flirting with some sort of devil worship or if the rituals were a lark, a bit of creepy theater done solely for amusement, or maybe as prelude to one of her sex orgies.

Joe asked Val: "You know about these rituals?"

"I saw one," she said. "You know those masks hanging in the sunroom? She made us all wear one while she pretended to be some high priestess calling on ancient gods for power and wealth. I thought it was all just part of the stoned revelry, seeing as how we were all blitzed on reefer and booze."

"Was Liz in on it?"

"Yes. She thought it was a real gas. She hammed it up good. I remember thinking she could've been a good actress herself, the way she threw herself into the dumb drama."

"So Chago was peeping the show, taking it all in and then decided D'Amore was ripe for his con."

Val nodded, then asked Frida if she had any idea where Chago lived. Frida answered with an emphatic no. "I'm a-scared," Frida added, "Chago keel me next time."

"No, there won't be a next time," said Joe. "We're going to get him, don't you worry. Do you know much about Palo? Chago's voodoo?"

Frida shrugged. "Palo *muy malo*." Then she crossed herself and bowed her head.

"Very bad," Val translated. "I don't think she knows more than that."

"*Gracias,* Frida," he said with a slight bow.

The phone rang and Joe dashed to the kitchen to pick it up. "Yeah."

"I've got a name and address for you," Tibbedeaux said. "The truck is registered to Alfred Alva Edison, Route 6, Dodd City."

Joe repeated the name. "Named after the light bulb genius, huh? Thanks. I'll be in touch." He hung up in a hurry.

Standing beside him, Val said, "We've got him?"

"Maybe. Truck's registered to a guy named Edison, not to Chago. Get your gun. I wanna get out of here before the cops come."

D'Amore appeared in the kitchen doorway, her cigarette-holder loaded and smoking. "Who was that?" she demanded.

"It was for me," he told her. "I've got the name and address of the guy who owns the pickup Chago drove off in."

"You saw him?" Her eyes went wide. She blanched.

"We blasted his truck but he got away."

"But not for long," Val added, saying it from the corner of her mouth like a gangster movie tough guy.

Having quickly digested the news, D'Amore said, "Remember what I told you. It won't do any good to give him to the police. You have to eliminate him."

"You aren't calling the shots, lady," Joe said. "You just give a good performance for the cops. We'll handle things in the real world."

As Joe and Val were heading out the door, Val suddenly stopped, said, "Hold on a sec," spun around and went back into the sunroom to retrieve the forked hickory stick with her hair affixed to it. She left the little black cauldron.

"I don't really believe in this voodoo shit," she said when they were climbing into the car, "but nobody gets a piece of me unless I offer it."

Joe said, "I'll keep that in mind."

She cut her eyes at him. Then she unwound the strand of red hair from the wood and tossed the hair out the window.

"You want Liz's . . . You want the blond lock?" she asked.

"No. I'm done trying to hold onto her. Can't hold onto a ghost."

She nodded. She threw the hickory twig out the window.

Joe gunned the engine.

CHAPTER THIRTEEN

Joe pulled a map of Florida from his glove box and gave it to Val. "Find Route 6," he said.

"Please?" Val cut her eyes at him.

"Please. *Pretty* please. Just find the damn thing, will ya?"

"You don't have to be rude."

"Sorry. But we don't have time for Emily Post. I wanna get this guy."

"No more than I do." She unfolded the map across her lap as Joe started the engine and pulled away from D'Amore's hacienda. The rain was letting up by the time they neared Dodd City's city limits.

"Turn right here," she told him.

"Left or right?"

"I said *right*, didn't I? *Right.*"

"Right, yeah." He turned right onto a dirt road fronting a cow pasture. Cows gazed at them with moony eyes. The car slewed over wet mud. Joe used the edge of his hand to wipe at the fog on the inside of the windshield, making blurry smears.

"I wonder who this Edison is," Val said. "Edison's definitely not a Cuban name. Why would Chago be driving his truck? I bet he stole it."

"Yeah, but it'd be stupid to be driving around in a stolen truck so close to where you boosted it. Unless you killed the guy you took it from."

Val shuddered. "I don't want to see any more dead people."

The car rattled the planks of a door-size wooden bridge spanning a small creek. In the trees ahead on the left stood a clapboard house with a rusted tin roof, set back a hundred or so feet from the road. A rust-flecked mailbox rested atop a leaning wooden post. There was no lawn to speak of, only sand, bushy scrub, and hearty weeds.

"Is that it?" Joe peered through the wiper-flogged windshield to read the letters on the mailbox. "'A. Edison.' That's our guy."

"I don't see the truck," she said. "He's not here. Chago I mean."

Joe stopped by the mailbox, rolled down his window and pulled the mailbox door open. It was empty, meaning that Mr. Edison was still alive or that Chago had been regularly removing the mail to allay the mailman's suspicion. *"Some-* body's been getting the mail," said Joe as he turned into the driveway and pulled up in front of the house.

"I don't care, I'm not going in," Val said. "I just know there's a stinking corpse in there."

"That's okay. It's better you stay out here and keep a lookout. Toot the horn if you see anybody coming."

She nodded as he got out of the car. "Don't be long," she called after him.

He stepped up onto the porch boards and rapped his knuckles against the front door. He rested his right hand on the butt of his holstered Colt, making a mental note to keep an extra box of ammo in his glove box. He'd fired two rounds at the truck and now he was down to three cartridges in the cylinder. Not good if you were heading into a shootout.

Over the sound of the diminishing rain on the tin roof he heard music inside the house. He recognized Tchaikovsky's "1812" by the noisy cannonade. Joe's father had been a lover of classical music and Joe had assimilated a rudimentary familiarity with the classics, though he preferred big band jazz and Mississippi delta blues.

He glanced back at the Buick. The rain-streaked windshield blurred Val's face and subdued the red hue of her hair. He didn't like the idea of leaving her alone in the car, but she was armed with 12-gauge firepower she wasn't afraid to use. He rapped again on the door, then opened it and stepped inside, sliding his gun out of the holster. "Anybody home?" he called loud enough to be heard over the booming music.

A cadaverous man with a shock of white hair atop a bony head looked up from his armchair and grinned. It was a grin showing raw gums and no teeth, and it might've been comical except for the naked malice in it and the madness in the beady eyes above the toothless pie-hole. An old phonograph player sat on a small table beside the armchair, its needle grinding away at the thick black disc on the turntable.

Joe hid his pistol behind his leg. "Mr. Edison?" he said, unable to take his eyes from the old man's hideous grin.

A tongue flicked out to wet thin lips, and then the man spoke: "Yep. Just missed 'im. But he left a message fer ye."

"Chago was just here?"

"Just was," said Edison, still grinning. "Said to tell ya he's a-gonna kill your world."

"What?" Joe wasn't sure he'd heard the man's words correctly above the music.

Edison slapped his knee and hooted with perverse glee.

Joe crossed the room and shut off the phonograph. The bare floor creaked under his weight. The house smelled of stale pipe tobacco, mildew, boiled collard greens and onions. Beneath that odorous mix something else lurked, though he couldn't name it.

"Hey! I was listening to that," the old man protested.

"Give me that again," said Joe, discreetly slipping the .38 back into the holster.

"You deaf, boy? He said he's a-gonna kill your world."

"That's it? That's all he said?"

"Hell, ain't that enough? He'll do it too. Sure will. He's a pistol, that one is."

"That why you let him drive your truck?"

"*I* can't drive it no more. Not without winding up in a ditch. I'm blind as a bat. He runs errands fer me, drives me to the bank to cash my social security check."

"I'll bet he takes a cut of the cash, too. Does he live here with you?"

"Nah. Says he's got a little shack somewhere hereabouts. Ain't the kind to stay long in one place, doncha know."

"You know the man's a killer?"

Finally the grin faded from Edison's weathered face. "Don't surprise me. 'At's why I stay on his good side. Too late for you, I reckon."

"If I were you, old-timer, I'd find somebody else to run your errands. Chago's not gonna be around much longer."

Edison began to quiver and shake all over. Joe thought the old man was having some sort of seizure until he realized the man was laughing without making a sound.

"By the way," Joe said with some satisfaction, "your truck's all shot up. That's what you get for letting that son of a bitch drive it, you damned old fool."

"You think I had a choice? You're dumber 'n you look, boy. I ain't so blind I can't see what that one is. No sir." Edison lowered his voice and said, "He's a demon outta hell and he brung hell with 'im."

At that moment Joe knew what was lurking beneath the malodorous atmosphere of the house. In the close air was an unmistakable presence of malice, as thickly pungent as the reek of stale tobacco smoke and old grease. It was the spoor of Chago the demon. Chago the devil. Chago the black-magic murderer. Joe had caught scent of it before, he now realized. It had lingered in the bedroom where Liz died. It had fouled the air around the pool where Betty drowned. And it was strong here in the old man's room where Chago had most recently tarried long enough to leave a threatening message for Joe Dall. *He's a-gonna kill your world.*

Clenching his fists, Joe said: "If you see him before I do, tell him for me he's a piece of shit and I'm gonna flush him out of my world."

The old man started that hideous laughing again.

* * *

Joe couldn't get out of that reeking house fast enough. He burst through the front door and hurried to the car, greatly relieved to see Val through the rain-jeweled windshield. Just before he left Edison's company, Joe had been visited by a vivid visual premonition of finding Val slumped in the front seat of the Roadmaster with her throat cut. Thankfully, she was alive and well—though not in a good mood.

"What took you so long?" she demanded as he flopped behind the wheel and started the engine. "I was beginning to get worried."

"We just missed him," he told her. "It's like he knew we'd show up here. He left a message for me. Says he's gonna kill my world."

"What the hell does *that* mean?"

"Doesn't matter 'cause I'm gonna kill him first."

"First you have to find him," Val reminded him. "And the spooky son of a bitch seems real damn good at not being found."

"He knows we're closing in on him now so he'll stay on the move. He'll have to come out into the open to move against us and that's when we'll nail him. It's like a military operation where you draw the enemy out into the open."

"Yeah, well I don't know about you, GI Joe, but I'd feel better if we had a team of commandos and a tank or two."

"Don't need a tank," he said, suppressing a grin, "when we've got you."

CHAPTER FOURTEEN

They were sitting around a table in the Sundown. Dot left the "Closed" sign and the black wreath on the door so would-be customers wouldn't disturb their brainstorming war council. They were all smoking cigarettes and sipping non-alcoholic drinks. Val's shotgun rested in an empty chair to her right. She had changed out of her wet clothes into blue jeans and a burgundy pullover shirt. Her hair was in a smart ponytail again. Joe was also in fresh jeans. He had on a beige button-up shirt with two wide vertical orange stripes down the front. It wasn't something he would've bought for himself; Liz had picked it out for him when they were still Mr. and Mrs.

He brought Dot up to date on the Chago situation, with Val filling in a few details. The radio behind the bar played softly. A Perry Como tune. The Blue Ribbon clock ticked closer to 5.

"So, what do you think?" Joe asked. "Do we just wait for the guy to make his next move?"

Dot said, "You could stake out Edison's house but Chago would probably be expecting it and stay away from there."

"We don't have that kind of time to waste anyway," said Val. "We can't just sit around and wait for something to happen. I've got to be doing something."

"Yeah, but what?" Joe asked.

"*Some*thing." Val vented a stream of smoke toward the ceiling.

Dot said, "From what the guy said about killing your world, you probably won't have long to wait. If he means what he said."

"He means it, all right." Joe stabbed out his cigarette in the ashtray. "The son of a bitch believes he can do any damn thing he pleases and get away with it. And so far, he has."

Val slapped the tabletop. "If you'd shot *him* instead of shooting his tire . . ."

"I told you, I wasn't sure it was him. I have to be sure. Look him in the eye."

Dot said, "What do you think he means by *kill your world?* That's an odd thing to say. What's he really saying?"

Joe shrugged, then gestured at the surrounding lounge. "This is my world. Or what it's come down to. This place, the bungalow, you guys."

Val glanced uneasily at the shotgun. Then she looked at the door, the windows. Outside, the sky had cleared and the late-afternoon shadows were growing long.

Dot's expression turned stony, but Joe could see the fear behind it.

Val said, "He's probably pissed off enough to bring it on, since we blasted his truck."

Joe shook another smoke from his pack and lit it. "Dot, you should call the cops and tell 'em somebody threatened to torch the lounge. Say it was an anonymous threat you take seriously and you want them to keep an eye on the place."

"You really think that would do any good?" she asked him. "The most they would do is drive by here once or twice a day. More likely, they'd chalk it up as a prank call, not take it seriously. If Chago wants to come at me, the Dead City cops aren't going to stop him. And we don't know when he'll make his move."

"Hell, I'm sorry, Dot," he said. "Sorry I got you into this mess. I never—"

She put her fingertips to his lips and shook her head. "I was already in it, hon. Sherlock to your Watson, remember? I put myself in it. Don't waste another second worrying about that."

"And I was already in it," said Val. "Nobody to blame but myself."

"If we knew how to find the guy, we could take the fight to him before he makes his next move," Joe said, repeating himself. "There must be some way . . ."

"The guy's the Phantom, minus the purple tights and good intentions," Val said, frowning. "Gives me a case of the creeping willies."

"You're the only one of us who's actually seen him close-up and in the flesh," Dot said. "Is there anything about him that . . . Ah, I'm just grabbing at straws."

Joe leaned forward in his chair. "Tibbedeaux said he would give me anything I needed to find the killer. I could tell him we need some manpower to guard the lounge and catch the guy when he shows up."

"Think he'd go for it?" asked Dot.

"Sure he would. Why wouldn't he?"

"What, like security guards?" asked Val.

"More like a goon squad," said Joe.

Dot said, "But if Chago sees them he'll just wait and make his move after the goons give up and leave. He could wait for days."

"Yeah, but it could buy us some time to track him down," Joe said. "If we can figure out how to do it."

A sudden banging on the front door startled them. Val grabbed the shotgun. Joe popped out of his chair, the pistol in his hand. Dot knocked over her bottle of Coke.

A man's voice from the other side of the door: "Dall! You in there? Open up!"

"Shit, it's just Keefer," Joe said. "The monkey boy."

Dot and Val laughed nervously, glad for an excuse to relieve some of the tension. Joe went to the door, threw back the bolt and opened it.

Monroe Tibbedeaux came through the doorway. Keefer followed him in. A Mutt and Jeff cartoon come to life.

"Are you avoiding me, Joseph?" Tibbedeaux said with an edge of warning in his voice.

"No, sir. In fact, I was just about to call you."

His ex-father-in-law shot him a dubious look.

Wiping her spilled cola off the table with her trusty bar rag, Dot slipped into the role of hostess. "Mr. Tibbedeaux, can I get you gentleman a drink? On the house."

"Yes, thank you. I'll have Scotch. On the rocks. Nothing for Barry. He's driving."

"Pull up a chair," Joe told him, "and we'll fill you in. We know who the killer is."

He grabbed Joe's arm. "What the hell is this?" he said in a low voice. "A committee meeting? This is not the way I do things, dammit."

"The ladies are in this too. Just sit down and listen." Joe pulled his arm from the older man's grasp. Tibbedeaux glowered, but he took a seat at the table, while Keefer stood off in the background with his hands folded over his crotch, trying to appear unobtrusive in spite of his hulking stature.

When what Joe had told him sank in, Tibbedeaux said, "You know the killer?"

Joe turned his chair backward and straddled it, folding his arms on the chair-back. He thought this posture might lend him a little extra authority while he briefed the O.J. King. Joe began. "He's a Cuban known as Chago. We don't know if that's his real name or a nickname or alias. He claims to be some sort of voodoo man and he used his black-magic con to get in tight with Laura D'Amore. Lizabeth met him through

D'Amore. We think he killed her as a warning to D'Amore that she'd better not buck him. "

"Chago," Tibbedeaux repeated. "I found that name in Dix's notes."

Joe's eyes widened. "Your private detective."

"Dix is dead," Tibbedeaux said with gravity. "Heart attack, apparently. I found him dead in his hotel room."

Val and Joe exchanged edgy glances.

"I want to see those notes," Joe said. "You have them with you?"

Tibbedeaux snapped his fingers at Keefer and said, "Get my valise from the car."

Keefer hopped to. He went quietly out the door.

Dot stuck another cigarette between her lips and flipped open her Zippo.

"I don't allow . . . I can't tolerate smoke," said Tibbedeaux. "If you don't mind."

Dot clicked the lighter shut and removed the cigarette from her pursed lips. Val's eyes smoldered as she ground out her smoke in the ashtray. Joe hoped her volcanic temper wasn't about to erupt. Not that Tibbedeaux didn't have it coming. But a blowup would only hamper the business at hand.

"How did Dix find out about Chago?" Joe asked.

"Evidently from the Cuban gardener who works across the street from Lizabeth's house. He did some work for Lizabeth from time to time. Maybe you can make more sense of his notes than I could. Do you know where to find this man Chago?"

"No. He's a slippery son of a bitch. And today he killed another woman. And he's threatened all of us."

"He's a goddamn phantom," Val said.

"Minus the purple tights," Dot said with a tight smile, still enjoying Val's little joke. Humor was wherever you found it, in trying times.

Tibbedeaux gave her a baffled look that made it clear he didn't waste his time reading the funny papers. Then he turned his narrowed eyes on Joe. "He was close enough to threaten you and you let him get away?"

"He doesn't threaten to your face," Joe said. "He leaves voodoo symbols. Or has somebody else tell you what he said. I've never seen him face to face. I only saw the back of his head as he was getting away in his truck."

"We shot the truck but I don't think we hit him," Val said.

"Who's this other woman he killed?"

"Betty something or other," said Joe. "A friend of Miss D'Amore's. Just a kid, really."

Val added, "We found her floating in the swimming pool, but we know he did it. He left a voodoo charm around her neck. That's when we chased him into the woods and shot at him."

"You didn't call the police?"

"No," Joe said. "There was no proof he did it, and we never saw his face. D'Amore didn't want the cops involved. She said she wouldn't admit anything to them."

Joe glanced at the door and frowned. "What's keeping Keefer? He should've been back by now."

Val reached for her shotgun just as Keefer came back inside, a valise hanging from his beefy hand.

"I thought I saw somebody lurking behind the building," Keefer told them, explaining his tardiness. He shrugged his big shoulders. "But I guess it was just a shadow or something." He gave the valise to his boss.

"Chago *is* a shadow," said Joe, standing up and drawing his .38. "Keefer, come with me. Let's make sure nobody's out there."

Keefer glanced at his boss, who nodded approval.

Joe told him: "You go out the front door and circle the building clockwise. I'll go out the back door."

Keefer nodded, pulled his pistol from his shoulder rig and slipped out the front door. Joe went through the storeroom and quietly out the back of the building.

The day was sliding toward a red sunset. A stiff breeze blew in off the lake. Down at the manmade sandy crescent, a handful of kids played in the shallows. A skinny girl in a bikini was walking from the pier to the snack bar. Joe scanned the pines behind the lounge, and then cast his gaze on his bungalow and the surrounding fortress-wall of shadows thrown by taller pines. Shadows, but no phantom in a panama hat. No shot-up green truck. He crept around the back corner, moving clockwise, pistol at the ready.

Keefer came around the corner in front of Joe. He raised his pistol and pointed it at Joe's chest. Keefer grinned.

"Stop fucking around," Joe said. "Do you know what clockwise means?"

Keefer didn't lower his aim. His face shone crimson in the slanting sunlight. There was a devilish glint in his eyes, and in his face Joe read a look of pent-up boredom and frustration aching for explosive release. His faded gridiron glories no longer sustained him; he hungered for new thrills. He was a washed-up jock waiting for an apocalyptic snap-count.

Having glanced into the heart of the man, Joe brought his gun up, cocked the hammer and pointed his piece squarely at Keefer's head. They were poised precariously, madly, upon the brink of chaotic violence. With little more than a twitch of muscle, a moment of boyish whimsy would turn deadly.

Keefer narrowed his eyes, their mad mirth melting down to dead pools.

Joe began to squeeze the trigger just as Keefer lowered his gun and grinned again.

"Crazy cocksucker," said Joe, after he'd checked his trigger finger.

"Man! That was a kick," Keefer said, still grinning. "Like rushing toward the goal line at the end of the fourth quarter, one man standing in your way. Did you get that charge?"

"Yeah, I got it. But this ain't a fucking football field."

Pistols holstered, they walked side-by-side to the Sundown's front entrance, completing their circuit of the building. Keefer swaggered a little.

"You know," Joe said, "you might wanna think about finding a new job, Barry. This one's starting to make you a little crazy."

"Is that right? Dr. Freud? Dr. Hemorrhoid."

"See what I mean?" Joe aimed his index finger at the side of his own head and made a loony circle.

Keefer laughed, then slapped Joe's shoulder. "You're all right, Dall. For a fucking hemorrhoid." He laughed harder. Joe held the door and let Keefer go ahead of him because he didn't trust the big lunatic at his back.

Val was reaching again for her shotgun but drew her hand back when she saw it was Joe and Keefer coming through the door. Tibbedeaux was wearing his reading glasses and pointing something out to Dot in a notebook opened on the table.

"Nobody out there," Joe said as he approached their table.

"See what you can make of this, Joe," said Dot, indicating the spiral notebook—probably the same one that had kept Joe out of jail.

He pulled up a chair and looked at Homer Dix's shorthand scrawl on the lined paper. Val crowded in at his left elbow, trying to get a better look.

At the bottom of the page Dix had written:

Manuel Hernandez $20:
Chago
SR 21   Mmaids   Znd DR rt   1 1/2 mi > Shk at end

"Hernandez is Liz's neighbor's gardener," Dot explained, catching Joe up. "Dix must've paid him for information on Chago and wrote it down to keep up with expenses. What do you make of this other?"

Joe stared at Dix's chicken-scratch. Nat King Cole crooned softly from the radio. The ceiling fan ticked as its blades turned a lazy circle. Finally Joe said, "State Road 21. Isn't there a billboard for Weeki Wachee Springs out there, with mermaids on it?"

"Yeah, I think there is. But what's this other? Z-n-d? Zend? What the hell is that?"

Then Joe saw it. "That's a two. Second. Second dirt road on the right. And this *s–h–k* could be shorthand for shack. Two and a half miles to the shack at the end of the road."

"That's it!" Dot slapped the tabletop. "Why didn't I see that?"

Removing his glasses, Tibbedeaux said, "So we know where this Chago person lives. But how do you know he's the man we want? How certain are you?"

"It's all circumstantial evidence," Dot quickly volunteered. "Probably not enough to stand up in court, but enough so *we* know he's the killer. And we know now from the gardener that he must've seen Chago at your daughter's house. It all adds up to a lot more than coincidence."

"So if you're correct in your assessment, Miss Barker," Tibbedeaux said, "then it would do no good to call the police on this man."

"Afraid not," she said, nodding. "There wouldn't be enough to charge him, much less prosecute."

"You seem very knowledgeable in criminal matters. Why is that? If you don't mind my asking."

"It's a hobby," Dot told him.

"It's a passion," Joe said. "She probably knows more about

crime than half the criminal lawyers in Florida."

Pocketing his glasses, Tibbedeaux suddenly stood. "Joe, I need a word in private. Walk outside with me."

They went out into the deepening twilight. Beneath wind-rattled palm fronds in front of the lounge, Tibbedeaux said, "You've done well, son. I was right to recruit you to the task. But now we've come down to the crux of the matter. I was hoping we could avoid it, but I don't see any other way. Before you extinguish that torch we spoke of, justice requires—demands—one final act. You know what I'm talking about, don't you, Joseph?"

Everything snapped into place. And there was the snapshot: the real reason the man had provided Joe with a detective license and put a gun in his hand. "You want me to kill him."

Tibbedeaux stared into Joe's eyes. "Can you do it?"

Joe stared back, stony-eyed. "Yeah," he said, his voice sounding hollow in his ears.

"You're sure."

"Oh yeah, I'm sure. Not only for what he did to Lizabeth but for what he plans to do to my friends. He has to die. There's no way around it. He's a dead man."

Tibbedeaux put a hand on Joe's shoulder and said, "Thank you, Joe. You'll be generously rewarded. I promise you."

"Here's what I want from you. I want you to hire some men to guard the Sundown. Right away. Tonight. Chago said he's going to *kill my world,* and this is probably where he'll start. I don't want him to torch this place or hurt my friends before I have a chance to get him."

"All right. I'll call in some of my off-duty manpower from the plant. They'll be glad to get the overtime and I'm sure most of them have hunting rifles and the like. Anything else?"

Joe thought for a minute, then said, "If things go wrong, I'll need a damn good lawyer."

"Only the best. But if you're careful and cunning enough, you won't need one."

Joe nodded grimly.

"You want Keefer with you when you . . . eliminate the problem? He's a good man who knows how to keep his lips tight."

"No. I'm solo on this."

Tibbedeaux nodded. He stuck out his hand.

Joe shook it. It didn't feel like a dead fish this time. There was actually warm strength in it.

The older man's eyes misted with raw emotion.

CHAPTER FIFTEEN

Joe went behind the bar, popped the cap off a cold bottle of beer and gulped half the contents. Tibbedeaux was using the phone at the bar to call in his troops, and Val and Dot were still seated at the table, heads bent together, talking in low tones. Keefer had stationed himself by the door and was leaning against the wall, trying not to look like the big sore thumb he was. Joe walked over and sat with the women. In defiance of Tibbedeaux's wishes, he lit a smoke. The women followed his lead and fired their own cigarettes. Dot winked at him, silently acknowledging their united defiance of the Orange Juice King.

"What's the plan?" she asked him. "You think you can find the shack in the dark?"

"No," he said. "I'll go in just before dawn."

Val nodded. "Catch him sleeping. I bet the bastard keeps late hours. What with his voodoo bullshit and all."

"The drawback being that it gives him tonight to move against us," Joe said. "But with Tibbedeaux's men standing guard, we should be all right. Dot, I want you to stay with us in the bungalow tonight, in case he goes after you at your home."

"Safety in numbers," she said with a solemn nod. "You think he knows where I live?"

"We should assume he does. I have a feeling he's been watching all of us from the shadows."

"Snoopy bastard," said Val, smoke jetting from her flaring nostrils.

He reached across the table and touched the back of her hand. "You can't go out there with me," he said. "I have to do this on my own."

"The hell you say!" Her eyes flashed heat. "You need me, Joe. What if you freeze up again? *I'm* not afraid to pull the trigger."

"I didn't freeze up." He withdrew his hand. "I told you . . ."

Dot tried to intervene: "Hon, Joe's right. You've got no business going out there. You're—"

"Got no business?" Vehemently indignant, Val seemed to puff up like a feline ready for a serious spitting-and-clawing scrap. "The son of a bitch marked me for death with his hoodoo stick. Don't tell me I've got no business."

"I'm going there to kill him," Joe said with low-pitched urgency. "Some would call it murder. You don't want to be a part of that, to have to live with it the rest of your life."

"Don't tell me what I want, Joe. I *know* what I want, and you're not going to stop me. I'm going out there, with you or by myself. But I *am* going."

"Hon—" Dot started.

"Butt out," snapped Val. Then she softened her demeanor and said: "I know you mean well, but I know what I have to do. Understand?"

Dot nodded and took a draw from her Camel.

"I don't want you to get hurt," Joe said. "Anything can happen out there."

"Which is why you need me," Val said. "What if he's not alone? Did you think of that? He could have voodoo henchmen. Zombies or whatever."

Joe sighed. "I think Chago's a lone-wolf type of guy."

"I don't care. I'm going with you and that's the last word."

Joe stubbed out his smoke and nodded reluctant assent. He chugalugged the rest of his beer.

Having recovered and regrouped after the verbal slap from Val, Dot leaned forward and asked, "Do you think it's odd that Homer Dix died after learning about Chago?"

"Hell of a coincidence," Joe said. Val gave a grudging nod of agreement. Apparently she wasn't feeling very agreeable so soon after their little squabble.

With a hint of a smile Dot said, "Detective Handbook Rule Four: *Never trust coincidence.*"

"You think Chago voodooed him to death?" Joe queried. "Poisoned him or something?"

"I wouldn't be a bit surprised."

"But what about this?" Val tapped a fingernail on the detective's notebook. "If Chago killed him because Dix was getting too close to finding him, why didn't Chago take the notebook?"

Off the phone now, Monroe Tibbedeaux came over to the table, saying: "That and his few valuables were deposited in the hotel safe. The concierge gave them to me when I told him Dix worked for me." He resumed his seat at the table. "I was the one who found him. He missed a meeting with me and I was unable to get in touch with him, so I went to the hotel this morning to find him. There he was, on the floor, stone cold dead in his underwear. There was white powder on his chest and face. I thought it was talcum powder. Maybe it was something else."

"Voodoo dust," said Val, making a sour face.

Tibbedeaux shrugged, then suddenly changed the subject. "My men will be here within the hour and will stay through the night. They will be very well armed."

"Thank you," Dot said. "We really appreciate it."

Tibbedeaux stared into space a moment and then said, "I don't understand this voodoo scenario. Chago killed Lizabeth as a warning to this . . . this over-the-hill actress? What in hell did he want from her?"

"According to D'Amore, an introduction to her friends in Hollywood," said Joe. "He wants to work his con where the real money is. Greener pastures. If it is a con. He probably believes his own religious bunk. The guy may be bug-house nuts but he's no dummy."

"He's evil," said Val. "Pure and simple evil."

Joe glanced at the clock and then looked with admiration at Valentine Cooper. He'd been with her for almost twenty-four hours now, and she had been—and still was—a bracing tonic to him. She had unknowingly given him a jolt of therapeutic reality that was making it easier to live in a world without Lizabeth. Moreover, he realized that he was already gone on Val, ass-over-teakettle in love—or something very much like it. He still felt a responsibility to his ex-wife to mete out justice to her killer, but he no longer felt haunted by Lizabeth's ghostly presence. In short, he knew he could get over her and get on with his life now, thanks mostly to Val Cooper.

Tires crunched on the shell-and-sand parking lot in front of the lounge, and Dot got up, went to the window and looked out. "Customers," she said. "I should open for business now, folks. Hope you don't mind, but I need the revenue."

"Not at all," said Tibbedeaux, rising. "I believe we have the situation in hand. The cavalry is on the way and Joe knows his assignment. I'll take my leave. Ladies."

He and Keefer left, and Dot flipped the "Closed" sign, removed the funeral wreath and let in the evening's first customers, a middle-aged married couple who always arrived in good spirits and usually left bitterly bickering. Joe had a hunch they liked to patch things up in bed. Tina had the night off, so Dot played waitress.

A few minutes later Dot's new man sauntered in through the front door and she smiled warmly as she introduced him. "Everybody, this is Hubie Horn, Joe's replacement."

Joe recognized him as the friendly-faced beer drinker who always sat on the same bar stool and always had his hand in the beer nuts bowl. Joe shook his hand and said, "How's it going?"

Hubie grinned and said it was going okay. "Hear you're in a new line of work," he added. "Like Peter Gunn."

"Peter Gunn?" Joe wondered if Hubie was trying to be a wise guy.

"Yeah, you know, that private eye guy on TV."

Joe shrugged. "I don't watch much TV."

Hubie shrugged.

Joe said, "Dot'll probably make you into one too with her selected readings from all her detective magazines."

Hubie grinned. He glanced at Dot and his grin got bigger. She huddled with Hubie by the bar. Joe figured she was briefing him on the Sundown's full-alert status.

"I'm hungry," Val said. She'd put the shotgun behind the bar before the customers came in and now was digging a handful of beer nuts out of the bowl on the bar. "Is that snack shack down by the pier still open?"

Joe shook his head. "They closed at sunset. I can drive down to the fish camp and bring back something. You like fish? They have burgers if you don't."

"I love any kind of fish, as long as it's battered and fried. With lots of hushpuppies and sweet coleslaw." A smile wrinkled her nose and made her eyes shine.

"I'll phone ahead so they can have it ready."

Her smile broadened. It warmed him from the inside, out. He smiled back, thinking how strange the world sometimes was, how the death of the woman he'd loved had brought him together with a woman like Val Cooper.

Joe checked with Dot to see if she thought Hubie could hold things down while he made a supper run to the fish camp. "Sure, Joe," she answered. "I just told him the situation and he's with us all the way. And he's got his hunting rifle in his truck."

As he walked alone to his car, Joe felt a heightened sense of reality he hadn't felt since his first days in a combat zone. His world was once again a dangerous place, but now he had a clear-cut mission and he knew what he was fighting for. Unlike his fight in Korea, his stateside fight had become deeply personal.

And that made the stakes dizzyingly high.

* * *

Though he couldn't completely shake the feeling that he was deserting his post, he needed time alone to digest the recent events and sort out the demands made upon him, and the drive to the fish camp provided the necessary solitude. He was trying to make his peace with the fact that he was the designated killer. Tibbedeaux and D'Amore—separately but no less urgently—had charged him with the task of eliminating Chago. And why not? Joe Dall was the leatherneck war vet. Killing was what he was best at. His one true purpose in life. Since his discharge from the service he'd felt at sea, rudderless and at the mercy of unseen currents. His marriage to Lizabeth and his brief ill-fated employment as insurance salesman and later as bouncer/handyman seemed little more than dreams now—dreams of a soldier who's strayed from the battlefield and lost the way back to his unit. But then events conspired and a target presented itself to the seasoned warrior. Individuals higher up the chain of command gave the erstwhile commando his orders. Take out the target. Eliminate the threat. Kill the evil son of a bitch.

Fine, he could do that, roger-dodger. No problem.

But Joe didn't like being used. He resented taking orders from civilians, especially those he didn't entirely trust. He *wanted* to kill the man who'd murdered Lizabeth and now threatened to destroy his world, but he couldn't shed the feeling that he was being duped—that he was a mere chess-piece, a knight sent leaping without looking, at the behest of strategists with dark agendas he knew nothing about.

He took a mental step backward and tried to see the bigger picture.

Lizabeth was dead.

Betty was dead.

They both had D'Amore's mark inked in their flesh. Had they been deliberately marked for death? Or—more likely— had they been killed because of their close relationships with Laura D'Amore, their tattoos merely inadvertent symbols of that closeness?

Homer Dix was dead. Natural causes or some sort of voodoo-dust assassination? His investigation had led him right to Chago's door, but then he died before he had a chance to act on what he'd learned. Dead by coincidence or by diabolical design?

Val Cooper had been . . . what? Cursed? Marked for death with Chago's black-magic hickory stick? Val didn't have the tattoo. She'd passed up her chance for admission to D'Amore's Girlfriend Club. She was not in the inner circle, but she was no less a prime target.

Three people dead. All fingers pointing to Chago as the culprit. But what was the proof? How did Joe know the man was in fact the murderer? He and Val had seen a man in a panama hat fleeing the vicinity immediately after Betty died in the swimming pool. Mr. Panama Hat had fled in a truck belonging to Old Man Edison, who'd confirmed that Chago had the use of his truck. So unless Betty coincidentally drowned on her own, the circumstantial evidence was strong that Chago had killed her. And left his calling card, a death's-head talisman around her neck, according to D'Amore.

That brought him back to Lizabeth. What was the evidence that Chago had killed her? There was no physical evidence, unless you counted the strands of her hair wrapped around a twig stuck in an animal's heart. And Joe didn't know for a fact that the blond hair was hers, nor was there proof that Chago had been the one who'd left the cauldron. All he had on Chago was D'Amore's story of deadly extortion, a story to some extent collaborated by Val Cooper. And the likelihood that Chago had been spotted in or near Liz's house by the neighbor's gardener.

That was it in the proverbial nutshell. Was it enough to go on when the going led to killing a man? Suppose he apprehended Chago and turned him over to the police. What would be the outcome of that? The cops would surely look into Chago's background, but who knew what they would find? Neither Tibbedeaux nor D'Amore wanted the authorities digging up scandalous dirt, and neither of them would cooperate with such an investigation. Tibbedeaux would do all he could to thwart any official effort that might sully the family name. Val would also be reluctant to tell the cops what she knew. She would not do anything to besmirch her family's honor. Small-town scandals were more venomous than big-city ones. An urban setting tended to dilute the venom. If Val's involvement in D'Amore's sex orgies came out as part of the larger story of murder, she and her family would probably become Dodd City pariahs and be forced to leave town.

Any investigation would dead-end and Chago would walk, free to continue his campaign of black-magic terror and murder.

What it all came down to, Joe had no choice. He *had* to kill the man. Kill him and dispose of the corpse. Feed Chago to swamp gators. The dirty work fell to him and he was just the man for the job. Commando Joe, professional killer.

CHAPTER SIXTEEN

"You didn't eat much," said Val, looking up from her food on the kitchen table. They'd left the lounge and brought their fish-camp paper-plate dinners to the bungalow. Tibbedeaux's men were already outside, quietly patrolling the area with deer rifles.

"Not hungry," said Joe as he tossed his greasy plate into the trash can.

"You're thinking about tomorrow," she said. "About what we have to do."

"That and other things."

"Such as?" She finished off a deep-fat-fried hushpuppy and licked her fingers.

Joe sat back down at the table and lit a smoke. "Besides killing a man?"

Val frowned, nodded.

"That I don't like being used. That Laura D'Amore brought all this on and she's getting off too easy. That she's more than an innocent victim in this whole thing."

"You're blaming her for what happened to Liz. And Betty."

"Yeah, I guess maybe I am. But it's more than that. I keep thinking she's dirtier than we know, that she's hiding something big." He shrugged. "Maybe I just don't like the snooty bitch. Maybe that's all it is."

"Maybe. We'll probably never know for sure. And I'm not going to worry about it. I'm not doing a damn thing for her.

I'm doing it for myself. For Liz. For you."

"We're going out there to kill a man," he said in earnest. "This is no game. Have you really let that sink in? You go with me, you'll be party to murder, even if you don't pull the trigger. We get caught, you'll go to prison, same as me. Imagine what that will do to your good name."

"I'm not an idiot, Joe," she said, reaching for a cigarette. "I know what we're going to do. And I would appreciate it if you wouldn't try to talk me out of doing it. It's settled. I'm with you all the way." She took a sip of iced tea. "We just have to make sure nobody ever finds out what we did."

"That's another thing," he said. "I don't like the idea of D'Amore having anything on us."

"I don't trust the woman either, but she won't be able to prove anything. And she won't blab to anybody because she'd be telling on herself. Conspiracy to commit murder, I believe it's called."

Joe nodded, then leaned back and stared at her.

"*What?*" She shifted uncomfortably in her seat. Took a draw from her smoke.

"I'm just wondering who the hell you are. You're not like any woman I've ever met. You're so . . ."

"Hardheaded?"

"Yeah, that too, but you're . . . tough-minded. You're not the country club brat I used to think you were, like Liz's other friends. You're more like a guy. Not physically, physically you're"—he whistled—"a knockout."

A smile teased the corners of her mouth. "Why shouldn't a woman be tough? Me, I was always a tomboy. I think I patterned myself after the Stimson men. They were *men's* men. Gentlemen brawlers. My dad was a career naval officer who went on to make his fortune as a real estate developer. He's the one who taught me to stand up for myself. Even as a kid

I wasn't afraid to take on playground bullyboys. I held my own in any scrap, standing up for the little guys. The night of the senior prom I broke this football player's nose to save the honor of a girl I hardly even knew. I thought I was some kind of Supergirl without the cape. A crusader for truth and justice. And the American way."

Joe chuckled. "I can see that. Bet you were hell on wheels."

"Then you see it's against my nature to back down from a fight against this evil human turd." She chortled. "I can curse like a sailor too."

"I noticed." He grinned.

Outside, an owl hooted. Joe wondered why Tibbedeaux's makeshift security squad hadn't scared the bird off. He stood. "Think I'll go out and check the perimeter. I don't have a lot of confidence in Tibbedeaux's juice boys."

"I'll come with you." She stubbed out her cigarette, stood and retrieved her shotgun from the counter by the stove.

They went out the front door. The fog had thickened. The lounge's lights were hazy blobs of yellow. The trunks of the pines were dark ghostly columns reaching upward into thick mists and disappearing there as if blotted out of existence.

"How can those guys see anybody in this pea soup?" Val asked. "This is not good."

"Let's hope they're experienced deer hunters that don't shoot if they aren't sure what they're shooting at."

They walked toward the thin stand of pine trees behind the bungalow. Joe drew his pistol and kept it angled safely at the ground.

"Halt!" A dark shape stepped out from behind a pine. A shape with a rifle.

"Don't shoot," said Joe. "We're the good guys. I work for Tibbedeaux too." It galled him to say that out loud, but it was better than getting shot by a nervous juice-plant man.

The man came forward, lowering his rifle. "You come outta that cottage?"

"Yeah. I live there. Appreciate you coming out here to help out."

"Overtime's always good."

"Keep a sharp eye. A real bad hombre might show up tonight. Don't let him slip up behind you in this damn fog. He's not above cutting a man's throat."

"No way. Can't see worth a damn but I got real good ears. No sumbitch'll creep up on Bubba Tolliver."

"Glad to hear it," said Joe. "How many of you out here?"

"Six. Good men and true."

"Swell. Carry on, Bubba." Joe graced him with a snappy salute. The man snapped one back.

As they walked away, Val said, "I feel a little better now. I was afraid they'd be guzzling beer on the job. Juicing juicers."

"Seems like a good old boy. Not a Marine, but he'll do."

Val suddenly stopped and cocked her ear at the bungalow. "Is that your phone?"

Joe stopped to listen. "Yeah. C'mon."

They jogged back to the bungalow and Joe snatched up the phone mid-ring. "Yeah?"

It was Dot telling him that she wouldn't be staying the night with them in the bungalow. She was going home with Hubie Horn after she closed up the lounge.

"How about that," he said. "Don't do anything I wouldn't do."

"Don't worry about me, Joe. You just be careful when you go out to that shack in the morning," she told him. "Shoot first and ask questions later."

"That from your Detective's Handbook?"

"No, that's from a hundred gangster movies, but it's still damned good advice."

"Yes ma'am. Have a good night."

Val gave him a questioning look as he cradled the phone. "Dot," he said. "She won't be joining our slumber party. She's going home with her new bouncer."

"Oh, so it's just the two of us then." She had a thoughtful expression on her face.

Joe tried to read her thoughts, then gave up and said, "Unless we have uninvited company."

"That would *really* piss me off." She propped the barrel of the shotgun casually on her shoulder and put her other hand on her hip. "Know what I mean?"

* * *

It began with an innocently affectionate goodnight kiss and it didn't end until they were lying, naked and wonderfully spent, in each other's arms.

"Goodness," she said with a contented sigh.

"Yeah," he whispered, inhaling the clean scent of her hair.

She stretched her arms over her head, her fingers touching the headboard, her breasts rising on her ribcage, nipples upthrust, as she finished off her languid head-to-toe stretch. Joe looked on in awe, as if he were witnessing the rise of new natural wonders of the world.

"I feel . . .," she said, her words coming out long and lazy, ". . . like we just sealed something . . . important."

"Whaddaya mean?" he asked. He had no clue what she was talking about.

"You know, like sealing a vow?" She brought her arms down, her breasts filling out again now that the languorous stretching was over. She laughed. "Don't panic, I'm not talking marriage vows. More like what blood brothers do when they cut their fingers or whatever and mix their blood. Get what I mean? Like we just sealed our . . . friendship. But more than friendship, really."

"Like . . . blood lovers. But without the blood."

"Blood lovers, yeah, something like that, but with fluids more intimate than blood."

"Hmmm."

She played her fingertips in the hair of his chest. She suddenly yanked a pinch of chest hair and said, "So don't you even think about slipping off without me in the morning."

"Hey, that hurt."

"Promise me," she said, grabbing more of his curly mat and pulling just enough to make it sting.

"I promise." He seized her wrist, twisted her arm and pulled her onto his chest. Those natural wonders of hers flattened against him. "You little hellcat."

They laughed. He poked her ribs. She tickled his armpit. They kissed. Caressed.

They sealed the promise with another bout of lovemaking.

CHAPTER SEVENTEEN

Lizabeth stood in the dark at the foot of the bed.

She was naked.

And dead. Yet *not* dead. She hovered in the eerie space between this world and the next, looking down at the entwined lovers. Joe came awake with a jerk of his leg and saw Lizabeth wink a cold eye as she faded into the bedroom's gloom. He winked back, letting her know he thought he finally understood.

He slapped the alarm clock to shut off its annoying ringing.

Her voice thick with sleep, Val said, "You always wake up like a horse out of the starting gate?"

"Sorry," he said. "I was . . . dreaming."

Her hands found him in the dark. "Lie with me a minute."

"It's four-thirty," he reminded her.

"One minute won't hurt."

He lay back down and pillowed his head on her bosom. He closed his eyes and breathed her intoxicating musk. She played her fingers in his hair.

"Wanna tell me about it?" she asked. "Your bad dream?"

"No. I prefer the real world." He kissed her breast.

"Mmmm. Me too since you put it like that."

He took her nipple in his mouth. She patted his head and said, "Okay, okay, time to get up. Before it's too late."

She sat up, dumping his head off her chest. "Time to get our minds on business," she added. She got up and padded into the bathroom. Joe slipped into his blue jeans and went into the kitchenette to make coffee.

They sat at the table and smoked while they sipped black coffee. They were both comfortable with the early morning silence, neither feeling compelled to make small talk. Joe re-checked his pistol to make sure the cylinder was packed with a full load. Val got a box of shells from her overnight bag and fed a couple into her shotgun to replace the ones she'd fired at Chago's truck.

At five o'clock they got in his Roadmaster and headed out.

* * *

The eastern sky was turning from purple to a deep electric blue as dawn drew near. When he turned onto the twin ruts of the dirt road at the billboard with the waving blond mermaids, Joe cut the headlights. The sandy road seemed to glow with its own light.

"You scared?" Val asked him.

"No. Well, I'm scared I'll screw up, but not scared of Chago. Same thing you feel in combat. You don't worry so much about getting hit as you do about doing something stupid that gets your buddies killed."

"I've never been in combat and I don't mind telling you, I'm scared shitless."

"That's okay. Shitless is good." He tried to laugh. He coughed instead.

"What if he's not there?"

"He's got to be there."

"But what if he's not? What do we do then? Wait for him?"

"My car would give us away. He'd see it before he got to the shack and turn tail. So you'd have to drive off and leave me there to wait for him."

"That's not the deal," she said. "You promised."

"I promised you could go to the shack with me, and you are," he reminded her. "But if he's not home, you'll have to get the car out of here. I don't see any other way. A battleplan has to be flexible because you can never be sure what the enemy's going to do."

She stared ahead at the ruts of the little-traveled road.

"You get that, don't you?" he asked because her sullen silence was beginning to spook him a little.

She nodded. "You could be waiting a long time for nothing. If he knew Dix was onto him, he could've pulled up stakes. He may never come back to the shack. And then all we can do is wait and see who he kills next."

"We don't wanna go in there thinking he might not be inside. We go in ready to take him down. No hesitation. We can't be distracted by what-ifs."

Joe glanced at the mileage counter. He stopped the car and turned off the motor. "We go the rest of the way on foot," he said. "Should be about half a mile from here. Ready?"

She nodded. She leaned across the seat, put a hand lightly on his thigh and kissed his lips. "For luck," she said.

* * *

The shack stood in the trees at the end of the dirt road. It looked to be a one-roomer with a single window in front, curtained with burlap. The slanted tin roof was streaked with rust. The green truck was not there.

Joe ordered himself to ignore the sinking sensation in the pit of his belly. He and Val exchanged glances as they advanced on the shack, keeping off the road ruts so their shoes wouldn't crunch rocks and sand. The sky was much brighter now, the sun coming up over a horizon they couldn't see from here because of all the trees and tropical greenery.

When they were about ten yards from the door, he put his

lips to Val's ear and whispered: "Wait here. I'm gonna make sure there's no back door."

She nodded. He crept to the back of the shack. There was no door back there, just another narrow window hung with a ragged curtain of burlap. The window was raised. He tried to look inside but the rusty screen and the burlap made it impossible to see anything of the shack's dark interior. They would have to go in blind.

He rejoined Val and whispered: "No rear entrance. If the door's locked, blast it with the shotgun. I go in first, you cover the door. Got it?"

She nodded grimly. Her hair shone crimson in the half-light.

They skulked to the door. Joe tried the rust-flaked door-knob. It turned with a soft click. The door swung open on creaking hinges. He heard Val draw a sharp breath behind him.

He went through the doorway with his gun raised, hammer cocked.

* * *

The naked girl came off the creaky bed with a shriek and made a wild dash for the door. Joe threw up his left hand and planted it in her chest and she tumbled backward and sat on the dirt floor. Joe quickly scanned the dim room. There was a black iron cauldron—a jumbo version of the one left at Val's beach-house door, the kind you'd expect to see a witch stirring—and a small wooden table and chair, but no Chago. The place reeked of incense and stale cigar smoke. An unlit lantern rested on the table. A beat-up steamer trunk sat in a corner.

The girl jumped to her feet, cursing in Spanish. Joe put his pistol in her face and told her to shut up. He pushed her down to a sitting position on the bed. Val came in behind him, saying, "Frida?"

The girl's resemblance to D'Amore's housekeeper was unmistakable, but this one was younger, with longer hair and a scar on her left cheek.

"Where's Chago?" Joe asked.

Making no effort to cover her nakedness, the girl blurted some more Spanish.

"You speak English?"

"Chago will keel you," she said.

"Not if I *keel* him first. Where is he?"

She shrugged. Her small breasts heaved with her rapid respirations.

"You're Frida's sister," said Val. "Aren't you?"

"I dun tell you nothin'."

Val stepped close to the girl, aiming the shotgun away from her. "Listen to me," she said. "Chago's killing people. He could kill your sister next. If you tell us where he is, we can stop him."

"If you don't," Joe added, "that makes you guilty of murder too. You wanna end up in the electric chair?"

She made a spitting sound to show her contempt.

"What's your name?" asked Val. "I'm Valentine and this is Joe."

Another dry spit.

Joe saw the machete on the floor by the bed. He holstered his pistol and picked up the machete. He grabbed the girl's wrist, pulled her to the small table and sat her in the chair. She eyed the blade warily.

"Now," he said, "I'll ask you again. If you don't tell me, I'll chop off a finger. Then I'll ask you again. No answer, I'll chop off another one. You understand? If you're as stubborn as you look, you won't have any fingers left, but that's all right, because then I'll start on your toes. Get it? When the toes are gone, I'll take off your hands. Then the arms, the legs. So if you don't want people calling you Stumpy, you'd better tell me now. Where is Chago?"

"Jesus, Joe," whispered Val.

The girl's eyes brimmed with tears. She shook her head and said, "I dun know."

Joe slapped her hand down on the table and pinned her wrist. She made a tight fist to hide her fingers, but he pried them open and bent her middle finger back until she cried out in pain. "See, you can't say *I don't know*," Joe said. "That's against the rules. *I don't know* will cost you a finger. What say we start with the pinky? This little one here."

The girl looked hard into his eyes, trying to decide if he bluffing. He looked hard back, showing her he meant what he said. She cursed him in Spanish.

He cocked the machete over his shoulder and then brought down the blade. She flinched and the blade took a splinter of flesh off the side of her little finger as it bit into the table. She yelped and tried to snake her hand from his grasp, but he held fast.

"Fina!" she said. "My name is Fina."

Joe raised the machete. "That's not what I asked you."

The girl pointed with her free hand at Val and said, "She did."

"Give her a chance, Joe. C'mon. Be a sport, huh?"

"Let's try again," he said. "And remember, you're one finger in the hole already. Where's Chago?"

"He went to see movie lady," Fina said, pouting.

"Laura D'Amore," he said.

Fina nodded.

"It's a little early for a social call," he said. "Why'd he go there?"

"I dun know. He dun tell me."

"When's he coming back here?"

Fina shrugged. "Not long, maybe. I dun know."

Joe released her hand. She stuck her bleeding finger in her mouth as if she could suck the pain away.

"How long's he been gone?"

"Um, half hour, maybe. I was sleepin', you know?"

Val stood over the iron cauldron. "What's this?" she asked the girl.

"*Prenda*," she answered. "For the *muertos*, um, ghosts, you know? Spirits of the dead. For Mama Wanga."

"Chago's mumbo-jumbo," said Joe.

"*Palo Mayombe*," Fina corrected him. "Mama Wanga ees, um, you know, a god?"

Val reached down into the cauldron and picked up the skull of a small animal. "He's got all kinds of weird crap in here."

"Dun touch that!" Fina shouted, a look of horror on her face.

"Is this where Chago gets his magic power?" asked Joe.

Fina shrugged, then grudgingly nodded. A tear trickled down her cheek, making the scar glisten.

Joe picked up the lantern and poured kerosene into the big black pot, saturating its bizarre contents. Bones, herbs, burlap pouches, strands of hair twined about forked sticks, pieces of cloth apparently cut from clothing, match boxes full of dirt, a wooden mask like the ones on D'Amore's walls, and a few objects Joe couldn't name. He picked up the mask, a demonic monkey face; he was sure it was from D'Amore's collection. He lit a cigarette, and then dropped the lighted match into the cauldron.

Fina gasped when the kerosene caught and flames leapt up from the bottom of the pot.

"Reckon that'll piss off Mama Wanga?" Joe asked the horrorstruck girl. She stared, slack-jawed, at the fire.

"Put your clothes on, for Christ's sake," Val told her.

Joe watched Fina slip into a cheap shift with a floral print. "So you told your boyfriend Chago your sister worked for the big movie star and you two decide to shake her down. You're in on this up to your pretty little tits, aren't you?"

"Joe," Val scolded him with her chastising tone.

"I dun shake nobody," Fina said. "Chago take me to Hollywood. America ees free country, no?"

"That's right, kid," he said. "But that doesn't mean you can go around killing people."

"I dint keel nobody." Fina nonchalantly slipped her feet into her flip-flops and combed her dark hair with her fingers. Val opened the steamer trunk and looked inside. She held up a glass jar filled with white powder. "Fina, what's this?"

"His roots, medicine, you know?"

Joe said, "His voodoo stuff. We'll take the trunk with us, have it analyzed. Dollars to donuts, this is the same powder that killed Dix."

Val put the jar back and closed the trunk. She wiped her hands on her jeans.

With his cigarette clamped between his teeth, Joe stuck the wooden mask under his left arm and unzipped his pants. "You ladies step outside," he said, "so I can put this fire out. Wouldn't want to piss off Smokey the Bear."

CHAPTER EIGHTEEN

Running flat-out on the Zephyrhills highway, the Buick
Roadmaster shook and shimmied like a mechanical drunk in
DTs. It was in desperate need of a wheel alignment, but Joe
wasn't thinking about auto maintenance; his thoughts were
of catching Chago at Chateau D'Amore and giving him a
tune-up for his trip to hell.

The monkey-demon mask was on the seat beside him. Val
picked it up, pulled its rope belt over her head and put it on.
She looked at him out of the narrow eye-holes in the wood.
Then she took it off and made a sour face. "Thing stinks,"
she said. "Like the shack."

The shack where they'd left Fina, standing in front of
it with her hands on her hips and a sullen pout on her lips.
Joe had told her, "If your boyfriend makes it back, tell him
I pissed on his magic the same way I'm gonna piss on his
dead face." That was in case they missed him at D'Amore's,
but Joe figured the odds were good they wouldn't miss him.
They would either meet him on the road or catch him at the
D'Amore compound.

"What would he be doing at Laura's this time of day?"
Val wondered aloud. "What's his next move?"

"There's nobody left to kill out there but Oscar. I don't see
him knocking off the housekeeper. D'Amore wouldn't give
a damn if he killed Frida. And Oscar's a big old boy. Chago
would have his hands full with him. But he could slit his

throat while he's sleeping. I figure he wants a heart-to-heart with Miss Torrid Town herself, to make her see the light once and for all."

"He ought to know by now she's not going to give him what he wants. What's she got to lose? He's already killed her lovers, and Oscar she just keeps around to make her feel safer, certainly not as a lover."

"I think Chago's down to playing his hole card," Joe said, putting it together as he said it. "If I'm Chago, I tell D'Amore if she doesn't give me what I want I'll take away her most prized possession."

"What? You mean . . . ?"

Joe nodded. "Her looks. Ask her if she wants her famous face carved up like a Halloween pumpkin. She knows he'd do it too."

"You could be right. From things she said, I think her plan is to worm her way back into the Hollywood in-crowd, kissing up to the studio bigwigs. She wants to make a few more movies before she's too old. I know she ran up a big phone bill with long-distance calls to California. She used to complain about the charges. Which is why she was not about to set Chago loose in Hollywood to queer her deal. Self-centered bitch."

"Which is also why she's so hot for me to eliminate her problem with a bullet. Not because she gives a shit about anybody else."

"Wouldn't break my heart if he cut up her face. *God*, did I really just say that?"

"He wouldn't have to cut her. She'd give in before that happened. But he'd have to get Oscar out of the way to have a clear shot at her. If we're right, Oscar's real close to being dead about now."

"We have to get there in time," she said. "I like Oscar. He's a nice guy."

"Yeah, he ain't bad for an overgrown zombie back-cracker."

After a moment, Val said, "Tell me something, Joe. Would you have really chopped off that girl's finger?"

"I was wondering that myself. I think, yeah, I probably would have. A woman lies down with the devil, she should expect to catch some hell. One way or another."

* * *

He slowed down as they drove past D'Amore's walled property. There was no sign of the green truck. The sun was already turning up the heat on the cloudless morning.

"He's not there," Val said, slumping in the passenger seat. "We missed him."

"Not necessarily," Joe said as he pulled to the side of the highway and parked in a spot that wouldn't be visible from the front of the house. "He's smart, he'd park in the woods like before and slip over the back wall. Same way we're going in."

"If he is still there, he's been in there a good while. I don't know, Joe, I think the slick son of a bitch's gone. He's probably back at the shack, fuming because you pissed in his voodoo pot."

Joe didn't think so. His soldier's sense was telling him the enemy was close. He threw open the car door. "Let's go see," he said.

They went on foot through a stand of trees and scrub brush to the right of the compound and came out behind the back wall. Val carried her shotgun in the crook of her right arm as casually as a bird hunter, but the severe expression on her face gave lie to the bird-hunting illusion. Joe slid the monkey-demon mask through the wrought-iron bars of the rear gate and then climbed up and over the iron. Val passed him the shotgun through the bars and scaled them, up and over, dropping quietly to her feet beside Joe. He handed her the scattergun and picked up the mask.

The swimming pool's filter hummed and gurgled. The air was acrid with chlorine. Wind stirred the surface of the water. The house was ominously quiet. The back of Joe's neck prickled, and he drew his Colt.

Val whispered, "You wanna tell me what you're gonna do with that mask?"

"Magic."

*　*　*

The back door wasn't locked. Joe guessed that Chago had picked the lock, saving him the trouble. He entered first. Val came in behind him. The kitchen lights were off, the morning sunlight glared in the windows and dimmed the interior with contrasting shadows. Muffled voices came from deeper in the house. The door to Frida's room was standing open; Joe looked in, saw she wasn't there. Her bed was unmade. He shook his head to tell Val the housekeeper wasn't in her room, then he pointed toward the hallway and the sunroom beyond, where he thought the voices were coming from. They crept toward it.

Then they were close enough to make out some of the words spoken by a man's guttural, accented voice and close enough to smell the stench of cigar smoke.

". . . spirit is mine now. She is a slave to me forever."

"You're an evil son of a bitch." D'Amore's voice, delivering the line with authentic rancor. But there was also a note of hysteria in it that Joe didn't like. It told him something bad was happening—or had already happened—in the room.

"Evil is for fairy tales," the man said with a thick Latin accent. "Like your moving pictures. Evil does not touch me. I walk outside all that."

Joe put the monkey mask against his face and snugged the rope behind his head. Then he stuck his head in the doorway to see what he could see. Through the eyeholes he saw Laura D'Amore ensconced on her creaking wicker throne, looking anything but regal. She was in a long black nightgown, her blue-black hair hanging to her shoulders in tangles she hadn't had time to brush out before being chivvied from her bed. Her eyes were wet, ready to rain tears. Fury twisted her face. Her tears, when they came, would be tears of bitter rage.

Chago stood with his back to Joe. He had on cutoff jeans, no shirt, and he had a knife in one hand, a cigar in the other. Black braids hung out from under his white panama halfway to his wide shoulders. He was short, maybe five-foot-six, with wiry muscles and little body hair. Compact but no doubt powerful.

At his feet lay Frida the housekeeper, an obscene gash in her throat and a pool of her blood on the floor. Her eyes were already death-glazed. Oscar Lamont was not in the room. Joe expected that Chago had already cut Oscar's throat while the big man slept.

"They belong to me now," Chago was saying. "Your little whores. Lizabeth. Betty. And this one, your little Cuban slave." He waved his blade at Frida's body. "I have their spirit power. Your soul is mine now. You will do what I tell you or I will fillet your famous face."

Val gave Joe a look, not so much of surprise as of wonder, wonder that he'd been right about Chago's hole-card move—slicing up D'Amore's meal ticket. She was wondering how he'd known. It was simple, really. When he put himself in Chago's place, it was exactly what he himself would've done after all else had failed. It occurred to him that he had a new rule of his own for Dot's detective handbook: *Think like a bad guy to catch a bad guy.*

Laura D'Amore made a mewling sound that was very much out of character. The woman was real close to losing control, slipping out of character and into absolute hysteria. Joe gave her a few more long seconds to contemplate her mortality, then he stepped out into the doorway and aimed his Colt at the back of Chago's head, at a point just above the hat brim.

D'Amore saw him then. Saw a man in a monkey-demon mask pointing a gun at the fiend in front of her. Surprise registered in her face, alerting Chago, who spun around to face the masked man.

Val stepped into the doorway to stand beside Joe. She brought the shotgun to her shoulder. Joe cocked the Colt's hammer.

Chago's mouth fell open when he recognized the monkey mask and realized the big iron pot at his shack had been raided, his mumbo-jumbo contaminated. It flashed through Joe's mind that Chago might think he was staring into the masked face of one of his pissed-off gods, come to punish him—except that the man knew Val and therefore would probably tumble to the identity of the man behind the mask.

Joe waited for him to make a move, hoping he would come at him with that wicked blade so he would feel fully justified in putting a bullet in his head. He wasn't sure Val had the patience to give Chago the next move. From the edge of his eye he saw she had the shotgun leveled at Chago's chest. She was probably close enough to cut the short man in half.

Chago grinned. He slowly raised his cigar and stoked it noisily, like he was blowing kisses to phantom fans.

"Shoot the son of a bitch!" said D'Amore. "You see what he did."

"No," said Chago, keeping the knife down by his leg. "You shoot me and your wife's soul goes with me. You let me go and I will let her go. You want her to be free, no?"

"Bullshit," said Val. "Let's kill the weasel right now."

Joe pulled off the mask and dropped it on the floor. "Your

magic's gone, asshole. I set a fire in your pot and pissed on the ashes. And Lizabeth is not my wife, not anymore. Looks like you've screwed the pooch, *amigo*."

Chago was handsome, in a craggy sort of way—sharp chin, beak nose, sinkhole sockets and jutting cheek bones—but when he heard what Joe had done to his repository of magic, Chago's face erupted with volcanic rage, his eyeballs bugging out, face flushing dark with hate, cigar smoke jetting from wide nostrils. His lips peeled back in a toothy snarl.

Joe had wanted to tell Chago the part about pissing on his face when he was dead, but he saw the guy was ready to blow so he just said, "Come on, cocksucker. Show me some magic. Let's see you catch this bullet in your teeth."

Chago dropped his stogie on the floor and flipped the knife into the air, caught the tip of the blade and started to throw it. Joe squeezed the trigger just as a human locomotive ran him down from behind.

* * *

Oscar Lamont, reeking of chloroform and charging like mortally wounded beef-on-the-hoof in a bullfight ring, lost his footing and crashed into the man and woman standing in the doorway to the sunroom, knocking them both to the floor. A shotgun went off and the big aquarium exploded, unleashing a small waterfall, followed by a gushing flood. Shards of glass and exotic fish washed over the floor. The fish snapped their tails, trying to jump back into deeper water which was no longer there.

The redheaded woman yelled at him: "Get off me, you goddamn whale!"

* * *

The Colt still in his fist, Joe rolled onto his back as Chago took a running jump and flew over them. Joe got off a shot at Chago's bare back, but the agile little guy kept going, not hit but losing his panama hat. Joe scrambled to his feet and went down the hallway after him.

"Don't let him get away!" D'Amore said, putting her lungs into it.

Voodoo braids dangling like live wires, Chago went tearing out the back door with Joe close on his heels. The man was fast and Joe didn't think he could catch him if he made it over the wall and broke into open territory.

Fast, but he couldn't outrun a bullet.

Chago raced along the edge of the swimming pool, glancing over his left shoulder to locate his pursuer.

Then a strange thing happened to Joe. It had happened a few times before, in combat, but never often enough to lose its strangeness. He'd thought about it a lot since the war, always amazed at what a man may think about while he's in the process of killing another human being. Like the time he was sighting down on the charging Red Chinese grunt, wondering just before firing the kill-shot what was in the enemy soldier's mind, curious to know if the guy was married, had kids, or if he knew he was about to be taken forever out of his life, and then wondering if the Commie believed in God or if it even mattered what he believed once he was dead. Joe had summarily concluded that the guy probably believed in the same God *he* did, the God of War.

Those strange thoughts always came lightning fast, but often without lightning's illumination.

The odd thoughts that intruded in intensified life-and-death situations fascinated Joe. Like the weird one flashing now as he chased Chago around the pool, knowing he would probably have to shoot the guy in the back to stop him. The peculiar thought centered on what Chago had said moments ago about evil, with a murdered girl at his feet. *Evil is for fairy tales. Evil does not touch me.* Joe was flipping those statements around in his mind, trying to understand their implications as he pursued the man who'd spoken them. Only seconds before having to shoot the guy in the back, Joe was puzzling out the nature of evil, wondering if it actually existed in the abstract or if it was nothing more than a subjective product of the mind. Odd, what a man thinks about while he's killing another man. Odder still where such thoughts often led. Where they led him now was to the likelihood that he himself was beyond good and evil—that the life he was about to take didn't matter, was no more important than the life of a lowly cockroach. There was no God of high and mighty morals to condemn the killing. *Thou shalt not kill* was a line from an adult fairy tale, nothing more. In a way, he hoped Chago was right in saying evil didn't touch him. Joe found it comforting to believe that when the .38 slug hit Chago in the back, *it* wouldn't be evil, nor the result of an evil act. It would simply *be*. Just one more meaningless death in the Darwinian universe. The amoral God of War would judge your combat skills, and nothing more.

Joe broke off his pursuit and his strange musings, stood with feet shoulder-width apart, used both hands to steady his aim and zeroed on a spot midway between Chago's shoulder blades. Five or six yards of pool-deck cement separated shooter from target. Joe cocked the hammer.

Maybe Chago heard the hammer click or maybe he just sensed what was coming; whichever the case, he suddenly stopped running, spun around with startling quickness, juked to his left and threw the knife.

The blade tumbled end over end, flashing erratic glints of sunlight as it hurtled toward Joe with hypnotic precision.

Joe fired and twisted at the waist, trying to make the knife miss him. The rushed shot missed Chago, but Chago's knife-throw was true, the point of the blade stabbing into Joe's left breast. Joe's feet tangled as he twisted and he went down on cement, losing his grip on the gun.

The world slowed down, and Joe, feeling oddly detached from the pain in his chest, took a moment to wonder if the blade had pierced his heart. If it had, he was as good as gone. He did have a sick feeling in his belly, but he could feel his heart pounding a steady beat and he was breathing all right, so his muscle and ribs must've taken the brunt of the hit. His heart was intact. He would live to fight another day, if he could reach his Colt before Chago did, but Chago was already coming on fast, going for the gun. There he went, bending down to snatch it up, a nasty grin on that craggy mug of his. Sonofabitch.

Joe sat up, got a firm grip on the knife's haft and yanked it out of his breast. It hurt more coming out than going in, and the bright morning went dark around the edges. Shit, he thought, don't let me pass out now.

Chago raised the pistol and pointed it down at the crown of Joe's head. The guy's shit-eating smirk pissed Joe off enough that he didn't pass out. He could run on pure rage long enough to finish the fight if he could just stop the guy from putting a slug in his brainpan. But Chago was more than an arm's length away, and Joe didn't have time or the knife-thrower's skill to tag the smirking bastard with his own knife. Shit.

Chago cocked the hammer and said, "Your soul is mine, *pendejo*."

Joe said, "Fuck you!" but the curse was lost in the booming explosion.

Chago's right hand, the gun still in it, went flying across the pool deck with a rooster-tail of blood trailing it. Chago screamed. Joe wasn't too surprised that the guy screamed like a girl.

Joe glanced over his shoulder and saw Valentine Cooper holding the shotgun, a little plume of white smoke snaking from the muzzle. God, but she was beautiful. And surely ferocious enough to make the God of War crack a big smile.

She worked the pump to jack another shell into the chamber.

Blood spurting from the stump of his wrist, Chago went after his detached hand; it was lying over by the flowerbed, still clutching the Colt. Then Joe realized the guy was going for the gun, not his hand.

Joe stood up—the knife still in his fist and his ears still ringing from the 12-gauge blast—and stumbled toward Chago. Val said something but he couldn't make it out. He deliberately put himself between her and Chago. He wanted to save her from killing the little punk and having to live with that, God of War be damned.

Chago was having trouble prying the pistol from his detached right hand with his left. He was cursing in Spanish, or maybe he was calling on Mama Wanga for a little help from on high—or wherever his gods hung out.

Joe's old hand-to-hand combat training took over now, the grizzled leatherneck intent on taking down the enemy combatant and swiftly dispatching him with the knife. But Chago was coming around with the Colt in his hand and pointing it at Joe's belly, so Joe went low, diving for Chago's knees.

Chago snapped off a shot that smacked the cement and whined off into the air.

Joe took Chago's legs out from under him and he fell across Joe's back.

Val yelled something unintelligible, at least to Joe's shell-shocked ears.

Chago hammered the pistol's handgrip on the back of Joe's head. Joe lashed blindly with the knife and felt the blade hit something solid, probably Chago's leg. Chago yelped and tried to backpedal far enough away for a clean shot, but Joe scrabbled after him on his hands and knees, desperate to crowd him and keep him off balance so he couldn't set himself for another shot. He fired anyway, and the slug clipped Joe's left shoulder as it zinged by.

Joe had his head up now, looking into his enemy's face and getting the range on him. Chago was trying to get his feet under him so he could stand up. His olive skin was ashen, his wrist still pumping blood, and he was wielding the gun clumsily with his left hand, trying to draw a bead on Joe but not able to because he had to concentrate too much on getting his legs under him. Give him another minute and the guy would probably pass out from blood loss and shock, but Joe knew he didn't have another minute. It was now or *Never mind, I'm dead.*

Joe made his move. He launched himself at Chago, thrusting the knife with the full power of his right arm.

The gun fired once more.

The knife blade sank into Chago's throat as he went over backward, his head bouncing on the cement.

Joe landed on Chago's chest and worked the blade in deeper, twisting it, feeling little resistance as it destroyed the man's throat, and then he ripped it free with a hooking motion that opened a big ugly gash where the Adam's apple had been.

Chago wheezed and gurgled, his eyes swelling up like little bloodshot balloons.

With his knees planted in Chago's chest, Joe watched the man die.

"I'm taking all your power, little man," he said, leaning close to Chago's face. "I'm freeing the souls of the ones you killed. You hear me, motherfucker? You got nothing. So get your ass to hell and when you get there tell Mama Wanga I said to go fuck herself."

Chago's eyes burned with emotions too dark and deep to name. They bore into Joe's but Joe didn't blink, didn't look away. Joe stared back hard and grinned. Chago tried to reach his remaining hand to his gaping throat wound but Joe kept his shoulder pinned to the deck.

The Cuban's complexion was losing its color, going from olive-skin dark to morgue-white with remarkable speed. His chest began to rise and fall faster, his breaths becoming shallower with each one. When the death rattle finally came, it was almost inaudible.

Joe watched until the light went out of the man's bulging eyes. Then he stood and dropped the knife, and Val was standing with him, slipping under his arm to give him support.

Laura D'Amore was standing by the back door, staring at Chago's corpse as if she couldn't believe the man was actually dead. Oscar Lamont stood by her, a dazed and sickened look on his face, his bald head shining in the bright morning sunlight.

"How bad are you hit?" asked Val, looking at the blood on the front of his shirt and his shoulder.

"I'm okay." He tried to smile to show he really was. "Like they say in the movies, it's just a flesh wound. Or two."

"Hey, Oscar," she said, "how about a little help here?"

Joe said, "Forget it. Oscar's still half in the bag. Chago chloroformed him."

"Let's get you inside and stop the bleeding," she said.

"Most of the blood is his." Joe jerked a thumb at Chago. He looked at the detached hand by the flowerbed, and then he grinned. "I hope you weren't trying to shoot the gun out of his hand with that scattergun."

She cut her eyes at him, and just for a second he thought she was going to hit him, but she surprised him with a smacking kiss on the cheek.

* * *

Joe was stretched out on a sofa in the sunroom, his bloody shirt on the floor where Val had tossed it. She was applying a hand-towel compress to the jagged wound in his pectoral muscle. The shoulder wound where the bullet had grazed his flesh wasn't deep and had already stopped bleeding. Val lit a cigarette and stuck it between his lips.

"I'm calling an ambulance," she said.

"No. I don't need one. No rush. You can drive me to the emergency room later. Just need some stitches and a tetanus shot. Call the cops and tell Bull Kelso to get his hulking ass out here."

"How much are we going to tell them?"

"Just the basics. We'll leave out the orgies for Liz's sake. And yours."

Val scowled at him. "D'Amore won't like this."

"You're damned right I won't," Laura D'Amore said as she stalked into the room. "I won't let you call the police. Oscar will dispose of the bodies and you won't say a word about what happened here."

Val put her hands on her hips and stuck out her chest. "Try and stop me," she said.

"I mean it, Valentine. I am not going to let you do this to me. The scandal sheets would ruin me forever, this time. They'll bury me."

"And queer your big comeback? Ask me if I care." Val walked over to one of the house's many phones—this one on a phone stand by the bay window—picked up the receiver and dialed the operator.

"Put that down," D'Amore said. She went toward Val. "This is *my* house, goddamn you."

"Stay away from me," Val warned her. "Hello, operator? Get me the Dodd City Police. Yes, it's an emergency."

Joe sat up on the sofa. He knew what was coming and wanted a ringside seat.

D'Amore jabbed her finger at the switch-hook, breaking the connection. "Put down that phone," she said through clenched teeth.

"Back off, bitch" Val said.

"Put it down right now!"

Val hung up the phone, balled a fist and popped D'Amore's jaw with an angry right cross. D'Amore went down in a dead heap. It wasn't the graceful fall she would've made in a movie, the other actor pulling the punch.

Val looked at Joe. "I warned her. You're my witness."

"Anything you say, doll face," Joe doing a passable impersonation of Humphrey Bogart, even getting that hinky twitch of the upper lip.

"Hope I didn't kill her."

"Nah, she's too mean to die that easy. She had that coming. I've wanted to deck her since I first met her."

Oscar lumbered into the room. He saw D'Amore on the floor and blurted: "My God, what happened?"

Joe said, "She fainted. Couldn't stand the sight of my blood. Never woulda guessed she was so sensitive."

Val flashed him a big grin.

CHAPTER NINETEEN

Joe raised his glass of bubbly to Dot and said, "Congratulations."

"No, Joe, you're supposed to congratulate the man," Val said. "You wish the bride-to-be good luck."

"You serious?" He cocked a brow.

"I am." She cocked one back at him.

"That's all right, Joe," said Dot, smiling big. "I'll take the congrats."

Joe shrugged. "Guess it makes sense, most of the men I know."

It was Sunday, so they had the Sundown all to themselves: Dot, Val and Joe sitting in a booth, drinking champagne, Dot in a rosy mood because of her engagement to Hubie Horn, the man who'd replaced Joe as the lounge bouncer.

"So where is the lucky guy?" he asked, looking up at the Blue Ribbon clock over the bar. It was a few minutes past six.

"He had a job to finish at the body shop," Dot said. "He'll be here soon."

"I hope he gets here before we drink up all the champagne," said Val, sipping her portion of pink bubbly from a long-stemmed glass.

"Honey, we're not going to run out. I've got a case in the back. Drink up and enjoy yourself. Lord knows, you deserve it. You both do." She gave Joe a kindly big-sister smile.

"Hell, Dot," he said, grinning, "we're just your run-of-the-mill small-town heroes."

"That's not the way the newspaper tells it." Dot lit a smoke. "According to O'Bannon's editorial, you two are the greatest thing since sliced bread on a hero sandwich."

"I was careful not to lay it on too thick when I talked to him," said Joe. "It was his idea to play up the bouncer-turned-private eye angle. He knew there was a lot I wasn't telling him, so he had to work with what he had, amp it up."

Dot asked, "Did you really mean what you said about setting up shop as a private dick in Miami?"

Joe nodded. "Tibbedeaux offered to set me up in Tampa, in the same building he has an office in, but I told him no thanks. I don't want any strings to the man." Tibbedeaux had made the offer after telling Joe that the various roots and herbs in Chago's steamer trunk had been analyzed by the state crime lab and that the white powder remained unidentified. The lab boys had identified another substance in Chago's apothecary, one that explained why Lizabeth hadn't fought back as she was strangled with her bra. The substance was curare, an alkaloid from a South American plant that causes paralysis in human's when administered in the proper dose. Apparently, the autopsy's lab tests hadn't been wide enough in scope to detect the presence of curare in Liz's system. Joe didn't like to think about why Chago had wanted Liz paralyzed or what sort of sick activities he might've done before he strangled her, poor Lizabeth conscious but unable to move. Joe knew she must have been absolutely terrified during her last moments. He wished he could kill the man again.

"Smart," said Val. "Any strings to the O. J. King would probably make you his puppet."

"I'm trying to talk Val into going in with me, get her P.I. license and be my business partner."

"Valentine Cooper, private eye," Val said, rolling her eyes. "Funny."

"I like it," said Dot, sucking on a Camel. "You can't deny that you two make a good team."

"I'll drink to that." Joe raised his glass and took a sip.

Val laughed, then she said, "I guess I shouldn't count on Laura D'Amore playing me if they ever make a movie about us."

"With her busted jaw wired up, she won't be playing anybody any time soon," said Joe.

"I didn't mean to break her jaw, but she wouldn't back off."

Joe said, "Cooper-Dall Investigations. I'm the brains, she's the muscle."

"Lord help us," said Val, flashing her jade-green eyes at him.

Playing off something Homer Dix had said, Joe lifted his glass again and said, "Dime-store Detectives. We work cheap."

"Hell no we don't," said Val. "Top dollar and nothing less. That's the deal."

Dot propped her elbows on the table and said, "I'll be available for consultation whenever you get a really tough case."

Joe wasn't sure, but he thought she was serious. "That's good to know," he said.

"In the meantime," Dot said, "here's the Golden Rule from The Detective's Handbook. *Detective work is thirty percent gray matter, seventy percent shoe leather.*"

Joe deadpanned as he looked at Val and said, "You're gonna need some good walking shoes, pard."

Val pointed a finger at him, cocked her thumb and dropped the hammer of her imaginary pistol.

She was smiling when she finger-shot him, so Joe took it as a good omen for their future prospects in the gumshoe business.

DEADCORE
4 HARDCORE ZOMBIE NOVELLAS

By Randy Chandler, Ben Cheetham, Edward M. Erdelac, and David James Keaton.

"Randy Chandler's *Dead Juju* is a wild, graphic ride—a fast-paced array of elements including religion, politics, race relations, news media, socio-economic classism, contumacy—all handled with skillful precision as Chandler gives us deft glimpses of humanity in all its chaotic, whacked out splendor."
—Walt Hicks, *Page Horrific*

"DEADCORE achieves all extremes. Violent, perverse, depraved and, as such, quite recommended." —*Fangoria*

"A wild ride and with an ending which leaves the readers as shocked as it does with its opening. *Dead Juju* opens DEADCORE with a visceral thrill which is hard to ignore and equally tough to stomach." —*Fantasy Book Critic*

THE DEATH PANEL
MURDER, MAYHEM, AND MADNESS

13 Hard boiled, violent tales of crime and horror from Randy Chandler, Tom Piccirilli, Scott Nicholson, Simon Wood, John Everson, and more.

"...be prepared to be blown away by some of the best genre short story fiction written in the last few years." —*Horror World*

"With sharp writing and a crisp design to match, the anthology makes a strong case for 2009's best. It's only Comet Press' third release, but already, the small-press label has distinguished itself as a reliable name brand. Pick it up, if you've got the balls."
—*Bookgasm*

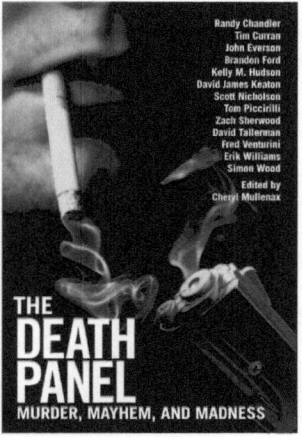

COMETPRESS

Comet Press is an independent publisher
of horror and dark crime.

Visit us on the web at:
www.cometpress.us

and follow us on twitter and facebook:

twitter.com/cometpress
facebook.com/cometpress

www.ingramcontent.com/pod-product-compliance
Lightning Source LLC
Chambersburg PA
CBHW022042240626
47154CB00007B/2532